Honoré de Balzac

The Gondreville Mystery

An Historical Mystery

Honoré de Balzac

The Gondreville Mystery

An Historical Mystery

ISBN/EAN: 9783955630263

Auflage: 1

Erscheinungsjahr: 2013

Erscheinungsort: Bremen, Deutschland

CONTENTS

PART I

Chapter I. Judas

The autumn of the year 1803 was one of the finest in the early part of that period of the present century which we now call "Empire." Rain had refreshed the earth during the month of October, so that the trees were still green and leafy in November. The French people were beginning to put faith in a secret understanding between the skies and Bonaparte, then declared Consul for life, – a belief in which that man owes part of his prestige; strange to say, on the day the sun failed him, in 1812, his luck ceased!

About four in the afternoon on the fifteenth of November, 1803, the sun was casting what looked like scarlet dust upon the venerable tops of four rows of elms in a long baronial avenue, and sparkling on the sand and grassy places of an immense *rond-point*, such as we often see in the country where land is cheap enough to be sacrificed to ornament. The air was so pure, the atmosphere so tempered that a family was sitting out of doors as if it were summer. A man dressed in a hunting-jacket of green drilling with green buttons, and breeches of the same stuff, and wearing shoes with thin soles and gaiters to the knee, was cleaning a gun with the minute care a skilful huntsman gives to the work in his leisure hours. This man had neither game nor game-bag, nor any of the accoutrements which denote either departure for a hunt or the return from it; and two women sitting near were looking at him as though beset by a terror they could ill-conceal. Any one observing the scene taking place in this leafy nook would have shuddered, as the old mother-in-law and the wife of the man we speak of were now shuddering. A huntsman does not take such minute precautions with his weapon to kill small game, neither does he use, in the department of the Aube, a heavy rifled carbine.

"Shall you kill a roe-buck, Michu?" said his handsome young wife, trying to assume a laughing air.

Before replying, Michu looked at his dog, which had been lying in the sun, its paws stretched out and its nose on its paws, in the charming attitude of a trained hunter. The animal had just raised its head and was snuffing the air, first down the avenue nearly a mile long which stretched before them, and then up the cross road where it entered the *rond-point* to the left.

"No," answered Michu, "but a brute I do not wish to miss, a lynx."

The dog, a magnificent spaniel, white with brown spots, growled.

"Hah!" said Michu, talking to himself, "spies! the country swarms with them."

Madame Michu looked appealingly to heaven. A beautiful fair woman with blue eyes, composed and thoughtful in expression and made like an antique statue, she seemed to be a prey to some dark and bitter grief. The husband's appearance may explain to a certain extent the evident fear of the two women. The laws of physiognomy are precise, not only in their application to character, but also in relation to the destinies of life. There is such a thing as prophetic physiognomy. If it were possible (and such a vital statistic would be of value to society) to obtain exact likenesses of those who perish on the scaffold, the science of Lavatar and also that of Gall would prove unmistakably that the heads of all such persons, even those who are innocent, show prophetic signs. Yes, fate sets its mark on the faces of those who are doomed to die a violent death of any kind. Now, this sign, this seal, visible to the eye of an observer, was imprinted on the expressive face of the man with the rifled carbine. Short and stout, abrupt and active in his motions as a monkey, though calm in temperament, Michu had a white face injected with blood, and features set close together like those of a Tartar, – a likeness to which his crinkled red hair conveyed a sinister expression. His eyes, clear and yellow as those of a tiger, showed depths behind them in which the glance of whoever examined the man might lose itself and never find either warmth or motion. Fixed, luminous, and rigid, those eyes terrified whoever gazed into them. The singular contrast between the immobility of the eyes and the activity of the body increased the chilling impression conveyed by a first sight of Michu. Action, always prompt in this man, was the outcome of a single thought; just as the life of animals is, without reflection, the outcome of instinct. Since 1793 he had trimmed his red beard to the shape of a fan. Even if he had not been (as he was during the Terror) president of a club of Jacobins, this peculiarity of his head would in itself have made him terrible to behold. His Socratic face with its blunt nose was surmounted by a fine forehead, so projecting, however, that it overhung the rest of the features. The ears, well detached from the head, had the sort of mobility which we find in those of wild animals, which are ever on the qui-vive. The mouth, half-open, as the custom usually is among country-people, showed teeth that were strong and white as almonds, but irregular. Gleaming red whiskers framed this face, which was white and yet mottled in spots. The hair, cropped close in front and allowed to grow long at the sides and on the back of the head, brought into relief, by its savage redness, all the strange and fateful peculiarities of this singular face. The neck which was short and thick, seemed to tempt the axe.

At this moment the sunbeams, falling in long lines athwart the group, lighted up the three heads at which the dog from time to time glanced up. The spot on which this scene took place was magnificently fine. The *rond-point* is at the entrance of the park of Gondreville, one of the finest estates in France, and by far the finest in the departments of the Aube; it boasts of long avenues of elms, a castle built from designs by Mansart, a park of fifteen hundred acres enclosed by a stone wall, nine large farms, a forest, mills, and meadows. This almost regal property belonged before the Revolution to the family of Simeuse. Ximeuse was a feudal estate in Lorraine; the name was pronounced Simeuse, and in course of time it came to be written as pronounced.

The great fortune of the Simeuse family, adherents of the House of Burgundy, dates from the time when the Guises were in conflict with the Valois. Richelieu first, and afterwards Louis XIV. remembered their devotion to the factious house of Lorraine, and rebuffed them. Then the Marquis de Simeuse, an old Burgundian, old Guiser, old leaguer, old *frondeur* (he inherited the four great rancors of the nobility against royalty), came to live at Cinq-Cygne. The former courtier, rejected at the Louvre, married the widow of the Comte de Cinq-Cygne, younger branch of the famous family of Chargeboeuf, one of the most illustrious names in Champagne, and now as celebrated and opulent as the elder. The marquis, among the richest men of his day, instead of wasting his substance at court, built the chateau of Gondreville, enlarged the estate by the purchase of others, and united the several domains, solely for the purposes of a hunting-ground. He also built the Simeuse mansion at Troyes, not far from that of the Cinq-Cygnes. These two old houses and the bishop's palace were long the only stone mansions at Troyes. The marquis sold Simeuse to the Duc de Lorraine. His son wasted the father's savings and some part of his great fortune under the reign of Louis XV., but he subsequently entered the navy, became a vice-admiral, and redeemed the follies of his youth by brilliant services. The Marquis de Simeuse, son of this naval worthy, perished with his wife on the scaffold at Troyes, leaving twin sons, who emigrated and were, at the time our history opens, still in foreign parts following the fortunes of the house of Conde.

The *rond-point* was the scene of the meet in the time of the "Grand Marquis" – a name given in the family to the Simeuse who built Gondreville. Since 1789 Michu lived in the hunting lodge at the entrance to the park, built in the reign of Louis XIV., and called the pavilion of Cinq-Cygne. The village of Cinq-Cygne is at the end of the forest of Nodesme (a corruption of Notre-Dame) which was reached through the fine avenue of four rows of elms where Michu's dog was now suspecting spies. After the death of the Grand Marquis this pavilion fell into disuse. The vice-admiral preferred the court and the sea to Champagne, and his son gave the dilapidated building to Michu for a dwelling.

This noble structure is of brick, with vermiculated stone-work at the angles and on the casings of the doors and windows. On either side is a gateway of finely wrought iron, eaten with rust and connected by a railing, beyond which is a wide and deep ha-ha, full of vigorous trees, its parapets bristling with iron arabesques, the innumerable sharp points of which are a warning to evil-doers.

The park walls begin on each side of the circumference of the *rond-point*; on the one hand the fine semi-circle is defined by slopes planted with elms; on the other, within the park, a corresponding half-circle is formed by groups of rare trees. The pavilion, therefore, stands at the centre of this round open space, which extends before it and behind it in the shape of two horse-shoes. Michu had turned the rooms on the lower floor into a stable, a kitchen, and a wood-shed. The only trace remaining of their ancient splendor was an antechamber paved with marble in squares of black and white, which was entered on the park side through a door with small leaded panes, such as might still be seen at Versailles before Louis-Philippe turned that Chateau into an asylum for the glories of France. The pavilion is divided inside by an old staircase of worm-eaten wood, full of character, which leads to the first story. Above that is an immense garret. This venerable edifice is covered by one of those vast roofs with four sides, a ridgepole decorated with leaden ornaments, and a round projecting window on each side, such as Mansart very justly delighted in; for in France, the Italian attics and flat roofs are a folly against which our climate protests. Michu kept his fodder in this garret. That portion of the park which surrounds the old pavilion is English in style. A hundred feet from the house a former lake, now a mere pond well stocked with fish, makes known its vicinity as much by a thin mist rising above the tree-tops as by the croaking of a thousand frogs, toads, and other amphibious gossips who discourse at sunset. The time-worn look of everything, the deep silence of the woods, the long perspective of the avenue, the forest in the distance, the rusty iron-work, the masses of stone draped with velvet mosses, all made poetry of this old structure, which still exists.

At the moment when our history begins Michu was leaning against a mossy parapet on which he had laid his powder-horn, cap, handkerchief, screw-driver, and rags, – in fact, all the utensils needed for his suspicious occupation. His wife's chair was against the wall beside the outer door of the house, above which could still be seen the arms of the Simeuse family, richly carved, with their noble motto, "Cy meurs." The old mother, in peasant dress, had moved her chair in front of Madame Michu, so that the latter might put her feet upon the rungs and keep them from dampness.

"Where's the boy?" said Michu to his wife.

"Round the pond; he is crazy about the frogs and the insects," answered the mother.

Michu whistled in a way that made his hearers tremble. The rapidity with which his son ran up to him proved plainly enough the despotic power of the bailiff of Gondreville. Since 1789, but more especially since 1793, Michu had been well-nigh master of the property. The terror he inspired in his wife, his mother-in-law, a servant-lad named Gaucher, and the cook named Marianne, was shared throughout a neighborhood of twenty miles in circumference. It may be well to give, without further delay, the reasons for this fear, – all the more because an account of them will complete the moral portrait of the man.

The old Marquis de Simeuse transferred the greater part of his property in 1790; but, overtaken by circumstances, he had not been able to put the estate of Gondreville into sure hands. Accused of corresponding with the Duke of Brunswick and the Prince of Cobourg, the marquis and his wife were thrust into prison and condemned to death by the revolutionary tribunal of Troyes, of which Madame Michu's father was then president. The fine domain of Gondreville was sold as national property. The head-keeper, to the horror of many, was present at the execution of the marquis and his wife in his capacity as president of the club of Jacobins at Arcis. Michu, the orphan son of a peasant, showered with benefactions by the marquise, who brought him up in her own home and gave him his place as keeper, was regarded as a Brutus by excited demagogues; but the people of the neighborhood ceased to recognize him after this act of base ingratitude. The purchaser of the estate was a man from Arcis named Marion, grandson of a former bailiff in the Simeuse family. This man, a lawyer before and after the Revolution, was afraid of the keeper;

he made him his bailiff with a salary of three thousand francs, and gave him an interest in the sales of timber; Michu, who was thought to have some ten thousand francs of his own laid by, married the daughter of a tanner at Troyes, an apostle of the Revolution in that town, where he was president of the revolutionary tribunal. This tanner, a man of profound convictions, who resembled Saint-Just as to character, was afterwards mixed up in Baboeuf's conspiracy and killed himself to escape execution. Marthe was the handsomest girl in Troyes. In spite of her shrinking modesty she had been forced by her formidable father to play the part of Goddess of Liberty in some republican ceremony.

The new proprietor came only three times to Gondreville in the course of seven years. His grandfather had been bailiff of the estate under the Simeuse family, and all Arcis took for granted that the citizen Marion was the secret representative of the present Marquis and his twin brother. As long as the Terror lasted, Michu, still bailiff of Gondreville, a devoted patriot, son-in-law of the president of the revolutionary tribunal of Troyes and flattered by Malin, representative from the department of the Aube, was the object of a certain sort of respect. But when the Mountain was overthrown and after his father-in-law committed suicide, he found himself a scape-goat; everybody hastened to accuse him, in common with his father-in-law, of acts to which, so far as he was concerned, he was a total stranger. The bailiff resented the injustice of the community; he stiffened his back and took an attitude of hostility. He talked boldly. But after the 18th Brumaire he maintained an unbroken silence, the philosophy of the strong; he struggled no longer against public opinion, and contented himself with attending to his own affairs, – wise conduct, which led his neighbors to pronounce him sly, for he owned, it was said, a fortune of not less than a hundred thousand francs in landed property. In the first place, he spent nothing; next, this property was legitimately acquired, partly from the inheritance of his father-in-law's estate, and partly from the savings of six-thousand francs a year, the salary he derived from his place with its profits and emoluments. He had been bailiff of Gondreville for the last twelve years and every one had estimated the probable amount of his savings, so that when, after the Consulate was proclaimed, he bought a farm for fifty thousand francs, the suspicions attaching to his former opinions lessened, and the community of Arcis gave him credit for intending to recover himself in public estimation. Unfortunately, at the very moment when public opinion was condoning his past a foolish affair, envenomed by the gossip of the country-side, revived the latent and very general belief in the ferocity of his character.

One evening, coming away from Troyes in company with several peasants, among whom was the farmer at Cinq-Cygne, he let fall a paper on the main road; the farmer, who was walking behind him, stooped and picked it up. Michu turned round, saw the paper in the man's hands, pulled a pistol from his belt and threatened the farmer (who knew how to read) to blow his brains out if he opened the paper. Michu's action was so sudden and violent, the tone of his voice so alarming, his eyes blazed so savagely, that the men about him turned cold with fear. The farmer of Cinq-Cygne was already his enemy. Mademoiselle de Cinq-Cygne, the man's employer, was a cousin of the Simeuse brothers; she had only one farm left for her maintenance and was now residing at her chateau of Cinq-Cygne. She lived for her cousins the twins, with whom she had played in childhood at Troyes and at Gondreville. Her only brother, Jules de Cinq-Cygne, who emigrated before the twins, died at Mayence, but by a privilege which was somewhat rare and will be mentioned later, the name of Cinq-Cygne was not to perish through lack of male heirs.

This affair between Michu and the farmer made a great noise in the arrondissement and darkened the already mysterious shadows which seemed to veil him. Nor was it the only circumstance which made him feared. A few months after this scene the citizen Marion, present owner of the Gondreville estate, came to inspect it with the citizen Malin. Rumor said that Marion was about to sell the property to his companion, who had profited by political events and had just been appointed on the Council of State by the First Consul, in return for his services on the 18th Brumaire. The shrewd heads of the little town of Arcis now perceived that Marion had been the agent of Malin in the purchase of the property, and not of the brothers Simeuse, as was first supposed. The all-powerful Councillor of State was the most important personage in Arcis. He had obtained for one of his political friends the prefecture of Troyes, and for a farmer at Gondreville the exemption of his son from the draft; in fact, he had done services to many. Consequently, the sale met with no opposition in the neighborhood where Malin then reigned, and where he still reigns supreme.

The Empire was just dawning. Those who in these days read the histories of the French Revolution can form no conception of the vast spaces which public thought traversed between events which now seem to have been so near together. The strong need of peace and tranquillity which every one felt after the violent tumults of the Revolution brought about a complete forgetfulness of important anterior facts. History matured rapidly under the advance of new and eager interests. No one, therefore, except Michu, looked into the past of this affair, which the community accepted as a simple matter. Marion, who had bought Gondreville for six hundred thousand francs in assignats, sold it for the value of a couple of million in coin; but the only payments actually made by Malin were for the costs of registration. Grevin, a seminary comrade of Malin, assisted the transaction, and the Councillor rewarded his help with the office of notary at Arcis. When the news of the sale reached the pavilion, brought there by a farmer whose farm, at Grouage, was situated between the forest and the park on the left of the noble avenue, Michu turned pale and left the house. He lay in wait for Marion, and finally met him alone in one of the shrubberies of the park.

"Is monsieur about to sell Gondreville?" asked the bailiff.

"Yes, Michu, yes. You will have a man of powerful influence for your master. He is the friend of the First Consul, and very intimate with all the ministers; he will protect you."

"Then you were holding the estate for him?"

"I don't say that," replied Marion. "At the time I bought it I was looking for a place to put my money, and I invested in national property as the best security. But it doesn't suit me to keep an estate once belonging to a family in which my father was – "

" – a servant," said Michu, violently. "But you shall not sell it! I want it; and I can pay for it."

"You?"

"Yes, I; seriously, in good gold, – eight hundred thousand francs."

"Eight hundred thousand francs!" exclaimed Marion. "Where did you get them?"

"That's none of your business," replied Michu; then, softening his tone, he added in a low voice: "My father-in-law saved the lives of many persons."

"You are too late, Michu; the sale is made."

"You must put it off, monsieur!" cried the bailiff, seizing his master by the hand which he held as in a vice. "I am hated, but I choose to be rich and powerful, and I must have Gondreville. Listen to me; I don't cling to life; sell me that place or I'll blow your brains out! – "

"But do give me time to get off my bargain with Malin; he's troublesome to deal with."

"I'll give you twenty-four hours. If you say a word about this matter, I'll chop your head off as I would chop a turnip."

Marion and Malin left the chateau in the course of the night. Marion was frightened; he told Malin of the meeting and begged him to keep an eye on the bailiff. It was impossible for Marion to avoid delivering the property to the man who had been the real purchaser, and Michu did not seem likely to admit any such reason. Moreover, this service done by Marion to Malin was to be, and in fact ended by being, the origin of the former's political fortune, and also that of his brother. In 1806 Malin had him appointed chief justice of an imperial court, and after the creation of tax-collectors his brother obtained the post of receiver-general for the department of the Aube. The State Councillor told Marion to stay in Paris, and he warned the minister of police, who gave orders that Michu should be secretly watched. Not wishing to push the man to extremes, Malin kept him on as bailiff, under the iron rule of Grevin the notary of Arcis.

From that moment Michu became more absorbed and taciturn than ever, and obtained the reputation of a man who was capable of committing a crime. Malin, the Councillor of State (a function which the First Consul raised to the level of a ministry), and a maker of the Code, played a great part in Paris, where he bought one of the finest mansions in the Faubuorg Saint-Germain after marrying the only daughter of a rich contractor named Sibuelle. He never came to Gondreville; leaving all matters concerning the property to the management of Grevin, the Arcis notary. After all, what had he to fear? – he, a former representative of the Aube, and president of a club of Jacobins. And yet, the unfavorable opinion of Michu held by the lower classes was shared by the bourgeoisie, and Marion, Grevin, and Malin, without giving any reason or compromising themselves on the subject, showed that they regarded him as an extremely dangerous man. The authorities, who were under instructions from the minister of police to watch the bailiff, did not of course lessen this belief. The neighborhood wondered that he kept his place, but supposed it was in consequence of the terror he inspired. It is easy now, after these explanations, to understand the anxiety and sadness expressed in the face of Michu's wife.

In the first place, Marthe had been piously brought up by her mother. Both, being good Catholics, had suffered much from the opinions and behavior of the tanner. Marthe could never think without a blush of having marched through the street of Troyes in the garb of a goddess. Her father had forced her to marry Michu, whose bad reputation was then increasing, and she feared him too much to be able to judge him. Nevertheless, she knew that he loved her, and at the bottom of her heart lay the truest affection for this awe-inspiring man; she had never known him to do anything that was not just; never did he say a brutal word, to her at least; in fact, he endeavored to forestall her every wish. The poor pariah, believing himself disagreeable to his wife, spent most of his time out of doors. Marthe and Michu, distrustful of each other, lived in what is called in these days an "armed peace." Marthe, who saw no one, suffered keenly from the ostracism which for the last seven years had surrounded her as the daughter of a revolutionary butcher, and the wife of a so-called traitor. More than once she had overheard the laborers of the adjoining farm (held by a man named Beauvisage, greatly attached to the Simeuse family) say as they passed the pavilion, "That's where Judas lives!" The singular resemblance between the bailiff's head and that of the thirteenth apostle, which his conduct appeared to carry out, won him that odious nickname throughout the neighborhood. It was this distress of mind, added to vague but constant fears for the future, which gave Marthe her thoughtful and subdued air. Nothing saddens so deeply as unmerited degradation from which there seems no escape. A painter could have made a fine picture of this family of pariahs in the bosom of their pretty nook in Champagne, where the landscape is generally sad.

"Francois!" called the bailiff, to hasten his son.

Francois Michu, a child of ten, played in the park and forest, and levied his little tithes like a master; he ate the fruits; he chased the game; he at least had neither cares nor troubles. Of all the family, Francois alone was happy in a home thus isolated from the neighborhood by its position between the park and the forest, and by the still greater moral solitude of universal repulsion.

"Pick up these things," said his father, pointing to the parapet, "and put them away. Look at me! You love your father and your mother, don't you?" The child flung himself on his father as if to kiss him, but Michu made a movement to shift the gun and pushed him back. "Very good. You have sometimes chattered about things that are done here," continued the father, fixing his eyes, dangerous as those of a wild-cat, on the boy. "Now remember this; if you tell the least little thing that happens here to Gaucher, or to the Grouage and Bellache people, or even to Marianne who loves us, you will kill your father. Never tattle again, and I will forgive what you said yesterday." The child began to cry. "Don't cry; but when any one questions you, say, as the peasants do, 'I don't know.' There are persons roaming about whom I distrust. Run along! As for you two," he added, turning to the women, "you have heard what I said. Keep a close mouth, both of you."

"Husband, what are you going to do?"

Michu, who was carefully measuring a charge of powder, poured it into the barrel of his gun, rested the weapon against the parapet and said to Marthe: –

"No one knows I own that gun. Stand in front of it."

Couraut, who had sprung to his feet, was barking furiously.

"Good, intelligent fellow!" cried Michu. "I am certain there are spies about – "

Man and beast feel a spy. Couraut and Michu, who seemed to have one and the same soul, lived together as the Arab and his horse in the desert. The bailiff knew the modulations of the dog's voice, just as the dog read his master's meaning in his eyes, or felt it exhaling in the air from his body.

"What do you say to that?" said Michu, in a low voice, calling his wife's attention to two strangers who appeared in a by-path making for the *rond-point*.

"What can it mean?" cried the old mother. "They are Parisians."

"Here they come!" said Michu. "Hide my gun," he whispered to his wife.

The two men who now crossed the wide open space of the *rond-point* were typical enough for a painter. One, who appeared to be the subaltern, wore top-boots, turned down rather low, showing well-made calves, and colored silk stockings of doubtful cleanliness. The breeches, of ribbed cloth, apricot color with metal buttons, were too large; they were baggy about the body, and the lines of their creases seemed to indicate a sedentary man. A marseilles waistcoat, overloaded with embroidery, open, and held together by one button only just above the stomach, gave to the wearer a dissipated look, – all the more so, because his jet black hair, in corkscrew curls, hid his forehead and hung down his cheeks. Two steel watch-chains were festooned upon his

13

breeches. The shirt was adorned with a cameo in white and blue. The coat, cinnamon-colored, was a treasure to caricaturists by reason of its long tails, which, when seen from behind, bore so perfect a resemblance to a cod that the name of that fish was given to them. The fashion of codfish tails lasted ten years; almost the whole period of the empire of Napoleon. The cravat, loosely fastened, and with numerous small folds, allowed the wearer to bury his face in it up to the nostrils. His pimpled skin, his long, thick, brick-dust colored nose, his high cheek-bones, his mouth, lacking half its teeth but greedy for all that and menacing, his ears adorned with huge gold rings, his low forehead, – all these personal details, which might have seemed grotesque in many men, were rendered terrible in him by two small eyes set in his head like those of a pig, expressive of insatiable covetousness, and of insolent, half-jovial cruelty. These ferreting and perspicacious blue eyes, glassy and glacial, might be taken for the model of that famous Eye, the formidable emblem of the police, invented during the Revolution. Black silk gloves were on his hands and he carried a switch. He was certainly some official personage, for he showed in his bearing, in his way of taking snuff and ramming it into his nose, the bureaucratic importance of an office subordinate, one who signs for his superiors and acquires a passing sovereignty by enforcing their orders.

The other man, whose dress was in the same style, but elegant and elegantly put on and careful in its smallest detail, wore boots *a la* Suwaroff which came high upon the leg above a pair of tight trousers, and creaked as he walked. Above his coat he wore a spencer, an aristocratic garment adopted by the Clichiens and the young bloods of Paris, which survived both the Clichiens and the fashionable youths. In those days fashions sometimes lasted longer than parties, – a symptom of anarchy which the year of our Lord 1830 has again presented to us. This accomplished dandy seemed to be thirty years of age. His manners were those of good society; he wore jewels of value; the collar of his shirt came to the tops of his ears. His conceited and even impertinent air betrayed a consciousness of hidden superiority. His pallid face seemed bloodless, his thin flat nose had the sardonic expression which we see in a death's head, and his green eyes were inscrutable; their glance was discreet in meaning just as the thin closed mouth was discreet in words. The first man seemed on the whole a good fellow compared with this younger man, who was slashing the air with a cane, the top of which, made of gold, glittered in the sunshine. The first man might have cut off a head with his own hand, but the second was capable of entangling innocence, virtue, and beauty in the nets of calumny and intrigue, and then poisoning them or drowning them. The rubicund stranger would have comforted his victim with a jest; the other was incapable of a smile. The first was forty-five years old, and he loved, undoubtedly, both women and good cheer. Such men have passions which keep them slaves to their calling. But the young man was plainly without passions and without vices. If he was a spy he belonged to diplomacy, and did such work from a pure love of art. He conceived, the other executed; he was the idea, the other was the form.

"This must be Gondreville, is it not, my good woman?" said the young man.

"We don't say 'my good woman' here," said Michu. "We are still simple enough to say 'citizen' and 'citizeness' in these parts."

"Ah!" exclaimed the young man, in a natural way, and without seeming at all annoyed.

Players of ecarte often have a sense of inward disaster when some unknown person sits down at the same table with them, whose manners, look, voice, and method of shuffling the cards, all, to their fancy, foretell defeat. The instant Michu looked at the young man he felt an inward and prophetic collapse. He was struck by a fatal presentiment; he had a sudden confused foreboding of the scaffold. A voice told him that that dandy would destroy him, although there was nothing whatever in common between them. For this reason his answer was rude; he was and he wished to be forbidding.

"Don't you belong to the Councillor of State, Malin?" said the younger man.

"I am my own master," answered Malin.

"Mesdames," said the young man, assuming a most polite air, "are we not at Gondreville? We are expected there by Monsieur Malin."

"There's the park," said Michu, pointing to the open gate.

"Why are you hiding that gun, my fine girl?" said the elder, catching sight of the carbine as he passed through the gate.

"You never let a chance escape you, even in the country!" cried his companion.

They both turned back with a sense of distrust which the bailiff understood at once in spite of their impassible faces. Marthe let them look at the gun, to the tune of Couraut's bark; she was so convinced that her husband was meditating some evil deed that she was thankful for the curiosity of the strangers.

Michu flung a look at his wife which made her tremble; he took the gun and began to load it, accepting quietly the fatal ill-luck of this encounter and the discovery of the weapon. He seemed no longer to care for life, and his wife fathomed his inward feeling.

"So you have wolves in these parts?" said the young man, watching him.

"There are always wolves where there are sheep. You are in Champagne, and there's a forest; we have wild-boars, large and small game both, a little of everything," replied Michu, in a truculent manner.

"I'll bet, Corentin," said the elder of the two men, after exchanging a glance with his companion, "that this is my friend Michu – "

"We never kept pigs together that I know of," said the bailiff.

"No, but we both presided over Jacobins, citizen," replied the old cynic, – "you at Arcis, I elsewhere. I see you've kept your Carmagnole civility, but it's no longer in fashion, my good fellow."

"The park strikes me as rather large; we might lose our way.

If you are really the bailiff show us the path to the chateau," said Corentin, in a peremptory tone.

Michu whistled to his son and continued to load his gun. Corentin looked at Marthe with indifference, while his companion seemed charmed by her; but the young man noticed the signs of her inward distress, which escaped the old libertine, who had, however, noticed and feared the gun. The natures of the two men were disclosed in this trifling yet important circumstance.

"I've an appointment the other side of the forest," said the bailiff. "I can't go with you, but my son here will take you to the chateau. How did you get to Gondreville? did you come by Cinq-Cygne?"

"We had, like yourself, business in the forest," said Corentin, without apparent sarcasm.

"Francois," cried Michu, "take these gentlemen to the chateau by the wood path, so that no one sees them; they don't follow the beaten tracks. Come here," he added, as the strangers turned to walk away, talking together as they did so in a low voice. Michu caught the boy in his arms, and kissed him almost solemnly with an expression which confirmed his wife's fears; cold chills ran down her back; she glanced at her mother with haggard eyes, for she could not weep.

"Go," said Michu; and he watched the boy until he was entirely out of sight. Couraut was barking on the other side of the road in the direction of Grouage. "Oh, that's Violette," remarked Michu. "This is the third time that old fellow has passed here today. What's in the wind? Hush, Couraut!"

A few moments later the trot of a pony was heard approaching.

Chapter II. A Crime Relinquished

Violette, mounted on one of those little nags which the farmers in the neighborhood of Paris use so much, soon appeared, wearing a round hat with a broad brim, beneath which his wood-colored face, deeply wrinkled, appeared in shadow. His gray eyes, mischievous and lively, concealed in a measure the treachery of his nature. His skinny legs, covered with gaiters of white linen which came to the knee, hung rather than rested in the stirrups, seemingly held in place by the weight of his hob-nailed shoes. Above his jacket of blue cloth he wore a cloak of some coarse woollen stuff woven in black and white stripes. His gray hair fell in curls behind his ears. This dress, the gray horse with its short legs, the manner in which Violette sat him, stomach projecting and shoulders thrown back, the big chapped hands which held the shabby bridle, all depicted him plainly as the grasping, ambitious peasant who desires to own land and buys it at any price. His mouth, with its bluish lips parted as if a surgeon had pried them open with a scalpel, and the innumerable wrinkles of his face and forehead hindered the play of features which were expressive only in their outlines. Those hard, fixed lines seemed menacing, in spite of the humility which country-folks assume and beneath which they conceal their emotions and schemes, as savages and Easterns hide theirs behind an imperturbable gravity. First a mere laborer, then the farmer of Grouage through a long course of persistent ill-doing, he continued his evil practices after conquering a position which surpassed his early hopes. He wished harm to all men and wished it vehemently. When he could assist in doing harm he did it eagerly. He was openly envious; but, no matter how malignant he might be, he kept within the limits of the law, – neither beyond it nor behind it, like a parliamentary opposition. He believed his prosperity depended on the ruin of others, and that whoever was above him was an enemy against whom all weapons were good. A character like this is very common among the peasantry.

Violette's present business was to obtain from Malin an extension of the lease of his farm, which had only six years longer to run. Jealous of the bailiff's means, he watched him narrowly. The neighbors reproached him for his intimacy with "Judas"; but the sly old farmer, wishing to obtain a twelve years' lease, was really lying in wait for an opportunity to serve either the government or Malin, who distrusted Michu. Violette, by the help of the game-keeper of Gondreville and others belonging to the estate, kept Malin informed of all Michu's actions. Malin had endeavored, fruitlessly, to win over Marianne, the Michus' servant-woman; but Violette and his satellites heard everything from Gaucher, – a lad on whose fidelity Michu relied, but who betrayed him for cast-off clothing, waistcoats, buckles, cotton socks and sugar-plums. The boy had no suspicion of the importance of his gossip. Violette in his reports blackened all Michu's actions and gave them a criminal aspect by absurd suggestions, – unknown, of course, to the bailiff, who was aware, however, of the base part played by the farmer, and took delight in mystifying him.

"You must have a deal of business at Bellache to be here again," said Michu.

"Again! is that meant as a reproach, Monsieur Michu? – Hey! I did not know you had that gun. You are not going to whistle for the sparrows on that pipe, I suppose – "

"It grew in a field of mine which bears guns," replied Michu. "Look! this is how I sow them."

The bailiff took aim at a viper thirty feet away and cut it in two.

"Have you got that bandit's weapon to protect your master?" said Violette. "Perhaps he gave it to you."

"He came from Paris expressly to bring it to me," replied Michu.

"People are talking all round the neighborhood of this jour-ney of his; some say he is in disgrace and has to retire from office; others that he wants to see things for himself down here. But anyway, why does he come, like the First Consul, without giving warning? Did you know he was coming?"

"I am not on such terms with him as to be in his confidence."

19

"Then you have not seen him?"

"I did not know he was here till I got back from my rounds in the forest," said Michu, reloading his gun.

"He has sent to Arcis for Monsieur Grevin," said Violette; "they are scheming something."

"If you are going round by Cinq-Cygne, take me up behind you," said the bailiff. "I'm going there."

Violette was too timid to have a man of Michu's strength on his crupper, and he spurred his beast. Judas slung his gun over his shoulder and walked rapidly up the avenue.

"Who can it be that Michu is angry with?" said Marthe to her mother.

"Ever since he heard of Monsieur Malin's arrival he has been gloomy," replied the old woman. "But it is getting damp here, let us go in."

After the two women had settled themselves in the chimney corner they heard Couraut's bark.

"There's my husband returning!" cried Marthe.

Michu passed up the stairs; his wife, uneasy, followed him to their bedroom.

"See if any one is about," he said to her, in a voice of some emotion.

"No one," she replied. "Marianne is in the field with the cow, and Gaucher – "

"Where is Gaucher?" he asked.

"I don't know."

"I distrust that little scamp. Go up in the garret, look in the hay-loft, look everywhere for him."

Marthe left the room to obey the order. When she returned she found Michu on his knees, praying.

"What is the matter?" she said, frightened.

The bailiff took his wife round the waist and drew her to him, saying in a voice of deep feeling: "If we never see each other again remember, my poor wife, that I loved you well. Follow minutely the instructions which you will find in a letter buried at the foot of the larch in that copse. It is enclosed in a tin tube. Do not touch it until after my death. And remember, Marthe, whatever happens to me, that in spite of man's injustice, my arm has been the instrument of the justice of God."

Marthe, who turned pale by degrees, became white as her own linen; she looked at her husband with fixed eyes widened by fear; she tried to speak, but her throat was dry. Michu disappeared like a shadow, having tied Couraut to the foot of his bed where the dog, after the manner of all dogs, howled in despair.

Michu's anger against Monsieur Marion had serious grounds, but it was now concentrated on another man, far more criminal in his eyes, – on Malin, whose secrets were known to the bailiff, he being in a better position than others to understand the conduct of the State Councillor. Michu's father-in-law had had, politically speaking, the confidence of the former representative to the Convention, through Grevin.

Perhaps it would be well here to relate the circumstances which brought the Simeuse and the Cinq-Cygne families into connection with Malin, – circumstances which weighed heavily on the fate of Mademoiselle de Cinq-Cygne's twin cousins, but still more heavily on that of Marthe and Michu.

The Cinq-Cygne mansion at Troyes stands opposite to that of Simeuse. When the populace, incited by minds that were as shrewd as they were cautious, pillaged the hotel Simeuse, discovered the marquis and marchioness, who were accused of corresponding with the nation's enemies, and delivered them to the national guards who took them to prison, the crowd shouted, "Now for the Cinq-Cygnes!" To their minds the Cinq-Cygnes were as guilty as other aristocrats. The brave and worthy Monsieur de Simeuse in the endeavor to save his two sons, then eighteen years of age, whose courage was likely to compromise them, had confided them, a few hours before the storm broke, to their aunt, the Comtesse de Cinq-Cygne. Two servants attached to the Simeuse family accompanied the young men to her house. The old marquis, who was anxious that his name should not die out, requested that what was happening might be concealed from his sons, even in the event of dire disaster. Laurence, the only daughter of the Comtesse de Cinq-Cygne, was then twelve years of age; her cousins both loved her and she loved them equally. Like other twins the Simeuse brothers were so alike that for a long while their mother dressed them in different colors to know them apart. The first comer, the eldest, was named Paul-Marie, the other Marie-Paul. Laurence de Cinq-Cygne, to whom their danger was revealed, played her woman's part well though still a mere child. She coaxed and petted her cousins and kept them occupied until the very moment when the populace surrounded the Cinq-Cygne mansion. The two brothers then knew their danger for the first time, and looked at each other. Their resolution was instantly taken; they armed their own servants and those of the Comtesse de Cinq-Cygne, barricaded the doors, and stood guard at the windows, after closing the wooden blinds, with the five men-servants and the Abbe d'Hauteserre, a relative of the Cinq-Cygnes. These eight courageous champions poured a deadly fire into the crowd. Every shot killed or wounded an assailant. Laurence, instead of wringing her hands, loaded the guns with extraordinary coolness, and passed the balls and powder to those who needed them. The Comtesse de Cinq-Cygne was on her knees.

"What are you doing, mother?" said Laurence.

"I am praying," she answered, "for them and for you."

Sublime words, – said also by the mother of Godoy, prince of the Peace, in Spain, under similar circumstances.

In a moment eleven persons were killed and lying on the ground among a number of wounded. Such results either cool or excite a populace; either it grows savage at the work or discontinues it. On the present occasion those in advance recoiled; but the crowd behind them were there to kill and rob, and when they saw their own dead, they cried out: "Murder! Murder! Revenge!"

The wiser heads went in search of the representative to the Convention, Malin. The twins, by this time aware of the disastrous events of the day, suspected Malin of desiring the ruin of their family, and of causing the arrest of their parents, and the suspicion soon became a certainty. They posted themselves beneath the porte-cochere, gun in hand, intending to kill Malin as soon as he made his appearance; but the countess lost her head; she imagined her house in ashes and her daughter assassinated, and she blamed the young men for their heroic defence and compelled them to desist. It was Laurence who opened the door slightly when Malin summoned the household to admit him. Seeing her, the representative relied upon the awe he expected to inspire in a mere child, and he entered the house. To his first words of inquiry as to why the family were making such a resistance, the girl replied: "If you really desire to give liberty to France how is it that you do not protect us in our homes? They are trying to tear down this house, monsieur, to murder us, and you say we have no right to oppose force to force!"

Malin stood rooted to the ground.

"You, the son of a mason employed by the Grand Marquis to build his castle!" exclaimed Marie-Paul, "you have let them drag our father to prison – you have believed calumnies!"

"He shall be released at once," said Malin, who thought himself lost when he saw each youth clutch his weapon convulsively.

"You owe your life to that promise," said Marie-Paul, solemnly. "If it is not fulfilled to-night we shall find you again."

"As to that howling populace," said Laurence, "If you do not send them away, the next blood will be yours. Now, Monsieur Malin, leave this house!"

The Conventionalist did leave it, and he harangued the crowd, dwelling on the sacred rights of the domestic hearth, the habeas corpus and the English "home." He told them that the law and the people were sovereigns, that the law *was* the people, and that the people could only act through the law, and that power was vested in the law. The particular law of personal necessity made him eloquent, and he managed to disperse the crowd. But he never forgot the contemptuous expression of the two brothers, nor the "Leave this house!" of Mademoiselle de Cinq-Cygne. Therefore, when it was a question of selling the estates of the Comte de Cinq-Cygne, Laurence's brother, as national property, the sale was rigorously made. The agents left nothing for Laurence but the chateau, the park and gardens, and one farm called that of Cinq-Cygne. Malin instructed the appraisers that Laurence had no rights beyond her legal share, – the nation taking possession of all that belonged to her brother, who had emigrated and, above all, had borne arms against the Republic.

The evening after this terrible tumult, Laurence so entreated her cousins to leave the country, fearing treachery on the part of Malin, or some trap into which they might fall, that they took horse that night and gained the Prussian outposts. They had scarcely reached the forest of Gondreville before the hotel Cinq-Cygne was surrounded; Malin came himself to arrest the heirs of the house of Simeuse. He dared not lay hands on the Comtesse de Cinq-Cygne, who was in bed with a nervous fever, nor on Laurence, a child of twelve. The servants, fearing the severity of the Republic, had disappeared. The next day the news of the resistance of the brothers and their flight to Prussia was known to the neighborhood. A crowd of three thousand persons assembled before the hotel de Cinq-Cygne, which was demolished with incredible rapidity. Madame de Cinq-Cygne, carried to the hotel Simeuse, died there from the effects of the fever aggravated by terror.

Michu did not appear in the political arena until after these events, for the marquis and his wife remained in prison over five months. During this time Malin was away on a mission. But when Monsieur Marion sold Gondreville to the Councillor of State, Michu understood the latter's game, – or rather, he thought he did; for Malin was, like Fouche, one of those personages who are of such depth in all their different aspects that they are impenetrable when they play a part, and are never understood until long after their drama is ended.

In all the chief circumstances of Malin's life he had never

failed to consult his faithful friend Grevin, the notary of Arcis, whose judgment on men and things was, at a distance, clear-cut and precise. This faculty is the wisdom and makes the strength of second-rate men. Now, in November, 1803, a combination of events (already related in the "Depute d'Arcis") made matters so serious for the Councillor of State that a letter might have compromised the two friends. Malin, who hoped to be appointed senator, was afraid to offer his explanations in Paris. He came to Gondreville, giving the First Consul only one of the reasons that made him wish to be there; that reason gave him an appearance of zeal in the eyes of Bonaparte; whereas his journey, far from concerning the interests of the State, related to his own interests only. On this particular day, as Michu was watching the park and expecting, after the manner of a red Indian, a propitious moment for his vengeance, the astute Malin, accustomed to turn all events to his own profit, was leading his friend Grevin to a little field in the English garden, a lonely spot in the park, favorable for a secret conference. There, standing in the centre of the grass plot and speaking low, the friends were at too great a distance to be overheard if any one were lurking near enough to listen to them; they were also sure of time to change the conversation if others unwarily approached.

"Why couldn't we have stayed in a room in the chateau?" asked Grevin.

"Didn't you take notice of those two men whom the prefect of police has sent here to me?"

Though Fouche made himself in the matter of the Pichegru, Georges, Moreau, and Polignac conspiracy the soul of the Consular cabinet, he did not at this time control the ministry of police, but was merely a councillor of State like Malin.

"Those men," continued Malin, "are Fouche's two arms. One, that dandy Corentin, whose face is like a glass of lemonade, vinegar on his lips and verjuice in his eyes, put an end to the insurrection at the West in the year VII. in less than fifteen days. The other is a disciple of Lenoir; he is the only one who preserves the great traditions of the police. I had asked for an agent of no great account, backed by some official personage, and they send me those past-masters of the business! Ah, Grevin, Fouche wants to pry into my game. That's why I left those fellows dining at the chateau; they may look into everything for all I care; they won't find Louis XVIII. nor any sign of him."

"But see here, my dear fellow, what game are you playing?" cried Grevin.

"Ha, my friend, a double game is a dangerous one, but this, taking Fouche into account, is a triple one. He may have nosed the fact that I am in the secrets of the house of Bourbon."

"You?"

"I," replied Malin.

"Have you forgotten Favras?"

The words made an impression on the councillor.

"Since when?" asked Grevin, after a pause.

"Since the Consulate for life."

"I hope there's no proof of it?"

"Not that!" said Malin, clicking his thumb-nail against his teeth.

In few words the Councillor of State gave a clear and succinct account of the critical position in which Bonaparte was about to hold England, by threatening her with invasion from the camp at Boulogne; he explained to Grevin the bearings of that project, which was unobserved by France and Europe but suspected by Pitt; also the critical position in which England was about to put Bonaparte. A powerful coalition, Prussia, Austria, and Russia, paid by English gold, was pledged to furnish seven hundred thousand men under arms. At the same time a formidable conspiracy was throwing a network over the whole of France, including among its members montagnards, chouans, royalists, and their princes.

"Louis XVIII. held that as long as there were three Consuls

anarchy was certain, and that he could at some opportune moment take his revenge for the 13th Vendemiaire and the 18th
Fructidor," said Malin, "but the Consulate for life has unmasked
Bonaparte's intentions – he will soon be emperor. The late sub-
lieutenant means to create a dynasty! This time his life is in actual
danger; and the plot is far better laid than that of the Rue Saint-
Nicaise. Pichegru, Georges, Moreau, the Duc d'Enghien, Polignac
and Riviere, the two friends of the Comte d'Artois are in it."

"What an amalgamation!" cried Grevin.

"France is being silently invaded; no stone is left unturned;
the thing will be carried with a rush. A hundred picked men,
commanded by Georges, are to attack the Consular guard and the
Consul hand to hand."

"Well then, denounce them."

"For the last two months the Consul, his minister of police,
the prefect and Fouche, hold some of the clues of this vast conspiracy; but they don't know its full extent, and at this particular
moment they are leaving nearly all the conspirators free, so as to
discover more about it."

"As to rights," said the notary, "the Bourbons have much
more right to conceive, plan, and execute a scheme against Bonaparte, than Bonaparte had on the 18th Brumaire against the Republic, whose product he was. He murdered his mother on that
occasion, but these royalists only seek to recover what was theirs.
I can understand that the princes and their adherents, seeing the
lists of the *emigres* closed, mortgages suppressed, the Catholic
faith restored, anti-revolutionary decrees accumulating, should
begin to see that their return is becoming difficult, not to say impossible. Bonaparte being the sole obstacle now in their way, they
want to get rid of him – nothing simpler. Conspirators if defeated
are brigands, if successful, heroes; and your perplexity seems to
me very natural."

"The matter now is," said Malin, "to make Bonaparte fling
the head of the Duc d'Enghien at the Bourbons, just as the Convention flung the head of Louis XVI. at the kings, so as to commit

him as fully as we are to the Revolution; *or else*, we must upset the idol of the French people and their future emperor, and seat the true throne upon his ruins. I am at the mercy of some event, some fortunate pistol-shot, some infernal machine which does its work. Even I don't know the whole conspiracy; they don't tell me all; but they have asked me to call the Council of State at the critical moment and direct its action towards the restoration of the Bourbons."

"Wait," said the notary.

"Impossible! I am compelled to make my decision at once."

"Why?"

"Well, the Simeuse brothers are in the conspiracy; they are here in the neighborhood; I must either have them watched, let them compromise themselves, and so be rid of them, or else I must privately protect them. I asked the prefect for underlings and he has sent me lynxes, who came through Troyes and have got the gendarmerie to support them."

"Gondreville is your real object," said Grevin, "and this conspiracy your best chance of keeping it. Fouche, Talleyrand, and those two fellows have nothing to do with that. Therefore play fair with them. What nonsense! those who cut Louis XVI.'s head off are in the government; France is full of men who have bought national property, and yet you talk of bringing back those who would require you to give up Gondreville! If the Bourbons were not imbeciles they would pass a sponge over all we have done. Warn Bonaparte, that's my advice."

"A man of my rank can't denounce," said Malin, quickly.

"Your rank!" exclaimed Grevin, smiling.

"They have offered to make me Keeper of the Seals."

"Ah! Now I understand your bewilderment, and it is for me to see clear in this political darkness and find a way out for you. Now, it is quite impossible to foresee what events may happen to bring back the Bourbons when a General Bonaparte is in possession of eighty line of battle ships and four hundred thousand men. The most difficult thing of all in expectant politics is to know when a power that totters will fall; but, my old man, Bonaparte's power is not tottering, it is in the ascendant. Don't you think that Fouche may be sounding you so as to get to the bottom of your mind, and then get rid of you?"

"No; I am sure of my go-between. Besides, Fouche would never, under those circumstances, send me such fellows as these; he would know they would make me suspicious."

"They alarm me," said Grevin. "If Fouche does not distrust you, and is not seeking to probe you, why does he send them? Fouche doesn't play such a trick as that without a motive; what is it?"

"What decides me," said Malin, "is that I should never be easy with those two Simeuse brothers in France. Perhaps Fouche, who knows how I am placed towards them, wants to make sure they don't escape him, and hopes through them to reach the Condes."

"That's right, old fellow; it is not under Bonaparte that the present possessor of Gondreville can be ousted."

Just then Malin, happening to look up, saw the muzzle of a gun through the foliage of a tall linden.

"I was not mistaken, I thought I heard the click of a trigger," he said to Grevin, after getting behind the trunk of a large tree, where the notary, uneasy at his friend's sudden movement, followed him.

"It is Michu," said Grevin; "I see his red beard."

"Don't let us seem afraid," said Malin, who walked slowly away, saying at intervals: "Why is that man so bitter against the owners of this property? It was not you he was covering. If he overheard us he had better ask the prayers of the congregation! Who the devil would have thought of looking up into the trees!"

"There's always something to learn," said the notary. "But he was a good distance off, and we spoke low."

"I shall tell Corentin about it," replied Malin.

Chapter III. The Mask Thrown Off

A few moments later Michu returned home, his face pale, his features contracted.

"What is the matter?" said his wife, frightened.

"Nothing," he replied, seeing Violette whose presence silenced him.

Michu took a chair and sat down quietly before the fire, into which he threw a letter which he drew from a tin tube such as are given to soldiers to hold their papers. This act, which enabled Marthe to draw a long breath like one relieved of a great burden, greatly puzzled Violette. The bailiff laid his gun on the mantelshelf with admirable composure. Marianne the servant, and Marthe's mother were spinning by the light of a lamp.

"Come, Francois," said the father, presently, "it is time to go to bed."

He lifted the boy roughly by the middle of his body and carried him off.

"Run down to the cellar," he whispered, when they reached the stairs. "Empty one third out of two bottles of the Macon wine, and fill them up with the Cognac brandy which is on the shelf. Then mix a bottle of white wine with one half brandy. Do it neatly, and put the three bottles on the empty cask which stands by the cellar door. When you hear me open the window in the kitchen come out of the cellar, run to the stable, saddle my horse, mount it, and go and wait for me at Poteaudes-Gueux – That little scamp hates to go to bed," said Michu, returning; "he likes to do as grown people do, see all, hear all, and know all. You spoil my people, pere Violette."

"Goodness!" cried Violette, "what has loosened your tongue? I never heard you say as much before."

"Do you suppose I let myself be spied upon without taking notice of it? You are on the wrong side, pere Violette. If, instead of serving those who hate me, you were on my side I could do better for you than renew that lease of yours."

"How?" said the peasant, opening wide his avaricious eyes.

"I'll sell you my property cheap."

"Nothing is cheap when we have to pay," said Violette, sententiously.

"I want to leave the neighborhood, and I'll let you have my farm of Mousseau, the buildings, granary, and cattle for fifty thousand francs."

"Really?"

"Does that suit you?"

"Hang it! I must think – "

"We'll talk about it – I shall want earnest money."

"I have no money."

"Well, a note."

"Can't give it."

"Tell me who sent you here to-day."

"I am on my way back from where I spent this afternoon, and I only stopped in to say good-evening."

"Back without your horse? What a fool you must take me for! You are lying, and you shall not have my farm."

"Well, to tell you the truth, it was monsieur Grevin who sent me. He said 'Violette, we want Michu; do you go and get him; if he isn't at home, wait for him.' I saw I should have to stay here all this evening."

"Are those sharks from Paris still at the chateau?"

"Ah! that I don't know; but there were people in the salon."

"You shall have my farm; we'll settle the terms now. Wife, go and get some wine to wash down the contract. Take the best Roussillon, the wine of the ex-marquis, – we are not babes. You'll find a couple of bottles on the empty cask near the door, and a bottle of white wine."

"Very good," said Violette, who never got drunk. "Let us drink."

"You have fifty thousand francs beneath the floor of your bedroom under your bed, pere Violette; you will give them to me two weeks after we sign the deed of sale before Grevin – " Violette stared at Michu and grew livid. "Ah! you came here to spy upon a Jacobin who had the honor to be president of the club at Arcis, and you imagine he will let you get the better of him! I have eyes, I saw where your tiles have been freshly cemented, and I concluded that you did not pry them up to plant wheat there. Come, drink."

Violette, much troubled, drank a large glass of wine without noticing the quality; terror had put a hot iron in his stomach, the brandy was not hotter than his cupidity. He would have given many things to be safely home and able to change the hiding-place of his treasure. The three women smiled.

"Do you like that wine?" said Michu, refilling his glass.

"Yes, I do."

After a good half-hour's decision on the time when the buyer might take possession, and on the various punctilios which the peasantry bring forward when concluding a bargain, – in the midst of assertions and counter-assertions, the filling and empty-ing of glasses, the giving of promises and denials, Violette sud-denly fell forward with his head on the table, not tipsy, but dead-drunk. The instant that Michu saw his eyes blur he opened the window.

"Where's that scamp, Gaucher?" he said to his wife.

"In bed."

"You, Marianne," said the bailiff to his faithful servant, "stand in front of his door and watch him. You, mother, stay down here, and keep an eye on this spy; keep your eyes and ears open and don't unfasten the door to any one but Francois. It is a question of life or death," he added, in a deep voice. "Every creature beneath my roof must remember that I have not quitted it this night; all of you must assert that – even though your heads were on the block. Come," he said to Marthe, "come, wife, put on your shoes, take your coat, and let us be off! No questions – I go with you."

For the last three quarters of an hour the man's demeanor and glance were of despotic authority, all-powerful, irresistible, drawn from the same mysterious source from which great generals on fields of battle who inflame an army, great orators inspiring vast audiences, and (it must be said) great criminals perpetrating bold crimes derive their inspiration. At such times invincible influence seems to exhale from the head and issue from the tongue; the gesture even can inject the will of the one man into others. The three women knew that some dreadful crisis was at hand; without warning of its nature they felt it in the rapid actions of the man, whose countenance shone, whose forehead spoke, whose brilliant eyes glittered like stars; they saw it in the sweat that covered his brow to the roots of his hair, while more than once his voice vibrated with impatience and fury. Marthe obeyed passively. Armed to the teeth and with his gun over his shoulder Michu dashed into the avenue, followed by his wife. They soon reached the cross-roads where Francois was in waiting hidden among the bushes.

"The boy is intelligent," said Michu, when he caught sight of him.

These were his first words. His wife had rushed after him, unable to speak.

"Go back to the house, hide in a thick tree, and watch the country and the park," he said to his son. "We have all gone to bed, no one is stirring. Your grandmother will not open the door until you ask her to let you in. Remember every word I say to you. The life of your father and mother depends on it. No one must know we did not sleep at home."

After whispering these words to the boy, who instantly disappeared in the forest like an eel in the mud, Michu turned to his wife.

"Mount behind me," he said, "and pray that God be with us. Sit firm, the beast may die of it." So saying he kicked the horse with both heels, pressing him with his powerful knees, and the animal sprang forward with the rapidity of a hunter, seeming to understand what his master wanted of him, and crossed the forest in fifteen minutes. Then Michu, who had not swerved from the shortest way, pulled up, found a spot at the edge of the woods from which he could see the roofs of the chateau of Cinq-Cygne lighted by the moon, tied his horse to a tree, and followed by his wife, gained a little eminence which overlooked the valley.

The chateau, which Marthe and Michu looked at together for a moment, makes a charming effect in the landscape. Though it has little extent and is of no importance whatever as architecture, yet archaeologically it is not without a certain interest. This old edifice of the fifteenth century, placed on an eminence, surrounded on all sides by a moat, or rather by deep, wide ditches always full of water, is built in cobble-stones buried in cement, the walls being seven feet thick. Its simplicity recalls the rough and warlike life of feudal days. The chateau, plain and unadorned, has two large reddish towers at either end, connected by a long main building with casement windows, the stone mullions of which, being roughly carved, bear some resemblance to vine-shoots. The stairway is outside the house, at the middle, in a sort of pentagonal tower entered through a small arched door. The interior of the ground-floor together with the rooms on the first storey were modernized in the time of Louis XIV., and the whole building is surmounted by an immense roof broken by casement windows with carved triangular pediments. Before the castle lies a vast green sward the trees of which had recently been cut down. On either side of the entrance bridge are two small dwellings where the gardeners live, connected across the road by a paltry iron railing without character, evidently modern. To right and left of the lawn, which is divided in two by a paved roadway, are the stables, cow-sheds, barns, wood-house, bakery, poultry-yard, and the offices, placed in what were doubtless the remains of two wings of the old building similar to those that were still standing. The two large towers, with their pepper-pot roofs which had not been rased, and the belfry of the middle tower, gave an air of distinction to the village. The church, also very old, showed near by its pointed steeple, which harmonized well with the solid masses of the castle. The moon brought out in full relief the various roofs and towers on which it played and sparkled.

Michu gazed at this baronial structure in a manner that upset all his wife's ideas about him; his face, now calm, wore a look of hope and also a sort of pride. His eyes scanned the horizon with a glance of defiance; he listened for sounds in the air. It was now nine o'clock; the moon was beginning to cast its light upon the margin of the forest and to illumine the little bluff on which they stood. The position struck him as dangerous and he left it, fearful of being seen. But no suspicious noise troubled the peace of the beautiful valley encircled on this side by the forest of Nodesme. Marthe, exhausted and trembling, was awaiting some explanation of their hurried ride. What was she engaged in? Was she to aid in a good deed or an evil one? At that instant Michu bent to his wife's ear and whispered: –

"Go the house and ask to speak to the Comtesse de Cinq-Cygne; when you see her beg her to speak to you alone. If no one can overhear you, say to her: 'Mademoiselle, the lives of your two cousins are in danger, and he who can explain the how and why is waiting to speak to you.' If she seems afraid, if she distrusts you, add these words: 'They are conspiring against the First Consul and the conspiracy is discovered.' Don't give your name; they distrust us too much."

Marthe raised her face towards her husband and said: –

"Can it be that you serve them?"

"What if I do?" he said, frowning, taking her words as a reproach.

"You don't understand me," cried Marthe, seizing his large hand and falling on her knees beside him as she kissed it and covered it with her tears.

"Go, go, you shall cry later," he said, kissing her vehemently.

When he no longer heard her step his eyes filled with tears.

He had distrusted Marthe on account of her father's opinions; he had hidden the secrets of his life from her; but the beauty of her simple nature had suddenly appeared to him, just as the grandeur of his had, as suddenly, revealed itself to her. Marthe had passed in a moment from the deep humiliation caused by the degradation of the man whose name she bore, to the exaltation given by a sense of his nobleness. The change was instantaneous, without transition; it was enough to make her tremble. She told him later that she went, as it were, through blood from the pavilion to the edge of the forest, and there was lifted to heaven, in a moment, among the angels. Michu, who had known he was not appreciated, and who mistook his wife's grieved and melancholy manner for lack of affection, and had left her to herself, living chiefly out of doors and reserving all his tenderness for his boy, instantly understood the meaning of her tears. She had cursed the part which her beauty and her father's will had forced her to take; but now happiness, in the midst of this great storm, played, with a beautiful flame like a vivid lightning about them. And it was lightning! Each thought of the last ten years of misconception, and they blamed themselves only. Michu stood motionless, his elbow on his gun, his chin on his hand, lost in deep reverie. Such a moment in a man's life makes him willing to accept the saddest moments of a painful past.

Marthe, agitated by the same thoughts as those of her husband, was also troubled in heart by the danger of the Simeuse brothers; for she now understood all, even the faces of the two Parisians, though she still could not explain to herself her husband's gun. She darted forward like a doe, and soon reached the road to the chateau. There she was surprised by the steps of a man following behind her; she turned, with a cry, and her husband's large hand closed her mouth.

"From the hill up there I saw the silver lace of the gendarmes' hats. Go in by the breach in the moat between Mademoiselle's tower and the stables. The dogs won't bark at you. Go through the garden and call the countess by the window; order them to saddle her horse, and ask her to come out through the breach. I'll be there, after discovering what the Parisians are planning, and how to escape them."

Danger, which seemed to be rolling like an avalanche upon them, gave wings to Marthe's feet.

Chapter IV. Laurence De Cinq-Cygne

The old Frank name of the Cinq-Cygnes and the Charge-boeufs was Duineff. Cinq-Cygne became that of the younger branch of the Chargeboeufs after the defence of a castle made, during their father's absence, by five daughters of that race, all remarkably fair, and of whom no one expected such heroism. One of the first Comtes de Champagne wished, by bestowing this pretty name, to perpetuate the memory of their deed as long as the family existed. Laurence, the last of her race, was, contrary to Salic law, heiress of the name, the arms, and the manor. She was therefore Comtesse de Cinq-Cygne in her own right; her husband would have to take both her name and her blazon, which bore for device the glorious answer made by the elder of the five sisters when summoned to surrender the castle, "We die singing." Worthy descendant of these noble heroines, Laurence was fair and lily-white as though nature had made her for a wager. The lines of her blue veins could be seen through the delicate close texture of her skin. Her beautiful golden hair harmonized delightfully with eyes of the deepest blue. Everything about her belonged to the type of delicacy. Within that fragile though active body, and in defiance as it were of its pearly whiteness, lived a soul like that of a man of noble nature; but no one, not even a close observer, would have suspected it from the gentle countenance and rounded features which, when seen in profile, bore some slight resemblance to those of a lamb. This extreme gentleness, though noble, had something of the stupidity of the little animal. "I look like a dreamy sheep," she would say, smiling. Laurence, who talked little, seemed not so much dreamy as dormant. But, did any important circumstance arise, the hidden Judith was revealed, sublime; and circumstances had, unfortunately, not been wanting.

At thirteen years of age, Laurence, after the events already related, was an orphan living in a house opposite to the empty space where so recently had stood one of the most curious specimens in France of sixteenth-century architecture, the hotel Cinq-Cygne. Monsieur d'Hauteserre, her relation, now her guardian, took the young heiress to live in the country at her chateau of

Cinq-Cygne. That brave provincial gentleman, alarmed at the death of his brother, the Abbe d'Hauteserre, who was shot in the open square as he was about to escape in the dress of a peasant, was not in a position to defend the interests of his ward. He had two sons in the army of the princes, and every day, at the slightest unusual sound, he believed that the municipals of Arcis were coming to arrest him. Laurence, proud of having sustained a siege and of possessing the historic whiteness of her swan-like ancestors, despised the prudent cowardice of the old man who bent to the storm, and dreamed only of distinguishing herself. So, she boldly hung the portrait of Charlotte Corday on the walls of her poor salon at Cinq-Cygne, and crowned it with oak-leaves. She corresponded by messenger with her twin cousins, in defiance of the law, which punished the act, when discovered, with death. The messenger, who risked his life, brought back the answers. Laurence lived only, after the catastrophes at Troyes, for the triumph of the royal cause. After soberly judging Monsieur and Madame d'Hauteserre (who lived with her at the chateau de Cinq-Cygne), and recognizing their honest, but stolid natures, she put them outside the lines of her own life. She had, moreover, too good a mind and too sound a judgment to complain of their natures; always kind, amiable, and affectionate towards them, she nevertheless told them none of her secrets. Nothing forms a character so much as the practice of constant concealment in the bosom of a family.

After she attained her majority Laurence allowed Monsieur d'Hauteserre to manage her affairs as in the past. So long as her favorite mare was well-groomed, her maid Catherine dressed to please her, and Gothard the little page was suitably clothed, she cared for nothing else. Her thoughts were aimed too high to come down to occupations and interests which in other times than these would doubtless have pleased her. Dress was a small matter to her mind; moreover her cousins were not there to see her. She wore a dark-green habit when she rode, and a gown of some common woollen stuff with a cape trimmed with braid when she walked; in the house she was always seen in a silk wrapper. Gothard, the little groom, a brave and clever lad of fifteen, attended her wherever she went, and she was nearly always out of doors, riding or hunting over the farms of Gondreville, without objection being made by either Michu or the farmers. She rode admirably well, and her cleverness in hunting was thought miraculous. In the country she was never called anything but "Mademoiselle" even during the Revolution.

Whoever has read the fine romance of "Rob Roy" will remember that rare woman for whose making Walter Scott's imagination abandoned its customary coldness, – Diana Vernon. The recollection will serve to make Laurence understood if, to the noble qualities of the Scottish huntress you add the restrained exaltation of Charlotte Corday, surpassing, however, the charming vivacity which rendered Diana so attractive. The young countess had seen her mother die, the Abbe d'Hauteserre shot down, the Marquis de Simeuse and his wife executed; her only brother had died of his wounds; her two cousins serving in Conde's army might be killed at any moment; and, finally, the fortunes of the Simeuse and the Cinq-Cygne families had been seized and wasted by the Republic without being of any benefit to the nation. Her grave demeanor, now lapsing into apparent stolidity, can be readily understood.

Monsieur d'Hauteserre proved an upright and most careful guardian. Under his administration Cinq-Cygne became a sort of farm. The good man, who was far more of a close manager than a knight of the old nobility, had turned the park and gardens to profit, and used their two hundred acres of grass and woodland as pasturage for horses and fuel for the family. Thanks to his severe economy the countess, on coming of age, had recovered by his investments in the State funds a competent fortune. In 1798 she possessed about twenty thousand francs a year from those sources, on which, in fact, some dividends were still due, and twelve thousand francs a year from the rentals at Cinq-Cygne, which had lately been renewed at a notable increase. Monsieur and Madame d'Hauteserre had provided for their old age by the purchase of an annuity of three thousand francs in the Tontines Lafarge. That fragment of their former means did not enable them to live elsewhere than at Cinq-Cygne, and Laurence's first act on coming to her majority was to give them the use for life of the wing of the chateau which they occupied.

The Hauteserres, as niggardly for their ward as they were for themselves, laid up every year nearly the whole of their annuity for the benefit of their sons, and kept the young heiress on miserable fare. The whole cost of the Cinq-Cygne household never exceeded five thousand francs a year. But Laurence, who condescended to no details, was satisfied. Her guardian and his wife, unconsciously ruled by the imperceptible influence of her strong character, which was felt even in little things, had ended by admiring her whom they had known and treated as a child, – a sufficiently rare feeling. But in her manner, her deep voice, her commanding eye, Laurence held that inexplicable power which rules all men, – even when its strength is mere appearance. To vulgar minds real depth is incomprehensible; it is perhaps for that reason that the populace is so prone to admire what it cannot understand. Monsieur and Madame d'Hauteserre, impressed by the habitual silence and erratic habits of the young girl, were constantly expecting some extraordinary thing of her.

Laurence, who did good intelligently and never allowed herself to be deceived, was held in the utmost respect by the peasantry although she was an aristocrat. Her sex, name, and great misfortunes, also the originality of her present life, contributed to give her authority over the inhabitants of the valley of Cinq-Cygne. She was sometimes absent for two days, attended by Gothard, but neither Monsieur nor Madame d'Hauteserre questioned her, on her return, as to the reasons of her absence. Please observe, however, that there was nothing odd or eccentric about Laurence. What she was and what she did was masked, as it were, by a feminine and even fragile appearance. Her heart was full of extreme sensibility, though her head contained a stoical firmness and the virile gift of resolution. Her clear-seeing eyes knew not how to weep; but no one would have imagined that the delicate white wrist with its tracery of blue veins could defy that of the boldest horseman. Her hand, so noble, so flexible, could handle gun or pistol with the ease of a practised marksman. She always wore when out of doors the coquettish little cap with visor and green veil which women wear on horseback. Her delicate fair face, thus protected, and her white throat tied with a black cravat, were never injured by her long rides in all weathers.

Under the Directory and at the beginning of the Consulate, Laurence had been able to escape the observation of others; but since the government had become a more settled thing, the new authorities, the prefect of the Aube, Malin's friends, and Malin himself had endeavored to undermine her in the community. Her preoccupying thought was the overthrow of Bonaparte, whose ambition and its triumphs excited the anger of her soul, – a cold, deliberate anger. The obscure and hidden enemy of a man at the pinnacle of glory, she kept her gaze upon him from the depths of her valley and her forests, with relentless fixity; there were times when she thought of killing him in the roads about Malmaison or Saint-Cloud. Plans for the execution of this idea may have been the cause of many of her past actions, but having been initiated, after the peace of Amiens, into the conspiracy of the men who expected to make the 18th Brumaire recoil upon the First Consul, she had thenceforth subordinated her faculties and her hatred to their vast and well laid scheme, which was to strike at Bonaparte externally by the vast coalition of Russia, Austria, and Prussia (vanquished at Austerlitz) and internally by the coalition of men politically opposed to each other, but united by their common hatred of a man whose death some of them were meditating, like Laurence herself, without shrinking from the word assassination. This young girl, so fragile to the eye, so powerful to those who knew her well, was at the present moment the faithful guide and assistant of the exiled gentlemen who came from England to take part in this deadly enterprise.

Fouche relied on the co-operation of the *emigres* everywhere beyond the Rhine to lure the Duc d'Enghien into the plot. The presence of that prince in the Baden territory, not far from Strasburg, gave much weight later to the accusation. The great question of whether the prince really knew of the enterprise, and was waiting on the frontier to enter France on its success, is one of those secrets about which, as about several others, the house of Bourbon has maintained an unbroken silence. As the history of that period recedes into the past, impartial historians will declare the imprudence, to say the least, of the Duc d'Enghien in placing himself close to the frontier at a time when a vast conspiracy was about to break forth, the secret of which was undoubtedly known to every member of the Bourbon family.

The caution which Malin displayed in talking with Grevin in the open air, Laurence applied to her every action. She met the emissaries and conferred with them either at various points in the Nodesme forest, or beyond the valley of the Cinq-Cygne, between the villages of Sezanne and Brienne. Often she rode forty miles on a stretch with Gothard, and returned to Cinq-Cygne without the least sign of weariness or pre-occupation on her fair young face.

Some years earlier, Laurence had seen in the eyes of a little cow-boy, then nine years old, the artless admiration which children feel for everything that is out of the common way. She made him her page, and taught him to groom a horse with the nicety and care of an Englishman. She saw in the lad a desire to do well, a bright intelligence, and a total absence of sly motives; she tested his devotion and found he had not only mind but nobility of character; he never dreamed of reward. The young girl trained this soul that was still so young; she was good to him, good with dignity; she attached him to her by attaching herself to him, and by herself polishing a nature that was half wild, without destroying its freshness or its simplicity. When she had sufficiently tested the almost canine fidelity she had nurtured, Gothard became her intelligent and ingenuous accomplice. The little peasant, whom no one could suspect, went from Cinq-Cygne to Nancy, and often returned before any one had missed him from the neighborhood. He knew how to practise all the tricks of a spy. The extreme distrust and caution his mistress had taught him did not change his natural self. Gothard, who possessed all the craft of a woman, the candor of a child, and the ceaseless observation of a conspirator, hid every one of these admirable qualities beneath the torpor and dull ignorance of a country lad. The little fellow had a silly, weak, and clumsy appearance; but once at work he was active as a fish; he escaped like an eel; he understood, as the dogs do, the merest glance; he nosed a thought. His good fat face, both round and red, his sleepy brown eyes, his hair, cut in the peasant fashion, his clothes, and his slow growth gave him the appearance of a child of ten.

The two young d'Hauteserres and the twin brothers Simeuse, under the guidance of their cousin Laurence, who had been watching over their safety and that of the other *emigres* who accompanied them from Strasburg to Bar-sur-Aube, had just passed through Alsace and Lorraine, and were now in Champagne while other conspirators, not less bold, were entering France by the cliffs of Normandy. Dressed as workmen the d'Hauteserres and the Simeuse twins had walked from forest to forest, guided on their way by relays of persons, chosen by Laurence during the last three months from among the least suspected of the Bourbon adherents living in each neighborhood. The *emigres* slept by day and travelled by night. Each brought with him two faithful soldiers; one of whom went before to warn of danger, the other behind to protect a retreat. Thanks to these military precautions, this valuable detachment had at last reached, without accident, the forest of Nodesme, which was chosen as the rendezvous. Twenty-seven other gentlemen had entered France from Switzerland and crossed Burgundy, guided towards Paris with the same caution.

Monsieur de Riviere counted on collecting five hundred men, one hundred of whom were young nobles, the officers of this sacred legion. Monsieur de Polignac and Monsieur de Riviere, whose conduct as chiefs of this advance was most remarkable, afterwards preserved an impenetrable secrecy as to the names of those of their accomplices who were not discovered. It may be said, therefore, now that the Restoration has made matters clearer, that Bonaparte never knew the extent of the danger he then ran, any more than England knew the peril she had escaped from the camp at Boulogne; and yet the police of France was never more intelligently or ably managed.

At the period when this history begins, a coward – for cowards are always to be found in conspiracies which are not confined to a small number of equally strong men – a sworn confederate, brought face to face with death, gave certain information, happily insufficient to cover the extent of the conspiracy, but precise enough to show the object of the enterprise. The police had therefore, as Malin told Grevin, left the conspirators at liberty, though all the while watching them, hoping to discover the ramifications of the plot. Nevertheless, the government found its hand to a certain extent forced by Georges Cadoudal, a man of action who took counsel of himself only, and who was hiding in Paris with twenty-five *chouans* for the purpose of attacking the First Consul.

Laurence combined both hatred and love within her breast. To destroy Bonaparte and bring back the Bourbons was to recover Gondreville and make the fortune of her cousins. The two sentiments, one the counterpart of the other, were sufficient, more especially at twenty-three years of age, to excite all the faculties of her soul and all the powers of her being. So, for the last two months, she had seemed to the inhabitants of Cinq-Cygne more beautiful than at any other period of her life. Her cheeks became rosy; hope gave pride to her brow; but when old d'Hauteserre read the Gazette at night and discussed the conservative course of the First Consul she lowered her eyes to conceal her passionate hopes of the coming fall of that enemy of the Bourbons.

No one at the chateau had the faintest idea that the young countess had met her cousins the night before. The two sons of Monsieur and Madame d'Hauteserre had passed the preceding night in Laurence's own room, under the same roof with their father and mother; and Laurence, after knowing them safely in bed had gone between one and two o'clock in the morning to a rendezvous with her cousins in the forest, where she hid them in the deserted hut of a wood-dealer's agent. The following day, certain of seeing them again, she showed no signs of her joy; nothing about her betrayed emotion; she was able to efface all traces of pleasure at having met them again; in fact, she was impassible. Catherine, her pretty maid, daughter of her former nurse, and Gothard, both in the secret, modelled their behavior upon hers. Catherine was nineteen years old. At that age a girl is a fanatic and would let her throat be cut before betraying a thought of one she loves. As for Gothard, merely to inhale the perfume which the countess used in her hair and among her clothes he would have born the rack without a word.

47

Chapter V. Royalist Homes and Portraits under the Consulate

At the moment when Marthe, driven by the imminence of the peril, was gliding with the rapidity of a shadow towards the breach of which Michu had told her, the salon of the chateau of Cinq-Cygne presented a peaceful sight. Its occupants were so far from suspecting the storm that was about to burst upon them that their quiet aspect would have roused the compassion of any one who knew their situation. In the large fireplace, the mantel of which was adorned with a mirror with shepherdesses in paniers painted on its frame, burned a fire such as can be seen only in chateaus bordering on forests. At the corner of this fireplace, on a large square sofa of gilded wood with a magnificent brocaded cover, the young countess lay as it were extended, in an attitude of utter weariness. Returning at six o'clock from the confines of Brie, having played the part of scout to the four gentlemen whom she guided safely to their last halting-place before they entered Paris, she had found Monsieur and Madame d'Hauteserre just finishing their dinner. Pressed by hunger she sat down to table without changing either her muddy habit or her boots. Instead of doing so at once after dinner, she was suddenly overcome with fatigue and allowed her head with its beautiful fair curls to drop on the back of the sofa, her feet being supported in front of her by a stool. The warmth of the fire had dried the mud on her habit and on her boots. Her doeskin gloves and the little peaked cap with its green veil and a whip lay on the table where she had flung them. She looked sometimes at the old Boule clock which stood on the mantelshelf between the candelabra, perhaps to judge if her four conspirators were asleep, and sometimes at the card-table in front of the fire where Monsieur and Madame d'Hauteserre, the cure of Cinq-Cygne, and his sister were playing a game of boston.

Even if these personages were not embedded in this drama, their portraits would have the merit of representing one of the aspects of the aristocracy after its overthrow in 1793. From this point of view, a sketch of the salon at Cinq-Cygne has the raciness of history seen in dishabille.

Monsieur d'Hauteserre, then fifty-two years of age, tall, spare, high-colored, and robust in health, would have seemed the embodiment of vigor if it were not for a pair of porcelain blue eyes, the glance of which denoted the most absolute simplicity. In his face, which ended in a long pointed chin, there was, judging by the rules of design, an unnatural distance between his nose and mouth which gave him a submissive air, wholly in keeping with his character, which harmonized, in fact, with other details of his appearance. His gray hair, flattened by his hat, which he wore nearly all day, looked much like a skull-cap on his head, and defined its pear-shaped outline. His forehead, much wrinkled by life in the open air and by constant anxieties, was flat and expressionless. His aquiline nose redeemed the face somewhat; but the sole indication of any strength of character lay in the bushy eyebrows which retained their blackness, and in the brilliant coloring of his skin. These signs were in some respects not misleading, for the worthy gentlemen, though simple and very gentle, was Catholic and monarchical in faith, and no consideration on earth could make him change his views. Nevertheless he would have let himself be arrested without an effort at defence, and would have gone to the scaffold quietly. His annuity of three thousand francs kept him from emigrating. He therefore obeyed the government *de facto* without ceasing to love the royal family and to pray for their return, though he would firmly have refused to compromise himself by any effort in their favor. He belonged to that class of royalists who ceaselessly remembered that they were beaten and robbed; and who remained thenceforth dumb, economical, rancorous, without energy; incapable of abjuring the past, but equally incapable of sacrifice; waiting to greet triumphant royalty; true to religion and true to the priesthood, but firmly resolved to bear in silence the shocks of fate. Such an attitude cannot be considered that of maintaining opinions, it becomes sheer obstinacy. Action is the essence of party. Without intelligence, but loyal, miserly as a peasant yet noble in demeanor, bold in his wishes but discreet in word and action, turning all things to profit, willing even to be made mayor of Cinq-Cygne, Monsieur d'Hauteserre was an admirable representative of those honorable gentlemen on whose brow God Himself has written the word *mites,* – Frenchmen who burrowed in their country homes and let the storms of the Revolution pass above their heads; who came once more to the surface under the Restoration, rich with their hidden savings, proud of their discreet attachment to the monarchy, and who, after 1830, recovered their estates.

Monsieur d'Hauteserre's costume, expressive envelope of his distinctive character, described to the eye both the man and his period. He always wore one of those nut-colored great-coats with small collars which the Duc d'Orleans made the fashion after his return from England, and which were, during the Revolution, a sort of compromise between the hideous popular garments and the elegant surtouts of the aristocracy. His velvet waistcoat with flowered stripes, the style of which recalled those of Robespierre and Saint-Just, showed the upper part of a shirt-frill in fine plaits. He still wore breeches; but his were of coarse blue cloth, with burnished steel buckles. His stockings of black spun-silk defined his deer-like legs, the feet of which were shod in thick shoes, held in place by gaiters of black cloth. He retained the former fashion of a muslin cravat in innumerable folds fastened by a gold buckle at the throat. The worthy man had not intended an act of political eclecticism in adopting this costume, which combined the styles of peasant, revolutionist, and aristocrat; he simply and innocently obeyed the dictates of circumstances.

Madame d'Hauteserre, forty years of age and wasted by emotions, had a faded face which seemed to be always posing for its portrait. A lace cap, trimmed with bows of white satin, contributed singularly to give her a solemn air. She still wore powder, in spite of a white kerchief, and a gown of puce-colored silk with tight sleeves and full skirt, the sad last garments of Marie-Antoinette. Her nose was pinched, her chin sharp, the whole face nearly triangular, the eyes worn-out with weeping; but she now wore a touch of rouge which brightened their grayness. She took snuff, and each time that she did so she employed all the pretty precautions of the fashionable women of her early days; the details of this snuff-taking constituted a ceremony which could be explained by one fact – she had very pretty hands.

For the last two years the former tutor of the Simeuse twins, a friend of the late Abbe d'Hauteserre, named Goujet, Abbe des Minimes, had taken charge of the parish of Cinq-Cygne out of friendship for the d'Hauteserres and the young countess. His sister, Mademoiselle Goujet, who possessed a little income of seven hundred francs, added that sum to the meagre salary of her brother and kept his house. Neither church nor parsonage had been sold during the Revolution on account of their small value. The abbe and his sister lived close to the chateau, for the wall of the parsonage garden and that of the park were the same in places. Twice a week the pair dined at the chateau, but they came every evening to play boston with the d'Hauteserres; for Laurence, unable to play a game, did not even know one card from another.

The Abbe Goujet, an old man with white hair and a face as white as that of an old woman, endowed with a kindly smile and a gentle and persuasive voice, redeemed the insipidity of his rather mincing face by a fine intellectual brow and a pair of keen eyes. Of medium height, and very well made, he still wore the old-fashioned black coat, silver shoe-buckles, breeches, black silk stockings, and a black waistcoat on which lay his clerical bands, giving him a distinguished air which detracted nothing from his dignity. This abbe, who became bishop of Troyes after the Restoration, had long made a study of young people and fully understood the noble character of the young countess; he appreciated her at her full value, and had shown her, from the first, a respectful deference which contributed much to her independence at Cinq-Cygne, for it led the austere old lady and the kind old gentleman to yield to the young girl, who by rights should have yielded to them. For the last six months the abbe had watched Laurence with the intuition peculiar to priests, the most sagacious of men; and although he did not know that this girl of twenty-three was thinking of overturning Bonaparte as she lay there twisting with slender fingers the frogged lacing of her riding-habit, he was well aware that she was agitated by some great project.

Mademoiselle Goujet was one of those unmarried women

whose portrait can be drawn in one word which will enable the least imaginative mind to picture her; she was ungainly. She knew her own ugliness and was the first to laugh at it, showing her long teeth, yellow as her complexion and her bony hands. She was gay and hearty. She wore the famous short gown of former days, a very full skirt with pockets full of keys, a cap with ribbons and a false front. She was forty years of age very early, but had, so she said, caught up with herself by keeping at that age for twenty years. She revered the nobility; and knew well how to preserve her own dignity by giving to persons of noble birth the respect and deference that were due to them.

This little company was a god-send to Madame d'Hauteserre, who had not, like her husband, rural occupations, nor, like Laurence, the tonic of hatred, to enable her to bear the dulness of a retired life. Many things had happened to ameliorate that life within the last six years. The restoration of Catholic worship allowed the faithful to fulfil their religious duties, which play more of a part in country life than elsewhere. Protected by the conservative edicts of the First Consul, Monsieur and Madame d'Hauteserre had been able to correspond with their sons, and no longer in dread of what might happen to them could even hope for the erasure of their names from the lists of the proscribed and their consequent return to France. The Treasury had lately made up the arrearages and now paid its dividends promptly; so that the d'Hauteserres received, over and above their annuity, about eight thousand francs a year. The old man congratulated himself on the sagacity of his foresight in having put all his savings, amounting to twenty thousand francs, together with those of his ward, in the public Funds before the 18th Brumaire, which, as we all know, sent those stocks up from twelve to eighteen francs.

The chateau of Cinq-Cygne had long been empty and denuded of furniture. The prudent guardian was careful not to alter its aspect during the revolutionary troubles; but after the peace of Amiens he made a journey to Troyes and brought back various relics of the pillaged mansions which he obtained from the dealers in second-hand furniture. The salon was furnished for the first time since their occupation of the house. Handsome curtains of white brocade with green flowers, from the hotel de Simeuse, draped the six windows of the salon, in which the family were now assembled. The walls of this vast room were entirely of wood, with panels encased in beaded mouldings with masks at the angles; the whole painted in two shades of gray. The spaces over the four doors were filled with those designs, painted in cameo of two colors, which were so much in vogue under Louis XV. Monsieur d'Hauteserre had picked up at Troyes certain gilded pier-tables, a sofa in green damask, a crystal chandelier, a card-table of marquetry, among other things that served him to restore the chateau. In 1792 all the furniture of the house had been taken or destroyed, for the pillage of the mansions in town was imitated in the valley. Each time that the old man went to Troyes he returned with some relic of the former splendor, sometimes a fine carpet for the floor of the salon, at other times part of a dinner service, or a bit of rare old porcelain of either Sevres or Dresden. During the last six months he had ventured to dig up the family silver, which the cook had buried in the cellar of a little house belonging to him at the end of one of the long faubourgs in Troyes.

That faithful servant, named Durieu, and his wife had followed the fortunes of their young mistress. Durieu was the factotum of the chateau, and his wife was the housekeeper. He was helped in the cooking by the sister of Catherine, Laurence's maid, to whom he was teaching his art and who gave promise of becoming an excellent cook. An old gardener, his wife, a son paid by the day, and a daughter who served as a dairy-woman, made up the household. Madame Durieu had lately and secretly had the Cinq-Cygne liveries made for the gardener's son and for Gothard. Though blamed for this imprudence by Monsieur d'Hauteserre, the housekeeper took great pleasure in seeing the dinner served on the festival of Saint-Laurence, the countess's fete-day, with almost as much style as in former times.

This slow and difficult restoration of departed things was the delight of Monsieur and Madame d'Hauteserre and the Durieus. Laurence smiled at what she thought nonsense. But the worthy old d'Hauteserre did not forget the more solid matters; he repaired the buildings, put up the walls, planted trees wherever there was a chance to make them grow, and did not leave an inch of unproductive land. The whole valley regarded him as an oracle in the matter of agriculture. He had managed to recover a hundred acres of contested land, not sold as national property, being in some way confounded with that of the township. This land he had turned into fields which afforded good pasturage for his horses and cattle, and he planted them round with poplars, which now, at the end of six years, were making a fine growth. He intended to buy back some of the lost estate, and to utilize all the out-buildings of the chateau by making a second farm and managing it himself.

Life at the chateau had thus become during the last two years prosperous and almost happy. Monsieur d'Hauteserre was off at daybreaks to overlook his laborers, for he employed them in all weathers. He came home to breakfast, mounted his farm pony as soon as the meal was over, and made his rounds of the estate like a bailiff, – getting home in time for dinner, and finishing the day with a game of boston. All the inhabitants of the chateau had their stated occupations; life was as closely regulated there as in a convent. Laurence alone disturbed its even tenor by her sudden journeys, her uncertain returns, and by what Madame d'Hauteserre called her pranks. But with all this peacefulness there existed at Cinq-Cygne conflicting interests and certain causes of dissension. In the first place Durieu and his wife were jealous of Catherine and Gothard, who lived in greater intimacy with their young mistress, the idol of the household, than they did. Then the two d'Hauteserres, encouraged by Mademoiselle Goujet and the abbe, wanted their sons as well as the Simeuse brothers to take the oath and return to this quiet life, instead of living miserably in foreign countries. Laurence scouted the odious compromise and stood firmly for the monarchy, militant and implacable. The four old people, anxious that their present peaceful existence should not be risked, nor their spot of refuge, saved from the furious waters of the revolutionary torrent, lost, did their best to convert Laurence to their cautious views, believing that her influence counted for much in the unwillingness of their sons and the Simeuse twins to return to France. The superb disdain with which she met the project frightened these poor people, who were not mistaken in their fears that she was meditating what they called knight-errantry. This jarring of opinion came to the surface after the explosion of the infernal machine in the rue Saint-Nicaise, the first royalist attempt against the conqueror of Marengo after his refusal to treat with the house of Bourbon. The d'Hauteserres considered it fortunate that Bonaparte escaped that danger, believing that the republicans had instigated it. But Laurence wept with rage when she heard he was safe. Her despair overcame her usual reticence, and she vehemently complained that God had deserted the sons of Saint-Louis.

"I," she exclaimed, "I could have succeeded! Have we no right," she added, seeing the stupefaction her words produced on the faces about her, and addressing the abbe, "no right to attack the usurper by every means in our power?"

"My child," replied the abbe, "the Church has been greatly blamed by philosophers for declaring in former times that the same weapons might be employed against usurpers which the usurpers themselves had employed to succeed; but in these days the Church owes far too much to the First Consul not to protect him against that maxim, – which, by the by, was due to the Jesuits."

"So the Church abandons us!" she answered, gloomily.

From that day forth whenever the four old people talked of submitting to the decrees of Providence, Laurence left the room. Of late, the abbe, shrewder than Monsieur d'Hauteserre, instead of discussing principles, drew pictures of the material advantages of the consular rule, less to convert the countess than to detect in her eyes some expression which might enlighten him as to her projects. Gothard's frequent disappearances, the long rides of his mistress, and her evident preoccupation, which, for the last few days, had appeared in her face, together with other little signs not to be hidden in the silence and tranquillity of such a life, had roused the fears of these submissive royalists. Still, as no event happened, and perfect quiet appeared to reign in the political atmosphere, the minds of the little household were soothed into peace, and the countess's long rides were one more attributed to her passion for hunting.

It is easy to imagine the deep silence which reigned at nine o'clock in the evening in the park, courtyards, and gardens of Cinq-Cygne, where at that particular moment the persons we have described were harmoniously grouped, where perfect peace pervaded all things, where comfort and abundance were again enjoyed, and where the worthy and judicious old gentleman was still hoping to convert his late ward to his system of obedience to the ruling powers by the argument of what we may call the continuity of prosperous results.

These royalists continued to play their boston, a game which spread ideas of independence under a frivolous form over the whole of France; for it was first invented in honor of the American insurgents, its very terms applying to the struggle which Louis XVI. encouraged. While making their "independences" and "poverties," the players kept an eye on the countess, who had fallen asleep, overcome by fatigue, with a singular smile on her lips, her last waking thought having been of the terror two words could inspire in the minds of the peaceful company by informing the d'Hauteserres that their sons had passed the preceding night under that roof. What young girl of twenty-three would not have been, as Laurence was, proud to play the part of Destiny? and who would not have felt, as she did, a sense of compassion for those whom she felt to be so far below her in loyalty?

"She sleeps," said the abbe. "I have never seen her so wearied."

"Durieu tells me her mare is almost foundered," remarked Madame d'Hauteserre. "Her gun has not been fired; the breech is clean; she has evidently not hunted."

"Oh! that's neither here nor there," said the abbe.

"Bah?" cried Mademoiselle Goujet; "when I was twenty-three and saw I should be an old maid all my life, I rushed about and fatigued myself in a dozen ways. I understand how the countess can scour the country for hours without thinking of the game. It is nearly twelve years now since she has seen her cousins, and you know she loves them. Well, if I were she, if I were as young and pretty, I'd make a straight line for Germany! Poor darling, perhaps she is thinking of the frontier, and that may be the reason why she rides so far towards it."

"You are rather giddy, Mademoiselle Goujet," said the abbe, smiling.

"Not at all," she replied. "I see you all uneasy about the goings on of a young girl, and I am explaining them to you."

"Her cousins will submit and return soon; they will all be rich, and she will end by calming down," said old d'Hauteserre.

"God grant it!" said his wife, taking out a gold snuff-box which had again seen the light under the Consulate.

"There is something stirring in the neighborhood," remarked Monsieur d'Hauteserre to the abbe. "Malin has been two days at Gondreville."

"Malin!" cried Laurence, roused by the name, though her sleep was sound.

"Yes," replied the abbe, "but he leaves to-night; everybody is conjecturing the motive of this hasty visit."

"That man," said Laurence, "is the evil genius of our two houses."

The countess had been dreaming of her cousins and the young Hauteserres; she saw them in peril. Her beautiful eyes grew fixed and glassy as her mind thus warned dwelled on the dangers they were about to incur in Paris. She rose suddenly and went to her bedroom without speaking. Her bedroom was the best in the house; next came a dressing-room and an oratory, in the tower which faced towards the forest. Soon after she had left the salon the dogs barked, the bell of the small gate rang, and Durieu rushed into the salon with a frightened face. "Here is the mayor!" he said. "Something is the matter."

Chapter VI. A Domiciliary Visit

The mayor, a former huntsman of the house of Simeuse, came occasionally to the chateau, where the d'Hauteserres showed him out of policy, a deference to which he attached great value. His name was Goulard; he had married a rich woman of Troyes, whose property, which was in the commune of Cinq-Cygne, he had further increased by the purchase of a fine abbey and its lands, in which he invested all his savings. The vast abbey of Val-des-Preux, standing about a mile from the chateau, he had turned into a dwelling that was almost as splendid as Gondreville; in it his wife and he were now living like rats in a cathedral. "Ah! Goulard, you have been greedy," Mademoiselle had said to him with a laugh the first time she received him at Cinq-Cygne. Though greatly attached to the Revolution and coldly received by the countess, the mayor always felt himself bound by ties of respect to the Cinq-Cygne and Simeuse families. He therefore shut his eyes to what went on at the chateau. He called shutting his eyes not seeing the portraits of Louis XVI., Marie Antoinette, and the royal children, and those of Monsieur, the Comte d'Artois, Cazales and Charlotte Corday, which filled the various panels of the salon; not resenting either the wishes freely expressed in his presence for the ruin of the Republic, or the ridicule flung at the five directors and all the other governmental combinations of that time. The position of this man, who, like many parvenus, having once made his fortune, reverted to his early faith in the old families, and sought to attach himself to them, was now being made use of by the two members of the Paris police whose profession had been so quickly guessed by Michu, and who, before going to Gondreville had reconnoitred the neighborhood.

The worthy described as the depositary of the best traditions of the old police, and Corentin phoenix of spies, were in fact employed on a secret mission. Malin was not mistaken in attributing a double purpose to those stars of tragic farces. But, before seeing them at work, it is advisable to show the head of which they were the arms. When Bonaparte became First Consul he found Fouche at the head of the police. The Revolution had frankly and with good reason made the management of the police into a special ministry. But after his return from Marengo, Bonaparte created the prefecture of police, placed Dubois in charge of it, and called Fouche to the Council of State, naming as his successor in the ministry a conventional named Cochon, since known as Comte de Lapparent. Fouche, who considered the ministry of police as by far the most important in a government of broad ideas and fixed policy, saw disgrace or at any rate distrust in the change. After Napoleon became aware of the immense superiority of this great statesman, as evidenced in the affair of the infernal machine and in the conspiracy with which we are now concerned, he returned him to the ministry of police. Later still, becoming alarmed at the powers Fouche displayed during his absence at the time of the affair at Walcheren, the Emperor gave that ministry to the Duc de Rovigo, and sent Fouche (Duc d'Otrante) as governor to the Illyrian provinces, – an appointment which was in fact an exile.

The singular genius of this man, Fouche, which had the power of inspiring Napoleon with a sort of fear, did not reveal itself all at once. This obscure conventional, one of the most extraordinary men of our time, and the most misjudged, was moulded, as it were, by the whirlwind of events. He raised himself under the Directory to the height from which men of genius could see the future and judge the past, and then, like certain commonplace actors who suddenly become admirable through the light of some vivid perception, he gave proofs of his dexterity during the rapid revolution of the 18th Brumaire. This man with the pallid face, educated to monastic dissimulation, possessing the secrets of the *montagnards* to whom he belonged, and those of the royalists to whom he ended by belonging, had slowly and silently studied the men, the events, and the interests on the political stage; he penetrated Napoleon's secrets, he gave him useful counsel and precious information. Satisfied with having proven his capacity and his usefulness, Fouche was careful not to disclose himself completely. He wished to remain at the head of affairs, but the Emperor's restless uneasiness about him cost him his place.

The ingratitude or rather the distrust shown by Napoleon after the affair at Walcheren, gives the key-note to the character of a man who, unfortunately for himself, was not a great *seigneur*, and whose conduct was modelled on that of Talleyrand. At that time neither his former colleagues nor his present ones had suspected the amplitude of his genius, which was purely ministerial, essentially governmental, just in its forecasts and incredibly sagacious. To-day, every impartial historian perceives that Napoleon's inordinate self-love was among the chief causes of his fall, a punishment which cruelly expiated his wrong-doing. In the mind of that distrustful sovereign lurked a constant jealousy for his own rising power, which influenced all his actions, and caused his secret hatred for men of talent, the precious legacy of the Revolution, with whom he might have made himself a cabinet capable of being a true repository for his thoughts. Talleyrand and Fouche were not the only ones who gave him umbrage. The misfortune of usurpers is that those who have given them a crown are as much their enemies as those from whom they snatch it. Napoleon's sovereignty was never convincingly felt by those who were once his superiors or his equals, nor by those who still held to the doctrine of rights; none of them regarded their oath of allegiance to him as binding.

Malin, an inferior man, incapable of comprehending Fouche's hidden genius, or of distrusting his own perceptions, burned himself, like a moth in a candle, by asking him confidentially to send agents to Gondreville, where, he said, he hoped to obtain certain clues to the conspiracy. Fouche, without alarming his friend by any questions, asked himself why Malin was going to Gondreville, and why he did not immediately and without loss of time, give the information he already possessed. The ex-Oratorian, fed from his youth up on trickery, and well aware of the double part played by a good many of the conventionals, said to himself: "From whom is Malin likely to obtain information when we ourselves know little or nothing?" Fouche concluded therefore that there was some either latent or prospective collusion, and took care to say nothing about it to the First Consul. He preferred to make Malin his instrument rather than destroy him. It was Fouche's habit to keep to himself a good part of the secrets he detected, and he thus obtained for his own purposes a power

over those concerned which was even greater than that of Bonaparte. This duplicity was one of the Emperor's charges against his
minister.

Fouche knew of the swindling transaction by which Malin
became possessed of Gondreville and which led him to keep his
eyes so anxiously on the Simeuse brothers. These gentlemen were
now serving in the army of Conde; Mademoiselle de Cinq-Cygne
was their cousin; possibly they were in her neighborhood, and
were sharers in the conspiracy; if so, it would implicate the house
of Conde to which they were devoted. Talleyrand and Fouche
were bent on casting light into this dark corner of the conspiracy
of 1803. All these considerations Fouche saw at a glance, rapidly
and with great clearness. But between Malin, Talleyrand, and
himself there were strong ties which forced him to the utmost
circumspection, and made him anxious to know the exact state of
things within the walls of Gondreville. Corentin was unreserv-
edly attached to Fouche, just as Monsieur de la Besnardiere was
to Talleyrand, Gentz to Monsieur de Metternich, Dundas to Pitt,
Duroc to Napoleon, Chavigny to Cardinal Richelieu. Corentin
was not the counsellor of his master, but his instrument, the Tris-
tan to this Louis XI. of low estate. Fouche had kept him in the
ministry of the police when he himself left it, so as to still keep an
eye and a finger in it. It was said that Corentin belonged to
Fouche by some unavowed relationship, for he rewarded him
lavishly after every service. Corentin had a friend in Peyrade, the
old pupil of the last lieutenant of police; but he kept a good many
of his secrets from him. Fouche gave Corentin an order to explore
the chateau of Gondreville, to get the plan of it into his memory,
and to know every hiding-place within its walls.

"We may be obliged to return there," said the ex-minister,
precisely as Napoleon told his lieutenants to explore the field of
Austerlitz on which he intended to fall back.

Corentin was also to study Malin's conduct, discover what
influence he had in the neighborhood, and observe the men he
employed. Fouche regarded it as certain that the Simeuse brothers were in that part of the country. By cautiously watching the
two officers, who were closely allied with the Prince de Conde,

Peyrade and Corentin could obtain precious light on the ramifications of the conspiracy beyond the Rhine. In any case, however, Corentin received the means, the orders, and the agents, to surround the chateau of Cinq-Cygne and watch the whole region, from the forest of Nodesme into Paris. Fouche insisted on the utmost caution, and would only allow a domiciliary visit to Cinq-Cygne in case Malin gave them positive information which made it necessary. By way of instructions he explained to Corentin the otherwise inexplicable personality of Michu, who had been watched by the police for the last three years. Corentin's idea was that of his master: "Malin knows all about the conspiracy – But," he added to himself, "perhaps Fouche does, too; who knows?"

Corentin, having started for Troyes before Malin, had made arrangements with the commandant of the gendarmerie in that town, who picked out a number of his most intelligent men and placed them under orders of an able captain. Corentin chose Gondreville as the place of rendezvous, and directed the captain to send some of his men at night in four detachments to different points of the valley of Cinq-Cygne at sufficient distance from each other to cause no alarm. These four pickets were to form a square and close in around the chateau of Cinq-Cygne. By leaving Corentin alone at Gondreville during his consultation in the fields with Grevin, Malin had enabled him to fulfil part of Fouche's orders and explore the house. When the Councillor of State returned home he told Corentin so positively that the d'Hauteserre and Simeuse brothers were in the neighborhood and probably at Cinq-Cygne that the two agents despatched the captain with the rest of his company, who, fortunately for the four gentlemen, crossed the forest on their way to the chateau during the time when Michu was making Violette drunk. Malin had told Corentin and Peyrade of the escape he had from lying in wait for him. The two agents related the incident of the gun they had seen the bailiff load, and Grevin had sent Violette to obtain information as to what was going on at Michu's house. Corentin advised the notary to take Malin to his own house in the little town of Arcis, and let him sleep there as a measure of precaution. At the moment when Michu and his wife were rushing through the forest on their way to Cinq-Cygne, Peyrade and Corentin were starting from Gondreville for Cinq-Cygne in a shabby wicker carriage, drawn by one post-horse driven by the corporal of Arcis, one of the shrewdest men in the Legion, whom the commandant at Troyes advised them to employ.

"The surest way to seize them all is to warn them," said Peyrade to Corentin. "At the moment when they are well frightened and are trying to save their papers or to escape we'll fall upon them like a thunderbolt. The gendarmes surround the chateau now and are as good as a net. We sha'n't lose one of them!"

"You had better send the mayor to warn them," said the corporal. "He is friendly to them and wouldn't like to see them harmed; they won't distrust him."

Just as Goulard was preparing to go to bed, Corentin, who stopped the vehicle in a little wood, went to his house and told him, confidentially, that in a few moments an emissary from the government would require him to enter the chateau of Cinq-Cygne and arrest the brothers d'Hauteserre and Simeuse; and in case they had already disappeared he would have to ascertain if they had slept there the night before, search Mademoiselle de Cinq-Cygne's papers, and, possibly, arrest both the masters and servants of the household.

"Mademoiselle de Cinq-Cygne," said Corentin, "is undoubtedly protected by some great personages, for I have received private orders to warn her of this visit, and to do all I can to save her without compromising myself. Once on the ground, I shall no longer be able to do so, for I am not alone; go to the chateau yourself and warn them."

The mayor's visit at that time of night was all the more bewildering to the card-players when they saw the agitation of his face.

"Where is the countess?" were his first words.

"She has gone to bed," said Madame d'Hauteserre.

The mayor, incredulous, listened to noises that were heard on the upper floor.

"What is the matter with you, Goulard?" said Monsieur d'Hauteserre.

Goulard was dumb with surprise as he noted the tranquil ease of the faces about him. Observing the peaceful and innocent game of cards which he had thus interrupted, he was unable to imagine what the Parisian police meant by their suspicions.

At that moment Laurence, kneeling in her oratory, was praying fervently for the success of the conspiracy. She prayed to God to send help and succor to the murderers of Bonaparte. She implored Him ardently to destroy that fatal being. The fanaticism of Harmodius, Judith, Jacques Clement, Ankarstroem, of Charlotte Corday and Limoelan, inspired this pure and virgin spirit. Catherine was preparing the bed, Gothard was closing the blinds, when Marthe Michu coming under the windows flung a pebble on the glass and was seen at once.

"Mademoiselle, here's some one," said Gothard, seeing a woman.

"Hush!" said Marthe, in a low voice. "Come down and speak to me."

Gothard was in the garden in less time than a bird would have taken to fly down from a tree.

"In a minute the chateau will be surrounded by the gendarmerie. Saddle mademoiselle's horse without making any noise and take it down through the breach in the moat between the stables and this tower."

Marthe quivered when she saw Laurence, who had followed Gothard, standing beside her.

"What is it?" asked Laurence, quietly.

"The conspiracy against the First Consul is discovered," replied Marthe, in a whisper. "My husband, who seeks to save your two cousins, sends me to ask you to come and speak to him."

Laurence drew back and looked at Marthe. "Who are you?" she said.

"Marthe Michu."

"I do not know what you want of me," replied the countess, coldly.

"Take care, you will kill them. Come with me, I implore you in the Simeuse name," said Marthe, clasping her hands and stretching them towards Laurence. "Have you papers here which may compromise you? If so, destroy them. From the heights over there my husband has just seen the silver-laced hats and the muskets of the gendarmerie."

Gothard had already clambered to the hay-loft and seen the same sight; he heard in the stillness of the evening the sound of their horses' hoofs. Down he slipped into the stable and saddled his mistress's mare, whose feet Catherine, at a word from the lad, muffled in linen.

"Where am I to go?" said Laurence to Marthe, whose look and language bore the unmistakable signs of sincerity.

"Through the breach," she replied; "my noble husband is there. You shall learn the value of a 'Judas'!"

Catherine went quickly into the salon, picked up the hat, veil, whip, and gloves of her mistress, and disappeared. This sudden apparition and action were so striking a commentary on the mayor's inquiry that Madame d'Hauteserre and the abbe exchanged glances which contained the melancholy thought: "Farewell to all our peace! Laurence is conspiring; she will be the death of her cousins."

"But what do you really mean?" said Monsieur d'Hauteserre to the mayor.

"The chateau is surrounded. You are about to receive a domiciliary visit. If your sons are here tell them to escape, and the Simeuse brothers too, if they are with them."

"My sons!" exclaimed Madame d'Hauteserre, stupefied.

"We have seen no one," said Monsieur d'Hauteserre.

"So much the better," said Goulard; "but I care too much for the Cinq-Cygne and Simeuse families to let any harm come to them. Listen to me. If you have any compromising papers – "

"Papers!" repeated the old gentleman.

"Yes, if you have any, burn them at once," said the mayor. "I'll go and amuse the police agents."

Goulard, whose object was to run with the royalist hare and hold with the republican hounds, left the room; at that moment the dogs barked violently.

"There is no longer time," said the abbe, "here they come! But who is to warn the countess? Where is she?"

"Catherine didn't come for her hat and whip to make relics of them," remarked Mademoiselle Goujet.

Goulard tried to detain the two agents for a few moments, assuring them of the perfect ignorance of the family at Cinq-Cygne.

"You don't know these people!" said Peyrade, laughing at him.

The two agents, insinuatingly dangerous, entered the house at once, followed by the corporal from Arcis and one gendarme. The sight of them paralyzed the peaceful card-players, who kept their seats at the table, terrified by such a display of force. The noise produced by a dozen gendarmes whose horses were stamping on the terrace, was heard without.

"I do not see Mademoiselle de Cinq-Cygne," said Corentin.

"She is probably asleep in her bedroom," said Monsieur d'Hauteserre.

"Come with me, ladies," said Corentin, turning to pass through the ante-chamber and up the staircase, followed by Mademoiselle Goujet and Madame d'Hauteserre. "Rely upon me," he whispered to the old lady. "I am in your interests. I sent the mayor to warn you. Distrust my colleague and look to me. I can save every one of you."

"But what is it all about?" said Mademoiselle Goujet.

"A matter of life and death; you must know that," replied Corentin.

Madame d'Hauteserre fainted. To Mademoiselle Goujet's great astonishment and Corentin's disappointment, Laurence's room was empty. Certain that no one could have escaped from the park or the chateau, for all the issues were guarded, Corentin stationed a gendarme in every room and ordered others to search the farm buildings, stables, and sheds. Then he returned to the salon, where Durieu and his wife and the other servants had rushed in the wildest excitement. Peyrade was studying their faces with his little blue eye, cold and calm in the midst of the uproar. Just as Corentin reappeared alone (Mademoiselle Goujet remaining behind to take care of Madame d'Hauteserre) the tramp of horses was heard, and presently the sound of a child's weeping. The horses entered by the small gate; and the general suspense was put an end to by a corporal appearing at the door of the salon pushing Gothard, whose hands were tied, and Catherine whom he led to the agents.

"Here are some prisoners," he said; "that little scamp was escaping on horseback."

"Fool!" said Corentin, in his ear, "why didn't you let him alone? You could have found out something by following him."

Gothard had chosen to burst into tears and behave like an idiot. Catherine took an attitude of artless innocence which made the old agent reflective. The pupil of Lenoir, after considering the two prisoners carefully, and noting the vacant air of the old gentleman whom he took to be sly, the intelligent eye of the abbe who was still fingering the cards, and the utter stupefaction of the servants and Durieu, approached Corentin and whispered in his ear, "We are not dealing with ninnies."

Corentin answered with a look at the card-table; then he added, "They were playing at boston! Mademoiselle's bed was just being made for the night; she escaped in a hurry; it is a regular surprise; we shall catch them."

Chapter VII. A Forest Nook

A breach has always a cause and a purpose. Here is the explanation of how the one which led from the tower called that of Mademoiselle and the stables came to be made. After his installation as Laurence's guardian at Cinq-Cygne old d'Hauteserre converted a long ravine, through which the water of the forest flowed into the moat, into a roadway between two tracts of uncultivated land belonging to the chateau, by merely planting out in it about a hundred walnut trees which he found ready in the nursery. In eleven years these trees had grown and branched so as to nearly cover the road, hidden already by steep banks, which ran into a little wood of thirty acres recently purchased. When the chateau had its full complement of inhabitants they all preferred to take this covered way through the breach to the main road which skirted the park walls and led to the farm, rather than go round by the entrance. By dint of thus using it the breach in the sides of the moat had gradually been widened on both sides, with all the less scruple because in this nineteenth century of ours moats are no longer of the slightest use, and Laurence's guardian had often talked of putting this one to some other purpose. The constant crumbling away of the earth and stones and gravel had ended by filling up the ditch, so that only after heavy rains was the causeway thus constructed covered. But the bank was still so steep that it was difficult to make a horse descend it, and even more difficult to get him up upon the main road. Horses, however, seem in times of peril to share their masters' thought.

While the young countess was hesitating to follow Marthe, and asking explanations, Michu, from his vantage-ground watched the closing in of the gendarmes and understood their plan. He grew desperate as time went by and the countess did not come to him. A squad of gendarmes were marching along the park wall and stationing themselves as sentinels, each man being near enough to communicate with those on either side of them, by voice and eye. Michu, lying flat on his stomach, his ear to earth, gauged, like a red Indian, by the strength of the sounds the time that remained to him.

"I came too late!" he said to himself. "Violette shall pay dear for this! what a time it took to make him drunk! What can be done?"

He heard the detachment that was coming through the forest reach the iron gates and turn into the main road, where before long it would meet the squad coming up from the other direction.

"Still five or six minutes!" he said.

At that instant the countess appeared. Michu took her with a firm hand and pushed her into the covered way.

"Keep straight before you! Lead her to where my horse is," he said to his wife, "and remember that gendarmes have ears."

Seeing Catherine, who carried the hat and whip, and Gothard leading the mare, the man, keen-witted in presence of danger, bethought himself of playing the gendarmes a trick as useful as the one he had just played Violette. Gothard had forced the mare to mount the bank.

"Her feet muffled! I thank thee, boy," exclaimed the bailiff.

Michu let the mare follow her mistress and took the hat, gloves, and whip from Catherine.

"You have sense, boy, you'll understand me," he said. "Force your own horse up here, jump on him, and draw the gendarmes after you across the fields towards the farm; get the whole squad to follow you – And you," he added to Catherine, "there are other gendarmes coming up on the road from Cinq-Cygne to Gondre-ville; run in the opposite direction to the one Gothard takes, and draw them towards the forest. Manage so that we shall not be interfered with in the covered way."

Catherine and the boy, who were destined to give in this af-fair such remarkable proofs of intelligence, executed the manoeu-vre in a way to make both detachments of gendarmes believe that they held the game. The dim light of the moon prevented the pursuers from distinguishing the figure, clothing, sex, or number of those they followed. The pursuit was based on the maxim, "Always arrest those who are escaping," – the folly of which saying was, as we have seen, energetically declared by Corentin to the corporal in command. Michu, counting on this instinct of the gendarmes, was able to reach the forest a few moments after the countess, whom Marthe had guided to the appointed place.

"Go home now," he said to Marthe. "The forest is watched and it is dangerous to remain here. We need all our freedom."

Michu unfastened his horse and asked the countess to follow him.

"I shall not go a step further," said Laurence, "unless you give me some proof of the interest you seem to have in us – for, after all, you are Michu."

"Mademoiselle," he answered, in a gentle voice; "the part I am playing can be explained to you in two words. I am, unknown to the Marquis de Simeuse and his brother, the guardian of their property. On this subject I received the last instructions of their late father and their dear mother, my protectress. I have played the part of a virulent Jacobin to serve my dear young masters. Unhappily, I began this course too late; I could not save their parents." Here, Michu's voice broke down. "Since the young men emigrated I have sent them regularly the sums they needed to live upon."

"Through the house of Breintmayer of Strasburg?" asked the countess.

"Yes, mademoiselle; the correspondents of Monsieur Girel of Troyes, a royalist who, like me, made himself for good reasons, a Jacobin. The paper which your farmer picked up one evening and which I forced him to surrender, related to the affair and would have compromised your cousins. My life no longer belongs to me, but to them, you understand. I could not buy in Gondreville. In my position, I should have lost my head had the authorities known I had the money. I preferred to wait and buy it later. But that scoundrel of a Marion was the slave of another scoundrel, Malin. All the same, Gondreville shall once more belong to its rightful masters. That's my affair. Four hours ago I had Malin sighted by my gun; ha! he was almost gone then! Were he dead, the property would be sold and you could have bought it. In case of my death my wife would have brought you a letter which would have given you the means of buying it. But I overheard that villain telling his accomplice Grevin – another scoundrel like himself – that the Marquis and his brother were conspiring against the First Consul, that they were here in the neighborhood, and that he meant to give them up and get rid of them so as to keep Gondreville in peace. I myself saw the police spies; I laid aside my gun, and I have lost no time in coming here, thinking that you must be the one to know best how to warn the young men. That's the whole of it."

"You are worthy to be a noble," said Laurence, offering her hand to Michu, who tried to kneel and kiss it. She saw his motion and prevented it, saying: "Stand up!" in a tone of voice and with a look which made him amends for all the scorn of the last twelve years.

"You reward me as though I had done all that remains for me to do," he said. "But don't you hear them, those huzzars of the guillotine? Let us go elsewhere."

He took the mare's bridle, and led her a little distance.

"Think only of sitting firm," he said, "and of saving your head from the branches of the trees which might strike you in the face."

Then he mounted his own horse and guided the young girl for half an hour at full gallop; making turns and half turns, and striking into wood-paths, so as to confuse their traces, until they reached a spot where he pulled up.

"I don't know where I am," said the countess looking about her, – "I, who know the forest as well as you do."

"We are in the heart of it," he replied. "Two gendarmes are after us, but we are quite safe."

The picturesque spot to which the bailiff had guided Laurence was destined to be so fatal to the principal personages of this drama, and to Michu himself, that it becomes our duty, as an historian, to describe it. The scene became, as we shall see hereafter, one of noted interest in the judiciary annals of the Empire.

The forest of Nodesme belonged to the monastery of Notre-Dame. That monastery, seized, sacked, and demolished, had disappeared entirely, monks and property. The forest, an object of much cupidity, was taken into the domain of the Comtes de Champagne, who mortgaged it later and allowed it to be sold. In the course of six centuries nature covered its ruins with her rich and vigorous green mantle, and effaced them so thoroughly that the existence of one of the finest convents was no longer even indicated except by a slight eminence shaded by noble trees and circled by thick, impenetrable shrubbery, which, since 1794, Michu had taken great pains to make still more impenetrable by planting the thorny acacia in all the slight openings between the bushes. A pond was at the foot of the eminence and showed the existence of a hidden stream which no doubt determined in former days the site of the monastery. The late owner of the title to the forest of Nodesme was the first to recognize the etymology of the name, which dated back for eight centuries, and to discover that at one time a monastery had existed in the heart of the forest. When the first rumblings of the thunder of the Revolution were heard, the Marquis de Simeuse, who had been forced to look into his title by a lawsuit and so learned the above facts as it were by chance, began, with a secret intention not difficult to conceive, to search for some remains of the former monastery. The keeper, Michu, to whom the forest was well known, helped his master in the search, and it was his sagacity as a forester which led to the discovery of the site. Observing the trend of the five chief roads of the forest, some of which were now effaced, he saw that they all ended either at the little eminence or by the pond at the foot of it, to which points travellers from Troyes, from the valley of Arcis and that of Cinq-Cygne, and from Bar-sur-Aube doubtless came. The marquis wished to excavate the hillock but he dared not employ the people of the neighborhood. Pressed by circumstances, he abandoned the intention, leaving in Michu's mind a strong conviction that the eminence had either the treasure or the foundations of the former abbey. He continued, all alone, this archaeological enterprise; he sounded the earth and discovered a hollowness on the level of the pond between two trees, at the foot of the only craggy part of the hillock.

One fine night he came to the place armed with a pickaxe, and by the sweat of his brow uncovered a succession of cellars, which were entered by a flight of stone steps. The pond, which was three feet deep in the middle, formed a sort of dipper, the handle of which seemed to come from the little eminence, and went far to prove that a spring had once issued from the crags, and was now lost by infiltration through the forest. The marshy shores of the pond, covered with aquatic trees, alders, willow, and ash, were the terminus of all the wood-paths, the remains of former roads and forest by-ways, now abandoned. The water, flowing from a spring, though apparently stagnant, was covered with large-leaved plants and cresses, which gave it a perfectly green surface almost indistinguishable from the shores, which were covered with fine close herbage. The place is too far from human habitations for any animal, unless a wild one, to come there. Convinced that no game was in the marsh and repelled by the craggy sides of the hills, keepers and hunters had never explored or visited this nook, which belonged to a part of the forest where the timber had not been cut for many years and which Michu meant to keep in its full growth when the time came round to fell it.

At the further end of the first cellar was a vaulted chamber, clean and dry, built with hewn stone, a sort of convent dungeon, such as they called in monastic days the *in pace*. The salubrity of the chamber and the preservation of this part of the staircase and of the vaults were explained by the presence of the spring, which had been enclosed at some time by a wall of extraordinary thickness built in brick and cement like those of the Romans, and received all the waters. Michu closed the entrance to this retreat with large stones; then, to keep the secret of it to himself and make it impenetrable to others, he made a rule never to enter it except from the wooded height above, by clambering down the crag instead of approaching it from the pond.

Just as the fugitives arrived, the moon was casting her beautiful silvery light on the aged tree-tops above the crag, and flickering on the splendid foliage at the corners of the several paths, all of which ended here, some with one tree, some with a group of trees. On all sides the eye was irresistibly led along their vanishing perspectives, following the curve of a wood-path or the solemn stretch of a forest glade flanked by a wall of verdure that was nearly black. The moonlight, filtering through the branches of the crossways, made the lonely, tranquil waters, where they peeped between the crosses and the lily-pads, sparkle like diamonds. The croaking of the frogs broke the deep silence of this beautiful forest-nook, the wild odors of which incited the soul to thoughts of liberty.

"Are we safe?" said the countess to Michu.

"Yes, mademoiselle. But we have each some work to do. Do you go and fasten our horses to the trees at the top of the little hill; tie a handkerchief round the mouth of each of them," he said, giving her his cravat; "your beast and mine are both intelligent, they will understand they are not to neigh. When you have done that, come down the crag directly above the pond; but don't let your habit catch anywhere. You will find me below."

While the countess hid the horses and tied and gagged them, Michu removed the stones and opened the entrance to the caverns. The countess, who thought she knew the forest by heart, was amazed when she descended into the vaulted chambers. Michu replaced the stones above them with the dexterity of a mason. As he finished, the sound of horses' feet and the voices of the gendarmes echoed in the darkness; but he quietly struck a match, lighted a resinous bit of wood and led the countess to the *in pace*, where there was still a piece of the candle with which he had first explored the caves. An iron door of some thickness, eaten in several places by rust, had been put in good order by the bailiff, and could be fastened securely by bars slipping into holes in the wall on either side of it. The countess, half dead with fatigue, sat down on a stone bench, above which there still remained an iron ring, the staple of which was embedded in the masonry.

"We have a salon to converse in," said Michu. "The gendarmes may prowl as much as they like; the worst they could do would be to take our horses."

"If they do that," said Laurence, "it would be the death of my cousins and the Messieurs d'Hauteserre. Tell me now, what do you know?"

Michu related what he had overheard Malin say to Grevin.

"They are already on the road to Paris; they were to enter it to-morrow morning," said the countess when he had finished.

"Lost!" exclaimed Michu. "All persons entering or leaving the barriers are examined. Malin has strong reasons to let my masters compromise themselves; he is seeking to get them killed out of his way."

"And I, who don't know anything of the general plan of the affair," cried Laurence, "how can I warn Georges, Riviere, and Moreau? Where are they? – However, let us think only of my cousins and the d'Hauteserres; you must catch up with them, no matter what it costs."

"The telegraph goes faster than the best horse," said Michu; "and of all the nobles concerned in this conspiracy your cousins are the closest watched. If I can find them, they must be hidden here and kept here till the affair is over. Their poor father may have had a foreboding when he set me to search for this hiding-place; perhaps he felt that his sons would be saved here."

"My mare is from the stables of the Comte d'Artois, – she is the daughter of his finest English horse," said Laurence; "but she has already gone sixty miles, she would drop dead before you reached them."

"Mine is in good condition," replied Michu; "and if you did sixty miles I shall have only thirty to do."

"Nearer forty," she said, "they have been walking since dark. You will overtake them beyond Lagny, at Coupvrai, where they expected to be at daybreak. They are disguised as sailors, and will enter Paris by the river on some vessel. This," she added, taking half of her mother's wedding-ring from her finger, "is the only thing which will make them trust you; they have the other half. The keeper of Couvrai is the father of one of their soldiers; he has hidden them tonight in a hut in the forest deserted by charcoal-burners. They are eight in all, Messieurs d'Hauteserre and four others are with my cousins."

"Mademoiselle, no one is looking for the others! let them save themselves as they can; we must think only of the Messieurs de Simeuse. It is enough just to warn the rest."

"What! abandon the Hauteserres? never!" she said. "They must all perish or be saved together!"

"Only petty noblemen!" remarked Michu.

"They are only chevaliers, I know that," she replied, "but they are related to the Cinq-Cygne and Simeuse blood. Save them all, and advise them how best to regain this forest."

"The gendarmes are here, – don't you hear them? they are holding a council of war."

"Well, you have twice had luck to-night; go! bring my cousins here and hide them in these vaults; they'll be safe from all pursuit – Alas! I am good for nothing!" she cried, with rage; "I should be only a beacon to light the enemy – but the police will never imagine that my cousins are in the forest if they see me at my ease. So the question resolves itself into this: how can we get five good horses to bring them in six hours from Lagny to the forest, – five horses to be killed and hidden in some thicket."

"And the money?" said Michu, who was thinking deeply as he listened to the young countess.

"I gave my cousins a hundred louis this evening," she replied.

"I'll answer for them!" cried Michu. "But once hidden here you must not attempt to see them. My wife, or the little one, shall bring them food twice a week. But, as I can't be sure of what may happen to me, remember, mademoiselle, in case of trouble, that the main beam in my hay-loft has been bored with an auger. In the hole, which is plugged with a bit of wood, you will find a plan showing how to reach this spot. The trees which you will find marked with a red dot on the plan have a black mark at their foot close to the earth. Each of these trees is a sign-post. At the foot of the third old oak which stands to the left of each sign-post, two feet in front of it and buried seven feet in the ground, you will find a large metal tube; in each tube are one hundred thousand francs in gold. These eleven trees – there are only eleven – contain the whole fortune of the Simeuse brothers, now that Gondreville has been taken from them."

"It will take a hundred years for the nobility to recover from such blows," said Mademoiselle de Cinq-Cygne, slowly.

"Is there a pass-word?" asked Michu.

"'France and Charles' for the soldiers, 'Laurence and Louis' for the Messieurs d'Hauteserre and Simeuse. Good God! to think that I saw them yesterday for the first time in eleven years, and that now they are in danger of death – and what a death! Michu," she said, with a melancholy look, "be as prudent during the next fifteen hours as you have been grand and devoted during the last twelve years. If disaster were to overtake my cousins now I should die of it – No," she added, quickly, "I would live long enough to kill Bonaparte."

"There will be two of us to do that when all is lost," said Michu.

Laurence took his rough hand and wrung it warmly, as the English do. Michu looked at his watch; it was midnight.

"We must leave here at any cost," he said. "Death to the gendarme who attempts to stop me! And you, madame la comtesse, without presuming to dictate, ride back to Cinq-Cygne as fast as you can. The police are there by this time; fool them! delay them!"

The hole once opened, Michu flung himself down with his ear to the earth; then he rose precipitately. "The gendarmes are at the edge of the forest towards Troyes!" he said. "Ha, I'll get the better of them yet!"

He helped the countess to come out, and replaced the stones.

When this was done he heard her soft voice telling him she must see him mounted before mounting herself. Tears came to the eyes of the stern man as he exchanged a last look with his young mistress, whose own eyes were tearless.

"Fool them! yes, he is right!" she said when she heard him no longer. Then she darted towards Cinq-Cygne at full gallop.

Chapter VIII. Trials of the Police

Madame d'Hauteserre, roused by the danger of her sons, and not believing that the Revolution was over, but still fearing its summary justice, recovered her senses by the violence of the same distress which made her lose them. Led by an agonizing curiosity she returned to the salon, which presented a picture worthy of the brush of a genre painter. The abbe, still seated at the card-table and mechanically playing with the counters, was covertly observing Corentin and Peyrade, who were standing together at a corner of the fireplace and speaking in a low voice. Several times Corentin's keen eye met the not less keen glance of the priest; but, like two adversaries who knew themselves equally strong, and who return to their guard after crossing their weapons, each averted his eyes the instant they met. The worthy old d'Hauteserre, poised on his long thin legs like a heron, was standing beside the stout form of the mayor, in an attitude expressive of utter stupefaction. The mayor, though dressed as a bourgeois, always looked like a servant. Each gazed with a bewildered eye at the gendarmes, in whose clutches Gothard was still sobbing, his hands purple and swollen from the tightness of the cord that bound them. Catherine maintained her attitude of artless simplicity, which was quite impenetrable. The corporal, who, according to Corentin, had committed a great blunder in arresting these smaller fry, did not know whether to stay where he was or to depart. He stood pensively in the middle of the salon, his hand on the hilt of his sabre, his eye on the two Parisians. The Durieus, also stupefied, and the other servants of the chateau made an admirable group of expressive uneasiness. If it had not been for Gothard's convulsive snifflings those present could have heard the flies fly.

When Madame d'Hauteserre, pale and terrified, opened the door and entered the room, almost carried by Mademoiselle Goujet, whose red eyes had evidently been weeping, all faces turned to her at once. The two agents hoped as much as the household feared to see Laurence enter. This spontaneous movement of both masters and servants seemed produced by the sort of mechanism which makes a number of wooden figures perform the same gesture or wink the same eye.

Madame d'Hauteserre advanced by three rapid strides towards Corentin and said, in a broken voice but violently: "For pity's sake, monsieur, tell me what my sons are accused of. Do you really think they have been here?"

The abbe, who seemed to be saying to himself when he saw the old lady, "She will certainly commit some folly," lowered his eyes.

"My duty and the mission I am engaged in forbid me to tell you," answered Corentin, with a gracious but rather mocking air.

This refusal, which the detestable politeness of the vulgar fop seemed to make all the more emphatic, petrified the poor mother, who fell into a chair beside the Abbe Goujet, clasped her hands and began to pray.

"Where did you arrest that blubber?" asked Corentin, addressing the corporal and pointing to Laurence's little henchman.

"On the road that leads to the farm along the park walls; the little scamp had nearly reached the Closeaux woods," replied the corporal.

"And that girl?"

"She? oh, it was Oliver who caught her."

"Where was she going?"

"Towards Gondreville."

"They were going in opposite directions?" said Corentin.

"Yes," replied the gendarme.

"Is that boy the groom, and the girl the maid of the citizeness Cinq-Cygne?" said Corentin to the mayor.

"Yes," replied Goulard.

After Corentin had exchanged a few words with Peyrade in a whisper, the latter left the room, taking the corporal of gendarmes with him.

Just then the corporal of Arcis made his appearance. He went up to Corentin and spoke to him in a low voice: "I know these premises well," he said; "I have searched everywhere; unless those young fellows are buried, they are not here. We have sounded all the floors and walls with the butt end of our muskets."

Peyrade, who presently returned, signed to Corentin to come out, and then took him to the breach in the moat and showed him the sunken way.

"We have guessed the trick," said Peyrade.

"And I'll tell you how it was done," added Corentin. "That little scamp and the girl decoyed those idiots of gendarmes and thus made time for the game to escape."

"We can't know the truth till daylight," said Peyrade. "The road is damp; I have ordered two gendarmes to barricade it top and bottom. We'll examine it after daylight, and find out by the footsteps who went that way."

"I see a hoof-mark," said Corentin; "let us go to the stables."

"How many horses do you keep?" said Peyrade, returning to the salon with Corentin, and addressing Monsieur d'Hauteserre and Goulard.

"Come, monsieur le maire, you know, answer," cried Corentin, seeing that that functionary hesitated.

"Why, there's the countess's mare, Gothard's horse, and Monsieur d'Hauteserre's."

"There is only one in the stable," said Peyrade.

"Mademoiselle is out riding," said Durieu.

"Does she often ride about at this time of night?" said the libertine Peyrade, addressing Monsieur d'Hauteserre.

"Often," said the good man, simply. "Monsieur le maire can tell you that."

"Everybody knows she has her freaks," remarked Catherine;

"she looked at the sky before she went to bed, and I think the glitter of your bayonets in the moonlight puzzled her. She told me she wanted to know if there was going to be another revolution."

"When did she go?" asked Peyrade.

"When she saw your guns."

"Which road did she take?"

"I don't know."

"There's another horse missing," said Corentin.

"The gendarmes – took it – away from me," said Gothard.

"Where were you going?" said one of them.

"I was – following – my mistress to the farm," sobbed the boy.

The gendarme looked towards Corentin as if expecting an order. But Gothard's speech was evidently so true and yet so false, so perfectly innocent and so artful that the two Parisians again looked at each other as if to echo Peyrade's former words: "They are not ninnies."

Monsieur d'Hauteserre seemed incapable of a word; the mayor was bewildered; the mother, imbecile from maternal fears, was putting questions to the police agents that were idiotically innocent; the servants had been roused from their sleep. Judging by these trifling signs, and these diverse characters, Corentin came to the conclusion that his only real adversary was Mademoiselle de Cinq-Cygne. Shrewd and dexterous as the police may be, they are always under certain disadvantages. Not only are they forced to discover all that is known to a conspirator, but they must also suppose and test a great number of things before they hit upon the right one. The conspirator is always thinking of his own safety, whereas the police is only on duty at certain hours. Were it not for treachery and betrayals, nothing would be easier than to conspire successfully. The conspirator has more mind concentrated upon himself than the police can bring to bear with

all its vast facilities of action. Finding themselves stopped short
morally, as they might be physically by a door which they expected to find open being shut in their faces, Corentin and Peyrade saw they were tricked and misled, without knowing by
whom.

"I assert," said the corporal of Arcis, in their ear, "that if the
four young men slept here last night it must have been in the
beds of their father and mother, and Mademoiselle de Cinq-
Cygne, or those of the servants; or they must have spent the night
in the park. There is not a trace of their presence."

"Who could have warned them?" said Corentin, to Peyrade.
"No one but the First Consul, Fouche, the ministers, the prefect of
police, and Malin knew anything about it."

"We must set spies in the neighborhood," whispered Peyrade.

"And watch the spies," said the abbe, who smiled as he overheard the word and guessed all.

"Good God!" thought Corentin, replying to the abbe's smile
with one of his own; "there is but one intelligent being here, – he's
the one to come to an understanding with; I'll try him."

"Gentlemen – " said the mayor, anxious to give some proof of
devotion to the First Consul and addressing the two agents.

"Say 'citizens'; the Republic still exists," interrupted Corentin,
looking at the priest with a quizzical air.

"Citizens," resumed the mayor, "just as I entered this salon
and before I had opened my mouth Catherine rushed in and took
her mistress's hat, gloves, and whip."

A low murmur of horror came from the breasts of all the
household except Gothard. All eyes but those of the agent and the
gendarmes were turned threateningly on Goulard, the informer,
seeming to dart flames at him.

"Very good, citizen mayor," said Peyrade. "We see it all
plainly. Some one" (this with a glance of evident distrust at Cor-

entin) "warned the citizeness Cinq-Cygne in time."

"Corporal, handcuff that boy," said Corentin, to the gendarme, "and take him away by himself. And shut up that girl, too," pointing to Catherine. "As for you, Peyrade, search for papers," adding in his ear, "Ransack everything, spare nothing. – Monsieur l'abbe," he said, confidentially, "I have an important communication to make to you"; and he took him into the garden.

"Listen to me attentively, monsieur," he went on; "you seem to have the mind of a bishop, and (no one can hear us) you will understand me. I have no longer any hope except through you of saving these families, who, with the greatest folly, are letting themselves roll down a precipice where no one can save them. The Messieurs Simeuse and d'Hauteserre have been betrayed by one of those infamous spies whom governments introduce into all conspiracies to learn their objects, means, and members. Don't confound me, I beg of you, with the wretch who is with me. He belongs to the police; but I am honorably attached to the Consular cabinet, I am therefore behind the scenes. The ruin of the Simeuse brothers is not desired. Though Malin would like to see them shot, the First Consul, if they are here and have come without evil intentions, wishes them to be warned out of danger, for he likes good soldiers. The agent who accompanies me has all the powers, I, apparently, am nothing. But I see plainly what is hatching. The agent is pledged to Malin, who has doubtless promised him his influence, an office, and perhaps money if he finds the Simeuse brothers and delivers them up. The First Consul, who is a really great man, never favors selfish schemes – I don't want to know if those young men are here," he added, quickly, observing the abbe's gesture, "but I wish to tell you that there is only one way to save them. You know the law of the 6th Floreal, year X., which amnestied all the *emigres* who were still in foreign countries on condition that they returned home before the 1st Vendemiaire of the year XI., that is to say, in September of last year. But the Messieurs Simeuse having, like the Messieurs d'Hauteserre, served in the army of Conde, they come into the category of exceptions to this law. Their presence in France is therefore criminal, and suffices, under the circumstances in which we are, to make them suspected of collusion in a horrible plot. The First Consul saw the error of this exception which has made enemies for his government, and he wishes the Messieurs Simeuse to know that no steps will be taken against them, if they will send him a petition saying that they have re-entered France intending to submit to the laws, and agreeing to take oath to the Constitution. You can understand that the document ought to be in my hands before they are arrested, and be dated some days earlier. I would then be the bearer of it – I do not ask you where those young men are," he said again, seeing another gesture of denial from the priest. "We are, unfortunately, sure of finding them; the forest is guarded, the entrances to Paris and the frontiers are all watched. Pray listen to me; if these gentlemen are between the forest and Paris they must be taken; if they are in Paris they will be found; if they retreat to the frontier they will still be arrested. The First Consul likes the *ci-devants*, and cannot endure the republicans – simple enough; if he wants a throne he must needs strangle Liberty. Keep the matter a secret between us. This is what I will do; I will stay here till to-morrow and *be blind*; but beware of the agent; that cursed Provencal is the devil's own valet; he has the ear of Fouche just as I have that of the First Consul."

"If the Messieurs Simeuse are here," said the abbe, "I would give ten pints of my blood and my right arm to save them; but if Mademoiselle de Cinq-Cygne is in the secret she has not – and this I swear on my eternal salvation – betrayed it in any way, neither has she done me the honor to consult me. I am now very glad of her discretion, if discretion there be. We played cards last night as usual, at boston, in almost complete silence, until half-past ten o'clock, and we neither saw nor heard anything. Not a child can pass through this solitary valley without the whole community knowing it, and for the last two weeks no one has come from other places. Now the d'Hauteserre and the Simeuse brothers would make a party of four. Old d'Hauteserre and his wife have submitted to the present government, and they have made all imaginable efforts to persuade their sons to return to France; they wrote to them again yesterday. I can only say, upon my soul and conscience, that your visit has alone shaken my firm belief that these young men are living in Germany. Between ourselves, there is no one here, except the young countess, who does not do justice to the eminent qualities of the First Consul."

"Fox!" thought Corentin. "Well, if those young men are shot," he said, aloud; "it is because their friends have willed it – I wash my hands of the affair."

He had led the abbe to a part of the garden which lay in the moonlight, and as he said the last words he looked at him suddenly. The priest was greatly distressed, but his manner was that of a man surprised and wholly ignorant.

"Understand this, monsieur l'abbe," resumed Corentin; "the right of these young men to the estate of Gondreville will render them doubly criminal in the eyes of the middle class. I'd like to see them put faith in God and not in his saints – "

"Is there really a plot?" asked the abbe, simply.

"Base, odious, cowardly, and so contrary to the generous spirit of the nation," replied Corentin, "that it will meet with universal opprobrium."

"Well! Mademoiselle de Cinq-Cygne is incapable of baseness," cried the abbe.

"Monsieur l'abbe," replied Corentin, "let me tell you this; there is for us (meaning you and me) proof positive of her guilt; but there is not enough for the law. You see she took flight when we came; I sent the mayor to warn her."

"Yes, but for one who is so anxious to save them, you followed rather closely on his heels," said the abbe.

At those words the two men looked at each other, and all was said. Each belonged to those profound anatomists of thought to whom a mere inflexion of the voice, a look, a word suffices to reveal a soul, just as the Indians track their enemies by signs invisible to European eyes.

"I expected to draw something out of him, and I have only betrayed myself," thought Corentin.

"Ha! the sly rogue!" thought the priest.

Midnight rang from the old church clock just as Corentin and the abbe re-entered the salon. The opening and shutting of doors and closets could be heard from the bedrooms above. The gendarmes pulled open the beds; Peyrade, with the quick perception of a spy, handled and sounded everything. Such desecration excited both fear and indignation among the faithful servants of the house, who still stood motionless about the salon. Monsieur d'Hauteserre exchanged looks of commiseration with his wife and Mademoiselle Goujet. A species of horrible curiosity kept every one on the qui vive. Peyrade at length came down, holding in his hand a sandal-wood box which had probably been brought from China by Admiral de Simeuse. This pretty casket was flat and about the size of a quarto volume.

Peyrade made a sign to Corentin and took him into the embrasure of a window.

"I've an idea!" he said, "that Michu, who was ready to pay Marion eight hundred thousand francs in gold for Gondreville, and who evidently meant to shoot Malin yesterday, is the man who is helping the Simeuse brothers. His motive in threatening Marion and aiming at Malin must be the same. I thought when I saw him that he was capable of ideas; evidently he has but one; he discovered what was going on and he must have come here to warn them."

"Probably Malin talked about the conspiracy to his friend the notary, and Michu from his ambush overheard what was said," remarked Corentin, continuing the inductions of his colleague. "No doubt he has only postponed his shot to prevent an evil he thinks worse than the loss of Gondreville."

"He knew what we were the moment he laid eyes on us," said Peyrade. "I thought then that he was amazingly intelligent for a peasant."

"That proves that he is always on his guard," replied Corentin. "But, mind you, my old man, don't let us make a mistake. Treachery stinks in the nostrils, and primitive folks do scent it from afar."

"But that's our strength," said the Provencal.

"Call the corporal of Arcis," cried Corentin to one of the gendarmes. "I shall send him at once to Michu's house," he added to Peyrade.

"Our ear, Violette, is there," said Peyrade.

"We started without getting news from him. Two of us are not enough; we ought to have had Sabatier with us – Corporal," he said, when the gendarme appeared, taking him aside with Peyrade, "don't let them fool you as they did the Troyes corporal just now. We think Michu is in this business. Go to his house, put your eye on everything, and bring word of the result."

"One of my men heard horses in the forest just as they arrested the little groom; I've four fine fellows now on the track of whoever is hiding there," replied the gendarme.

He left the room, and the gallop of his horse which echoed on the paved courtyard died rapidly away.

"One thing is certain," said Corentin to himself, "either they have gone to Paris or they are retreating to Germany."

He sat down, pulled a note-book from the pocket of his spencer, wrote two orders in pencil, sealed them, and made a sign to one of the gendarmes to come to him.

"Be off at full gallop to Troyes, wake up the prefect, and tell him to start the telegraph as soon as there's light enough."

The gendarme departed. The meaning of this movement and Corentin's intentions were so evident that the hearts of the household sank within them; but this new anxiety was additional to another that was now martyrizing them; their eyes were fixed on the sandal-wood box! All the while the two agents were talking together they were each taking note of those eager looks. A sort of cold anger stirred the unfeeling hearts of these men who relished the power of inspiring terror. The police man has the instincts and emotions of a hunter: but where the one employs his powers of mind and body in killing a hare, a partridge, or a deer, the other is thinking of saving the State, or a king, and of winning a large reward. So the hunt for men is superior to the other class of hunting by all the distance that there is between animals and human beings. Moreover, a spy is forced to lift the part he plays to the level and the importance of the interests to which he is bound. Without looking further into this calling, it is easy to see that the man who follows it puts as much passionate ardor into his chase as another man does into the pursuit of game. Therefore the further these men advanced in their investigations the more eager they became; but the expression of their faces and their eyes continued calm and cold, just as their ideas, their suspicions, and their plans remained impenetrable. To any one who watched the effects of the moral scent, if we may so call it, of these blood-hounds on the track of hidden facts, and who noted and understood the movements of canine agility which led them to strike the truth in their rapid examination of probabilities, there was in it all something actually horrifying. How and why should men of genius fall so low when it was in their power to be so high? What imperfection, what vice, what passion debases them? Does a man become a police-agent as he becomes a thinker, writer, statesmen, painter, general, on the condition of knowing nothing but how to spy, as the others speak, write, govern, paint, and fight? The inhabitants of the chateau had but one wish, – that the thunderbolts of heaven might fall upon these miscreants; they were athirst for vengeance; and had it not been for the presence, up to this time, of the gendarmes there would undoubtedly have been an outbreak.

"No one, I suppose, has the key of this box?" said the cynical Peyrade, questioning the family as much by the movement of his huge red nose as by his words.

The Provencal noticed, not without fear, that the guards were no longer present; he and Corentin were alone with the family. The younger man drew a small dagger from his pocket, and began to force the lock of the box. Just then the desperate galloping of a horse was heard upon the road and then upon the pavement by the lawn; but most horrible of all was the fall and sighing of the animal, which seemed to drop all at once at the door of the middle tower. A convulsion like that which a thunderbolt might produce shook the spectators when Laurence, the trailing of whose riding-habit announced her coming, entered the room. The servants hastily formed into two lines to let her pass.

In spite of her rapid ride, the girl had felt the full anguish the discovery of the conspiracy must needs cause her. All her hopes were overthrown! she had galloped through ruins as her thoughts turned to the necessity of submission to the Consular government. Were it not for the danger which threatened the four gentlemen, and which served as a tonic to conquer her weariness and her despair, she would have dropped asleep on the way. The mare was almost killed in her haste to reach the chateau, and stand between her cousins and death. As all present looked at the heroic girl, pale, her features drawn, her veil aside, her whip in her hand, standing on the threshold of the door, whence her burning glance grasped the whole scene and comprehended it, each knew from the almost imperceptible motion which crossed the soured and bittered face of Corentin, that the real adversaries had met. A terrible duel was about to begin.

Noticing the box, now in the hands of Corentin, the countess raised her whip and sprang rapidly towards him. Striking his hands with so violent a blow that the casket fell to the ground, she seized it, flung it into the middle of the fire, and stood with her back to the chimney in a threatening attitude before either of the agents recovered from their surprise. The scorn which flamed from her eyes, her pale brow, her disdainful lips, were even more insulting than the haughty action which treated Corentin as though he were a venomous reptile. Old d'Hauteserre felt himself once more a cavalier; all his blood rushed to his face, and he grieved that he had no sword. The servants trembled for an instant with joy. The vengeance they had called down upon these men had come. But their joy was driven back within their souls by a terrible fear; the gendarmes were still heard coming and going in the garrets.

The *spy* – noun of strength, under which all shades of the police are confounded, for the public has never chosen to specify in language the varieties of those who compose this dispensary of social remedies so essential to all governments – the spy has this curious and magnificent quality: he never becomes angry; he possesses the Christian humility of a priest; his eyes are stolid with an indifference which he holds as a barrier against the world of fools who do not understand him; his forehead is adamant under insult; he pursues his ends like a reptile whose carapace is fractured only by a cannonball; but (like that reptile) he is all the more furious when the blow does reach him, because he believed his armor invulnerable. The lash of the whip upon his fingers was to Corentin, pain apart, the cannonball that cracked the shell. Coming from that magnificent and noble girl, this action, emblematic of her disgust, humiliated him, not only in the eyes of the people about him, but in his own.

Peyrade sprang to the hearth, caught Laurence's foot, raised it, and compelled her, out of modesty, to throw herself on the sofa, where she had lately lain asleep. The scene, like other contrasts in human things, was burlesque in the midst of terror. Peyrade scorched his hand as he dashed it into the fire to seize the box; but he got it, threw it on the floor and sat down upon it. These little actions were done with great rapidity and without a word being uttered. Corentin, recovering from the pain of the blow, caught Mademoiselle de Cinq-Cygne by both hands, and held her.

"Do not compel me to use force against you," he said, with withering politeness.

Peyrade's action had extinguished the fire by the natural process of suppressing the air.

"Gendarmes! here!" he cried, still occupying his ridiculous position.

"Will you promise to behave yourself?" said Corentin, insolently, addressing Laurence, and picking up his dagger, but not committing the great fault of threatening her with it.

"The secrets of that box do not concern the government," she answered, with a tinge of melancholy in her tone and manner. "When you have read the letters it contains you will, in spite of your infamy, feel ashamed of having read them – that is, if you can still feel shame at anything," she added, after a pause.

The abbe looked at her as if to say, "For God's sake, be calm!"

Peyrade rose. The bottom of the box, which had been nearly burned through, left a mark upon the floor; the lid was scorched and the sides gave way. The grotesque Scaevola, who had offered to the god of the Police and Terror the seat of his apricot breeches, opened the two sides of the box as if it had been a book, and slid three letters and two locks of hair upon the card-table. He was about to smile at Corentin when he perceived that the locks were of two shades of gray. Corentin released Mademoiselle de Cinq-Cygne's hands and went up to the table to read the letter from which the hair had fallen.

Laurence rose, moved to the table beside the spies, and said: – "Read it aloud; that shall be your punishment."

As the two men continued to read to themselves, she herself read out the following words: –

Dear Laurence, – My husband and I have heard of your noble conduct on the day of our arrest. We know that you love our dear twins as much, almost, as we love them ourselves. Therefore it is with you that we leave a token which will be both precious and sad to them. The executioner has come to cut our hair, for we are to die in a few moments; he has promised to put into your hands the only remembrance we are able to leave to our beloved orphans. Keep these last remains of us and give them to our sons in happier days. We have kissed these locks of hair and have laid our blessing upon them. Our last thought will be of our sons, of you, and of God. Love them, Laurence.

Berthe de Cinq-Cygne. Jean de Simeuse.

Tears came to the eyes of all the household as they listened to the letter.

Laurence looked at the agents with a petrifying glance and said, in a firm voice: –

"You have less pity than the executioner."

Corentin quietly folded the hair in the letter, laid the letter aside on the table, and put a box of counters on the top of it as if to prevent its blowing away. His coolness in the midst of the general emotion was horrible.

Peyrade unfolded the other letters.

"Oh, as for those," said Laurence, "they are very much alike. You hear the will; you can now hear of its fulfilment. In future I shall have no secrets from any one."

1794, Andernach. Before the battle.

My dear Laurence, – I love you for life, and I wish you to know it. But you ought also to know, in case I die, that my brother, Paul-Marie, loves you as much as I love you. My only consolation in dying would be the thought that you might some day make my brother your husband without being forced to see me die of jealousy – which must surely happen if, both of us being alive, you preferred him to me. After all, that preference seems natural, for he is, perhaps, more worthy of your love than I –

Marie-Paul.

"Here is the other letter," she said, with the color in her cheeks.

Andernach. Before the battle.

My kind Laurence, – My heart is sad; but Marie-Paul has a gayer nature, and will please you more than I am able to do. Some day you will have to choose between us – well, though I love you passionately –

"You are corresponding with *emigres*," said Peyrade, interrupting Laurence, and holding the letters between himself and the light to see if they contained between the lines any treasonable writing with invisible ink.

"Yes," replied Laurence, folding the precious letters, the paper of which was already yellow with time. "But by virtue of what right do you presume to violate my dwelling and my personal liberty?"

"Ah, that's the point!" cried Peyrade. "By what right, indeed! – it is time to let you know it, beautiful aristocrat," he added, taking a warrant from his pocket, which came from the minister of justice and was countersigned by the minister of the interior. "See, the authorities have their eye upon you."

"We might also ask you," said Corentin, in her ear, "by what right you harbor in this house the assassins of the First Consul. You have applied your whip to my hands in a manner that authorizes me to take my revenge upon your cousins, whom I came here to save."

At the mere movement of her lips and the glance which Laurence cast upon Corentin, the abbe guessed what that great artist was saying, and he made her a sign to be distrustful, which no one intercepted but Goulard. Peyrade struck the cover of the box to see if there were a double top.

"Don't break it!" she exclaimed, taking the cover from him.

She took a pin, pushed the head of one of the carved figures, and the two halves of the top, joined by a spring, opened. In the hollow half lay miniatures of the Messieurs de Simeuse, in the uniform of the army of Conde, two portraits on ivory done in Germany. Corentin, who felt himself in presence of an adversary worthy of his efforts, called Peyrade aside into a corner of the room and conferred with him.

"How could you throw *that* into the fire?" said the abbe, speaking to Laurence and pointing to the letter of the marquise which enclosed the locks of hair.

For all answer the young girl shrugged her shoulders significantly. The abbe comprehended then that she had made the sacrifice to mislead the agents and gain time; he raised his eyes to heaven with a gesture of admiration.

"Where did they arrest Gothard, whom I hear crying?" she asked him, loud enough to be overheard.

"I don't know," said the abbe.

"Did he reach the farm?"

"The farm!" whispered Peyrade to Corentin. "Let us send there."

"No," said Corentin; "that girl never trusted her cousins' safety to a farmer. She is playing with us. Do as I tell you, so that we mayn't have to leave here without detecting something, after committing the great blunder of coming here at all."

Corentin stationed himself before the fire, lifting the long pointed skirts of his coat to warm himself and assuming the air, manner, and tone of a gentleman who was paying a visit.

"Mesdames, you can go to bed, and the servants also. Monsieur le maire, your services are no longer needed. The sternness of our orders does not permit us to act otherwise than as we have done; but as soon as the walls, which seem to me rather thick, have been thoroughly examined, we shall take our departure."

The mayor bowed to the company and retired; but neither the abbe nor Mademoiselle Goujet stirred. The servants were too uneasy not to watch the fate of their young mistress. Madame d'Hauteserre, who, from the moment of Laurence's entrance, had studied her with the anxiety of a mother, rose, took her by the arm, led her aside, and said in a low voice, "Have you seen them?"

"Do you think I could have let your sons be under this roof without your knowing it?" replied Laurence. "Durieu," she added, "see if it is possible to save my poor Stella; she is still breathing."

"She must have gone a great distance," said Corentin.

"Forty miles in three hours," she answered, addressing the abbe, who watched her with amazement. "I started at half-past nine, and it was well past one when I returned."

She looked at the clock which said half-past two.

"So you don't deny that you have ridden forty miles?" said Corentin.

"No," she said. "I admit that my cousins, in their perfect innocence, expected not to be excluded from the amnesty, and were on their way to Cinq-Cygne. When I found that the Sieur Malin was plotting to injure them, I went to warn them to return to Germany, where they will be before the telegraph can have guarded the frontier. If I have done wrong I shall be punished for it."

This answer, which Laurence had carefully considered, was so probable in all its parts that Corentin's convictions were shaken. In that decisive moment, when every soul present hung suspended, as it were, on the faces of the two adversaries, and all eyes turned from Corentin to Laurence and from Laurence to Corentin, again the gallop of a horse, coming from the forest, resounded on the road and from there through the gates to the paved courtyard. Frightful anxiety was stamped on every face.

Peyrade entered, his eyes gleaming with joy. He went hastily to Corentin and said, loud enough for the countess to hear him: "We have caught Michu."

Laurence, to whom the agony, fatigue, and tension of all her intellectual faculties had given an unusual color, turned white and fell back almost fainting on a chair. Madame Durieu, Mademoiselle Goujet, and Madame d'Hauteserre sprang to help her, for she was suffocating. She signed to cut the frogging of her habit.

"Duped!" said Corentin to Peyrade. "I am certain now they are on their way to Paris. Change the orders."

They left the room and the house, placing one gendarme on guard at the door of the salon. The infernal cleverness of the two men had gained a terrible advantage by taking Laurence in the trap of a not uncommon trick.

Chapter IX. Foiled

At six o'clock in the morning, as day was dawning, Corentin and Peyrade returned. Having explored the covered way they were satisfied that horses had passed through it to reach the forest. They were now awaiting the report of the captain of gendarmerie sent to reconnoitre the neighborhood. Leaving the chateau in charge of a corporal, they went to the tavern at Cinq-Cygne to get their breakfast, giving orders that Gothard, who never ceased to reply to all questions with a burst of tears, should be set at liberty, also Catherine, who still continued silent and immovable. Catherine and Gothard went to the salon to kiss the hands of their mistress, who lay exhausted on the sofa; Durieu also went in to tell her that Stella would recover, but needed great care.

The mayor, uneasy and inquisitive, met Peyrade and Corentin in the village. He declared that he could not allow such important officials to breakfast in a miserable tavern, and he took them to his own house. The abbey was only three quarters of a mile distant. On the way, Peyrade remarked that the corporal of Arcis had sent no news of Michu or of Violette.

"We are dealing with very able people," said Corentin; "they are stronger than we. The priest no doubt has a finger in all this."

Just as the mayor's wife was ushering her guests into a vast dining-room (without any fire) the lieutenant of gendarmes arrived with an anxious air.

"We met the horse of the corporal of Arcis in the forest without his master," he said to Peyrade.

"Lieutenant," cried Corentin, "go instantly to Michu's house and find out what is going on there. They must have murdered the corporal."

This news interfered with the mayor's breakfast. Corentin and Peyrade swallowed their food with the rapidity of hunters halting for a meal, and drove back to the chateau in their wicker carriage, so as to be ready to start at the first call for any point where their presence might be necessary. When the two men reappeared in the salon into which they had brought such trouble, terror, grief, and anxiety, they found Laurence, in a dressing-gown, Monsieur d'Hauteserre and his wife, the abbe and his sister, sitting round the fire, to all appearance tranquil.

"If they had caught Michu," Laurence told herself, "they would have brought him with them. I have the mortification of knowing that I was not the mistress of myself, and that I threw some light upon the matter for those wretches; but the harm can be undone – How long are we to be your prisoners?" she asked sarcastically, with an easy manner.

"How can she know anything about Michu? No one from the outside has got near the chateau; she is laughing at us," said the two agents to each other by a look.

"We shall not inconvenience you long," replied Corentin. "In three hours from now we shall offer our regrets for having troubled your solitude."

No one replied. This contemptuous silence redoubled Corentin's inward rage. Laurence and the abbe (the two minds of their little world) had talked the man over and drawn their conclusions. Gothard and Catherine had set the breakfast-table near the fire and the abbe and his sister were sharing the meal. Neither masters nor servants paid the slightest attention to the two spies, who walked up and down the garden, the courtyard or the lawn, returning every now and then to the salon.

At half-past two the lieutenant reappeared.

"I found the corporal," he said to Corentin, "lying in the road which leads from the pavilion of Cinq-Cygne to the farm at Bellache. He has no wound, only a bad contusion of the head, caused, apparently, by his fall. He told me he had been lifted suddenly off his horse and flung so violently to the ground that he could not discover how the thing was done. His feet left the stirrups, which was lucky, for he might have been killed by the horse dragging him. We put him in charge of Michu and Violette – "

"Michu! is Michu in his own house?" said Corentin, glancing at Laurence.

The countess smiled ironically, like a woman obtaining her revenge.

"He is bargaining with Violette about the sale of some land," said the lieutenant. "They seemed to me drunk; and it's no wonder, for they have been drinking all night and discussing the matter, and they haven't come to terms yet."

"Did Violette tell you so?" cried Corentin.

"Yes," said the lieutenant.

"Nothing is right if we don't attend to it ourselves!" cried Peyrade, looking at Corentin, who doubted the lieutenant's news as much as the other did.

"At what hour did you get to Michu's house?" asked Corentin, noticing that the countess had glanced at the clock.

"About two," replied the lieutenant.

Laurence covered Monsieur and Madame d'Hauteserre and the abbe and his sister in one comprehensive glance, which made them fancy they were wrapped in an azure mantle; triumph sparkled in her eyes, she blushed, and the tears welled up beneath her lids. Strong under all misfortunes, the girl knew not how to weep except from joy. At this moment she was all glorious, especially to the priest, who was sometimes distressed by the virility of her character, and who now caught a glimpse of the infinite tenderness of her woman's nature. But such feelings lay in her soul like a treasure hidden at a great depth beneath a block of granite.

Just then a gendarme entered the salon to ask if he might bring in Michu's son, sent by his father to speak to the gentlemen from Paris. Corentin gave an affirmative nod. Francois Michu, a sly little chip of the old block, was in the courtyard, where Gothard, now at liberty, got a chance to speak to him for an instant under the eyes of a gendarme. The little fellow managed to slip something into Gothard's hand without being detected, and the latter glided into the salon after him till he reached his mistress, to whom he stealthily conveyed both halves of the wedding-ring, a sure sign, she knew, that Michu had met the four gentlemen and put them in safety.

"My papa wants to know what he's to do with the corporal, who ain't doing well," said Francois.

"What's the matter with him?" asked Peyrade.

"It's his head – he pitched down hard on the ground," replied the boy. "For a gindarme who knows how to ride it was bad luck – I suppose the horse stumbled. He's got a hole – my! as big as your fist – in the back of his head. Seems as if he must have hit some big stone, poor man! He may be a gindarme, but he suffers all the same – you'd pity him."

The captain of the gendarmerie now arrived and dismounted in the courtyard. Corentin threw up the window, not to lose time.

"What has been done?"

"We are back like the Dutchmen! We found nothing but five dead horses, their coats stiff with sweat, in the middle of the forest. I have kept them to find out where they came from and who owns them. The forest is surrounded; whoever is in it can't get out."

"At what hour do you suppose those horsemen entered the forest?"

"About half-past twelve."

"Don't let a hare leave that forest without your seeing it," whispered Corentin. "I'll station Peyrade at the village to help you; I am going to see the corporal myself – Go to the mayor's house," he added, still whispering, to Peyrade. "I'll send some able man to relieve you. We shall have to make use of the country-people; examine all faces." He turned towards the family and said in a threatening tone, "Au revoir!"

No one replied, and the two agents left the room.

"What would Fouche say if he knew we had made a domiciliary visit without getting any results?" remarked Peyrade as he helped Corentin into the osier vehicle.

"It isn't over yet," replied the other, "those four young men are in the forest. Look there!" and he pointed to Laurence who was watching them from a window. "I once revenged myself on a woman who was worth a dozen of that one and had stirred my bile a good deal less. If this girl comes in the way of my hatchet I'll pay her for the lash of that whip."

"The other was a strumpet," said Peyrade; "this one has rank."

"What difference is that to me? All's fish that swims in the sea," replied Corentin, signing to the gendarme who drove him to whip up.

Ten minutes later the chateau de Cinq-Cygne was completely evacuated.

"How did they get rid of the corporal?" said Laurence to Francois Michu, whom she had ordered to sit down and eat some breakfast.

"My father told me it was a matter of life and death and I mustn't let anybody get into our house," replied the boy. "I knew when I heard the horses in the forest that I'd got to do with them hounds of gindarmes, and I meant to keep 'em from getting in. So I took some big ropes that were in my garret and fastened one of 'em to a tree at the corner of the road. Then I drew the rope high enough to hit the breast of a man on horseback, and tied it to the tree on the opposite side of the way in the direction where I heard the horses. That barred the road. It didn't miss fire, I can tell you! There was no moon, and the corporal just pitched! – but he wasn't killed; they're tough, them gindarmes! I did what I could."

"You have saved us!" said Laurence, kissing him as she took him to the gate. When there, she looked about her and seeing no one she said cautiously, "Have they provisions?"

"I have just taken them twelve pounds of bread and four bottles of wine," said the boy. "They'll be snug for a week."

Returning to the salon, the girl was beset with mute questions in the eyes of all, each of whom looked at her with as much admiration as eagerness.

"But have you really seen them?" cried Madame d'Hauteserre.

The countess put a finger on her lips and smiled; then she left the room and went to bed; her triumph sure, utter weariness had overtaken her.

The shortest road from Cinq-Cygne to Michu's lodge was that which led from the village past the farm at Bellache to the *rond-point* where the Parisian spies had first seen Michu on the preceding evening. The gendarme who was driving Corentin took this way, which was the one the corporal of Arcis had taken. As they drove along, the agent was on the look-out for signs to show why the corporal had been unhorsed. He blamed himself for having sent but one man on so important an errand, and he drew from this mistake an axiom for the police Code, which he afterwards applied.

"If they have got rid of the corporal," he said to himself, "they have done as much by Violette. Those five horses have evidently brought the four conspirators and Michu from the neighborhood of Paris to the forest. Has Michu a horse?" he inquired of the gendarme who was driving him and who belonged to the squad from Arcis.

"Yes, and a famous little horse it is," answered the man, "a hunter from the stables of the ci-devant Marquis de Simeuse. There's no better beast, though it is nearly fifteen years old. Michu can ride him fifty miles and he won't turn a hair. He takes mighty good care of him and wouldn't sell him at any price."

"What does the horse look like?"

"He's brown, turning rather to black; white stockings above the hoofs, thin, all nerves like an Arab."

"Did you ever see an Arab?"

"In Egypt – last year. I've ridden the horses of the mamelukes. We have to serve twelve years in the cavalry, and I was on the Rhine under General Steingel, after that in Italy, and then I followed the First Consul to Egypt. I'll be a corporal soon."

"When I get to Michu's house go to the stable; if you have served twelve years in the cavalry you know when a horse is blown. Let me know the condition of Michu's beast."

"See! that's where our corporal was thrown," said the man, pointing to a spot where the road they were following entered the *rond-point*.

"Tell the captain to come and pick me up at Michu's, and I'll go with him to Troyes."

So saying Corentin got down, and stood about for a few minutes examining the ground. He looked at the two elms which faced each other, – one against the park wall, the other on the bank of the *rond-point*; then he saw (what no one had yet noticed) the button of a uniform lying in the dust, and he picked it up. Entering the lodge he saw Violette and Michu sitting at the table in the kitchen and talking eagerly. Violette rose, bowed to Corentin, and offered him some wine.

"Thank you, no; I came to see the corporal," said the young man, who saw with half a glance that Violette had been drunk all night.

"My wife is nursing him upstairs," said Michu.

"Well, corporal, how are you?" said Corentin who had run up the stairs and found the gendarme with his head bandaged, and lying on Madame Michu's bed; his hat, sabre, and shoulder-belt on a chair.

Marthe, faithful in her womanly instincts, and knowing nothing of her son's prowess, was giving all her care to the corporal, assisted by her mother.

"We expect Monsieur Varlet the doctor from Arcis," she said to Corentin; "our servant-lad has gone to fetch him."

"Leave us alone for a moment," said Corentin, a good deal surprised at the scene, which amply proved the innocence of the two women. "Where were you struck?" he asked the man, examining his uniform.

"On the breast," replied the corporal.

"Let's see your belt," said Corentin.

On the yellow band with a white edge, which a recent regulation had made part of the equipment of the guard now called National, was a metal plate a good deal like that of the foresters, on which the law required the inscription of these remarkable words: "Respect to persons and to properties." Francois's rope had struck the belt and defaced it. Corentin took up the coat and found the place where the button he had picked up upon the road belonged.

"What time did they find you?" asked Corentin.

"About daybreak."

"Did they bring you up here at once?" said Corentin, noticing that the bed had not been slept in.

"Yes."

"Who brought you up?"

"The women and little Michu, who found me unconscious."

"So!" thought Corentin: "evidently they didn't go to bed. The corporal was not shot at, nor struck by any weapon, for an assailant must have been at his own height to strike a blow. Something, some obstacle, was in his way and that unhorsed him. A piece of wood? not possible! an iron chain? that would have left marks. What did you feel?" he said aloud.

"I was knocked over so suddenly – "

"The skin is rubbed off under your chin," said Corentin quickly.

"I think," said the corporal, "that a rope did go over my face."

"I have it!" cried Corentin; "somebody tied a rope from tree to tree to bar the way."

"Like enough," replied the corporal.

Corentin went downstairs to the kitchen.

"Come, you old rascal," Michu was saying to Violette, "let's make an end of this. One hundred thousand francs for the place, and you are master of my whole property. I shall retire on my income."

"I tell you, as there's a God in heaven, I haven't more than sixty thousand."

"But don't I offer you time to pay the rest? You've kept me here since yesterday, arguing it. The land is in prime order."

"Yes, the soil is good," said Violette.

"Wife, some more wine," cried Michu.

"Haven't you drunk enough?" called down Marthe's mother. "This is the fourteenth bottle since nine o'clock yesterday."

"You have been here since nine o'clock this morning, haven't you?" said Corentin to Violette.

"No, beg your pardon, since last night I haven't left the place, and I've gained nothing after all; the more he makes me drink the more he puts up the price."

"In all markets he who raises his elbow raises a price," said Corentin.

A dozen empty bottles ranged along the table proved the truth of the old woman's words. Just then the gendarme who had driven him made a sign to Corentin, who went to the door to speak to him.

"There is no horse in the stable," said the man.

"You sent your boy on horseback to the chateau, didn't you?" said Corentin, returning to the kitchen. "Will he be back soon?"

"No, monsieur," said Michu, "he went on foot."

"What have you done with your horse, then?"

"I have lent him," said Michu, curtly.

"Come out here, my good fellow," said Corentin; "I've a word for your ear."

Corentin and Michu left the house.

"The gun which you were loading yesterday at four o'clock you meant to use in murdering the Councillor of State; but we can't take you up for that – plenty of intention, but no witnesses. You managed, I don't know how, to stupefy Violette, and you and your wife and that young rascal of yours spent the night out of doors to warn Mademoiselle de Cinq-Cygne and save her cousins, whom you are hiding here, – though I don't as yet know where. Your son or your wife threw the corporal off his horse cleverly enough. Well, you've got the better of us just now; you're a devil of a fellow. But the end is not yet, and you won't have the last word. Hadn't you better compromise? your masters would be the better for it."

"Come this way, where we can talk without being overheard," said Michu, leading the way through the park to the pond.

When Corentin saw the water he looked fixedly at Michu, who was no doubt reckoning on his physical strength to fling the spy into seven feet of mud below three feet of water. Michu replied with a look that was not less fixed. The scene was absolutely as if a cold and flabby boa constrictor had defied one of those tawny, fierce leopards of Brazil.

"I am not thirsty," said Corentin, stopping short at the edge of the field and putting his hand into his pocket to feel for his dagger.

"We shall never come to terms," said Michu, coldly.

"Mind what you're about, my good fellow; the law has its eye upon you."

"If the law can't see any clearer than you, there's danger to every one," said the bailiff.

"Do you refuse?" said Corentin, in a significant tone.

"I'd rather have my head cut off a thousand times, if that could be done, than come to an agreement with such a villain as you."

Corentin got into his vehicle hastily, after one more comprehensive look at Michu, the lodge, and Couraut, who barked at him. He gave certain orders in passing through Troyes, and then returned to Paris. All the brigades of gendarmerie in the neighborhood received secret instructions and special orders.

During the months of December, January, and February the search was active and incessant, even in remote villages. Spies were in all the taverns. Corentin learned some important facts: a horse like that of Michu had been found dead in the neighborhood of Lagny; the five horses burned in the forest of Nodesme had been sold, for five hundred francs each, by farmers and millers to a man who answered to the description of Michu. When the decree against the accomplices and harborers of Georges was put in force Corentin confined his search to the forest of Nodesme. After Moreau, the royalists, and Pichegru were arrested no strangers were ever seen about the place.

Michu lost his situation at that time; the notary of Arcis brought him a letter in which Malin, now made senator, requested Grevin to settle all accounts with the bailiff and dismiss him. Michu asked and obtained a formal discharge and became a free man. To the great astonishment of the neighborhood he went to live at Cinq-Cygne, where Laurence made him the farmer of all the reserved land about the chateau. The day of his installation as farmer coincided with the fatal day of the death of the Duc d'Enghien, when nearly the whole of France heard at the same time of the arrest, trial, condemnation, and death of the prince, – terrible reprisals, which preceded the trial of Polignac, Riviere, and Moreau.

PART II

Chapter X. One and the Same, Yet a Two-Fold Love

While the new farm-house was being built Michu the Judas, so-called, and his family occupied the rooms over the stables at Cinq-Cygne on the side of the chateau next to the famous breach. He bought two horses, one for himself and one for Francois, and they both joined Gothard in accompanying Mademoiselle de Cinq-Cygne in her many rides, which had for their object, as may well be imagined, the feeding of the four gentlemen and perpetual watching that they were still in safety. Francois and Gothard, assisted by Couraut and the countess's dogs, went in front and beat the woods all around the hiding-place to make sure that there was no one within sight. Laurence and Michu carried the provisions which Marthe, her mother, and Catherine prepared, unknown to the other servants of the household so as to restrict the secret to themselves, for all were sure that there were spies in the village. These expeditions were never made oftener than twice a week and on different days and at different hours, sometimes by day, sometimes by night.

These precautions lasted until the trial of Riviere, Polignac, and Moreau ended. When the senatus-consultum, which called the dynasty of Bonaparte to the throne and nominated Napoleon as Emperor of the French, was submitted to the French people for acceptance Monsieur d'Hauteserre signed the paper Goulard brought him. When it was made known that the Pope would come to France to crown the Emperor, Mademoiselle de Cinq-Cygne no longer opposed the general desire that her cousins and the young d'Hauteserres should petition to have their names struck off the list of *emigres*, and be themselves reinstated in their rights as citizens. On this, old d'Hauteserre went to Paris and consulted the ci-devant Marquis de Chargeboeuf who knew Talleyrand. That minister, then in favor, conveyed the petition to Josephine, and Josephine gave it to her husband, who was addressed as Emperor, Majesty, Sire, before the result of the popular vote was known. Monsieur de Chargeboeuf, Monsieur d'Hauteserre, and the Abbe Goujet, who also went to Paris, obtained an interview with Talleyrand, who promised them his support. Napoleon had already pardoned several of the principal actors in the great royalist conspiracy; and yet, though the four gentlemen were merely suspected of complicity, the Emperor, after a meeting of the Council of State, called the senator Malin, Fouche, Talleyrand, Cambaceres, Lebrun, and Dubois, prefect of police, into his cabinet.

"Gentlemen," said the future Emperor, who still wore the dress of the First Consul, "we have received from the Sieurs de Simeuse and d'Hauteserre, officers in the army of the Prince de Conde, a request to be allowed to re-enter France."

"They are here now," said Fouche.

"Like many others whom I meet in Paris," remarked Talleyrand.

"I think you have not met these gentlemen," said Malin, "for they are hidden in the forest of Nodesme, where they consider themselves at home."

He was careful not to tell the First Consul and Fouche how he himself had given them warning, by talking with Grevin within hearing of Michu, but he made the most of Corentin's reports and convinced Napoleon that the four gentlemen were sharers in the plot of Riviere and Polignac, with Michu for an accomplice. The prefect of police confirmed these assertions.

"But how could that bailiff know that the conspiracy was discovered?" said the prefect, "for the Emperor and the council and I were the only persons in the secret."

No one paid attention to this remark.

"If they have been hidden in that forest for the last seven months and you have not been able to find them," said the Emperor to Fouche, "they have expiated their misdeeds."

"Since they are my enemies as well," said Malin, frightened by the Emperor's clear-sightedness, "I desire to follow the magnanimous example of your Majesty; I therefore make myself their advocate and ask that their names be stricken from the list of *emigres.*"

"They will be less dangerous to you here than if they are exiled; for they will now have to swear allegiance to the Empire and the laws," said Fouche, looking at Malin fixedly.

"In what way are they dangerous to the senator?" asked Napoleon.

Talleyrand spoke to the Emperor for some minutes in a low voice. The reinstatement of the Messieurs de Simeuse and d'Hauteserre appeared to be granted.

"Sire," said Fouche, "rely upon it, you will hear of those men again."

Talleyrand, who had been urged by the Duc de Grandlieu, gave the Emperor pledges in the name of the young men on their honor as gentlemen (a term which had great fascination for Napoleon), to abstain from all attacks upon his Majesty and to submit themselves to his government in good faith.

"Messieurs d'Hauteserre and de Simeuse are not willing to bear arms against France, now that events have taken their present course," he said, aloud; "they have little sympathy, it is true, with the Imperial government, but they are just the men that your Majesty ought to conciliate. They will be satisfied to live on French soil and obey the laws."

Then he laid before the Emperor a letter he had received from the brothers in which these sentiments were expressed.

"Anything so frank is likely to be sincere," said the Emperor, returning the letter and looking at Lebrun and Cambaceres. "Have you any further suggestions?" he asked of Fouche.

"In your Majesty's interests," replied the future minister of police, "I ask to be allowed to inform these gentlemen of their reinstatement – when it is *really granted,*" he added, in a louder tone.

"Very well," said Napoleon, noticing an anxious look on Fouche's face.

The matter did not seem positively decided when the Council rose; but it had the effect of putting into Napoleon's mind a vague distrust of the four young men. Monsieur d'Hauteserre, believing that all was gained, wrote a letter announcing the good news. The family at Cinq-Cygne were therefore not surprised when, a few days later, Goulard came to inform the countess and Madame d'Hauteserre that they were to send the four gentlemen to Troyes, where the prefect would show them the decree reinstating them in their rights and administer to them the oath of allegiance to the Empire and the laws. Laurence replied that she would send the notification to her cousins and the Messieurs d'Hauteserre.

"Then they are not here?" said Goulard.

Madame d'Hauteserre looked anxiously after Laurence, who left the room to consult Michu. Michu saw no reason why the young men should not be released at once from their hiding-place. Laurence, Michu, his son, and Gothard therefore started as soon as possible for the forest, taking an extra horse, for the countess resolved to accompany her cousins to Troyes and return with them. The whole household, made aware of the good news, gathered on the lawn to witness the departure of the happy cavalcade. The four young men issued from their long confinement, mounted their horses, and took the road to Troyes, accompanied by Mademoiselle Cinq-Cygne. Michu, with the help of his son and Gothard, closed the entrance to the cellar, and started to return home on foot. On the way he recollected that he had left the forks and spoons and a silver cup, which the young men had been using, in the cave, and he went back for them alone. When he reached the edge of the pond he heard voices, and went straight to the entrance of the cave through the brushwood.

"Have you come for your silver?" said Peyrade, showing his big red nose through the branches.

Without knowing why, for at any rate his young masters were safe, Michu felt a sharp agony in all his joints, so keen was the sense of vague, indefinable coming evil which took possession of him; but he went forward at once, and found Corentin on the stairs with a taper in his hand.

"We are not very harsh," he said to Michu; "we might have seized your ci-devants any day for the last week; but we knew they were reinstated – You're a tough fellow to deal with, and you gave us too much trouble not to make us anxious to satisfy our curiosity about this hiding-place of yours."

"I'd give something," cried Michu, "to know how and by whom we have been sold."

"If that puzzles you, old fellow," said Peyrade, laughing, "look at your horses' shoes, and you'll see that you betrayed your-selves."

"Well, there need be no rancor!" said Corentin, whistling for the captain of gendarmerie and their horses.

"So that rascally Parisian blacksmith who shoed the horses in the English fashion and left Cinq-Cygne only the other day was their spy!" thought Michu. "They must have followed our tracks when the ground was damp. Well, we're quits now!"

Michu consoled himself by thinking that the discovery was of no consequence, as the young men were now safe, Frenchmen once more, and at liberty. Yet his first presentiment was a true one. The police, like the Jesuits, have the one virtue of never abandoning their friends or their enemies.

Old d'Hauteserre returned from Paris and was more than surprised not to be the first to bring the news. Durieu prepared a succulent dinner, the servants donned their best clothes, and the household impatiently awaited the exiles, who arrived about four o'clock, happy, – and yet humiliated, for they found they were to be under police surveillance for two years, obliged to present themselves at the prefecture every month and ordered to remain in the commune of Cinq-Cygne during the said two years. "I'll send you the papers for signature," the prefect said to them. "Then, in the course of a few months, you can ask to be relieved of these conditions, which are imposed on all of Pichegru's ac-complices. I will back your request."

These restrictions, fairly deserved, rather dispirited the young men, but Laurence laughed at them.

"The Emperor of the French," she said, "was badly brought up; he has not yet acquired the habit of bestowing favors graciously."

The party found all the inhabitants of the chateau at the gates, and a goodly proportion of the people of the village waiting on the road to see the young men, whose adventures had made them famous throughout the department. Madame d'Hauteserre held her sons to her breast for a long time, her face covered with tears; she was unable to speak and remained silent, though happy, through a part of the evening. No sooner had the Simeuse twins dismounted than a cry of surprise arose on all sides, caused by their amazing resemblance, – the same look, the same voice, the same actions. They both had the same movement in rising from their saddles, in throwing their leg over the crupper of their horses when dismounting, in flinging the reins upon the animal's neck. Their dress, precisely the same, contributed to this likeness. They wore boots *a la* Suwaroff, made to fit the instep, tight trousers of white leather, green hunting-jackets with metal buttons, black cravats, and buckskin gloves. The two young men, just thirty-one years of age, were – to use a term in vogue in those days – charming cavaliers, of medium height but well set up, brilliant eyes with long lashes, floating in liquid like those of children, black hair, noble brows, and olive skin. Their speech, gentle as that of a woman, fell graciously from their fresh red lips; their manners, more elegant and polished than those of the provincial gentlemen, showed that knowledge of men and things had given them that supplementary education which makes its possessor a man of the world.

Not lacking money, thanks to Michu, during their emigration, they had been able to travel and be received at foreign courts. Old d'Hauteserre and the abbe thought them rather haughty; but in their present position this may have been the sign of nobility of character. They possessed all the eminent little marks of a careful education, to which they added a wonderful dexterity in bodily exercises. Their only dissimilarity was in the region of ideas. The youngest charmed others by his gaiety, the eldest by his melancholy; but the contrast, which was purely spiritual, was not at first observable.

"Ah, wife," whispered Michu in Marthe's ear, "how could one help devoting one's self to those young fellows?"

Marthe, who admired them as a wife and mother, nodded her head prettily and pressed her husband's hand. The servants were allowed to kiss their new masters.

During their seven months' seclusion in the forest (which the young men had brought upon themselves) they had several times committed the imprudence of taking walks about their hiding-place, carefully guarded by Michu, his son, and Gothard. During these walks, taken usually on starlit nights, Laurence, reuniting the thread of their past and present lives, felt the utter impossibility of choosing between the brothers. A pure and equal love for each divided her heart. She fancied indeed that she had two hearts. On their side, the brothers dared not speak to themselves of their impending rivalry. Perhaps all three were trusting to time and accident. The condition of her mind on this subject acted no doubt upon Laurence as they entered the house, for she hesitated a moment, and then took an arm of each as she entered the salon followed by Monsieur and Madame d'Hauteserre, who were occupied with their sons. Just then a cheer burst from the servants, "Long live the Cinq-Cygne and the Simeuse families!" Laurence turned round, still between the brothers, and made a charming gesture of acknowledgement.

When these nine persons came to actually observe each other, – for in all meetings, even in the bosom of families, there comes a moment when friends observe those from whom they have been long parted, – the first glance which Adrien d'Hauteserre cast upon Laurence seemed to his mother and to the abbe to betray love. Adrien, the youngest of the d'Hauteserres, had a sweet and tender soul; his heart had remained adolescent in spite of the catastrophes which had nerved the man. Like many young heroes, kept virgin in spirit by perpetual peril, he was daunted by the timidities of youth. In this he was very different from his brother, a man of rough manners, a great hunter, an intrepid soldier, full of resolution, but coarse in fibre and without activity of mind or delicacy in matters of the heart. One was all soul, the other all action; and yet they both possessed in the same degree that sense of honor which is the vital essence of a gentleman. Dark, short, slim and wiry, Adrien d'Hauteserre gave an impression of strength; whereas Robert, who was tall, pale and fair, seemed weakly. Adrien, nervous in temperament, was stronger in soul; while his brother though lymphatic, was fonder of bodily exercise. Families often present these singularities of contrast, the causes of which it might be interesting to examine; but they are mentioned here merely to explain how it was that Adrien was not likely to find a rival in his brother. Robert's affection for Laurence was that of a relation, the respect of a noble for a girl of his own caste. In matters of sentiment the elder d'Hauteserre belonged to the class of men who consider woman as an appendage to man, limiting her sphere to the physical duties of maternity; demanding perfection in that respect, but regarding her mentally as of no account. To such men the admittance of woman as an actual sharer in society, in the body politic, in the family, meant the subversion of the social system. In these days we are so far removed from this theory of primitive people that almost all women, even those who do not desire the fatal emancipation offered by the new sects, will be shocked in merely hearing of it; but it must be owned that Robert d'Hauteserre had the misfortune to think in that way. Robert was a man of the middle-ages, Adrien a man of to-day. These differences instead of hindering their affection had drawn its bonds the closer. On the first evening after the return of the young men these shades of character were caught and understood by the abbe, Mademoiselle Goujet, and Madame d'Hauteserre, who, while playing their boston, were secretly foreseeing the difficulties of the future.

At twenty-three years of age, having passed through the many reflections of a long solitude and the anguish of a defeated enterprise, Laurence had become a woman, and felt within her an absorbing desire for affection. She now put forth all her graces of her mind and was charming; she revealed the hidden beauties of her tender heart with the simple candor of a child. For the last thirteen years she had been a woman only through suffering; she longed to obtain amends for it, and she showed herself as loving and winning as she had been, up to this time, strong and great.

The four elders, who were the last to leave the salon that night, admitted to each other that they felt uneasy at the new position of this charming girl. What power might not passion have on a young woman of her character and with her nobility of soul? The twin brothers loved her with one and the same love and a blind devotion; which of the two would Laurence choose? To choose one was to kill the other. Countess in her own right, she could bring her husband a title and certain prerogatives, together with a long lineage. Perhaps in thinking of these advantages the elder of the twins, the Marquis de Simeuse, would sacrifice himself to give Laurence to his brother, who, according to the old laws, was poor and without a title. But would the younger brother deprive the elder of the happiness of having Laurence for a wife? At a distance, this strife of love and generosity might do no harm, – in fact, so long as the brothers were facing danger the chances of war might end the difficulty; but what would be the result of this reunion? When Marie-Paul and Paul-Marie reached the age when passions rise to their greatest height could they share, as now, the looks and words and attentions of their cousin? must there not inevitably arise a jealousy between them the consequences of which might be horrible? What would then become of the unity of those beautiful lives, one in heart though twain in body? To these questionings, passed from one to another as they finished their game, Madame d'Hauteserre replied that in her opinion Laurence would not marry either of her cousins. The poor lady had experienced that evening one of those inexplicable presentiments which are secrets between the mother's heart and God.

Laurence, in her inward consciousness, was not less alarmed at finding herself tete-a-tete with her cousins. To the active drama of conspiracy, to the dangers which the brothers had incurred, to the pain and penalties of their exile, was now succeeding another sort of drama, of which she had never thought. This noble girl could not resort to the violent means of refusing to marry either of the twins; and she was too honest a woman to marry one and keep an irresistible passion for the other in her heart. To remain unmarried, to weary her cousins' love by no decision, and then to take the one who was faithful to her in spite of her caprices, was a solution of the difficulty not so much sought for by her as vaguely admitted. As she fell asleep that night she told herself the wisest course to follow was to let things take their chance. Chance is, in love, the providence of women.

The next morning Michu went to Paris, whence he returned a few days later with four fine horses for his new masters. In six weeks' time the hunting would begin, and the young countess sagely reflected that the violent excitements of that exercise would be a help against the tete-a-tetes of the chateau. At first, however, an unexpected result surprised the spectators of these strange loves and roused their admiration. Without any premeditated agreement the brothers rivalled each other in attentions to Laurence, with a sense of pleasure in so doing which appeared to suffice them. The relation between themselves and Laurence was just as fraternal as that between themselves. What could be more natural? After so long an absence they felt the necessity of studying her, of knowing her well and letting her know them, leaving to her the right of choice. They were sustained in this first trial by the mutual affection which made their double life one and the same life.

Love, like their own mother, was unable to distinguish between the brothers. Laurence was obliged (in order to know them apart and make no mistakes) to give them different cravats – to the elder a white one, to the younger black. Without this perfect resemblance, this identity of life, which misled all about them, such a situation would be justly thought impossible. It can, indeed, be explained only by the fact itself, which is one of those which men do not believe in unless they see them; and then the mind is more bewildered by having to explain them than by the actual sight which caused belief. If Laurence spoke, her voice echoed in two hearts equally faithful and loving with one tone. Did she give utterance to an intelligent, or witty, or noble thought, her glance encountered the delight expressed in two

117

glances which followed her every movement, interpreted her slightest wish, and beamed upon her ever with a new expression, gaiety in the one, tender melancholy in the other. In any matter that concerned their mistress the brothers showed an admirable quick-wittedness of heart coupled with instant action which (to use the abbe's own expression) approached the sublime. Often, if something had to be fetched, if it was a question of some little attention which men delight to pay to a beloved woman, the elder would leave that pleasure to the younger with a look at Laurence that was proud and tender. The younger, on the other hand, put all his own pride into paying such debts. This rivalry of noble natures in a feeling which leads men often to the jealous ferocity of the beasts amazed the old people who were watching it, and bewildered their ideas.

Such little details often drew tears to the eyes of the countess. A single sensation, which is perhaps all-powerful in some rare organizations, will give an idea of Laurence's emotions; it may be perceived by recalling the perfect unison of two fine voices (like those of Malibran and Sontag) in some harmonious *duo*, or the blending of two instruments touched by the hand of genius, their melodious tones entering the soul like the passionate sighing of one heart. Sometimes, seeing the Marquis de Simeuse buried in an arm-chair and glancing from time to time with deepest melancholy at his brother and Laurence who were talking and laughing, the abbe believed him capable of making the great sacrifice; presently, however, the priest would see in the young man's eyes the flash of an unconquerable passion. Whenever either of the brothers found himself alone with Laurence he might reasonably suppose himself the one preferred.

"I fancy then that there is but one of them," explained the countess to the abbe when he questioned her. That answer showed the priest her total want of coquetry. Laurence did not conceive that she was loved by two men.

"But, my dear child," said Madame d'Hauteserre one evening (her own son silently dying of love for Laurence), "you must choose!"

"Oh, let us be happy," she replied; "God will save us from ourselves."

Adrien d'Hauteserre buried within his breast the jealousy that was consuming him; he kept the secret of his torture, aware of how little he could hope. He tried to be content with the happiness of seeing the charming woman who during the few months this struggle lasted shone in all her brilliancy. In one sense Laurence had become coquettish, taking that dainty care of her person which women who are loved delight in. She followed the fashions, and went more than once to Paris to deck her beauty with *chiffons* or some choice novelty. Desirous of giving her cousins a sense of home and its every enjoyment, from which they had so long been severed, she made her chateau, in spite of the remonstrances of her late guardian, the most completely comfortable house in Champagne.

Robert d'Hauteserre saw nothing of this hidden drama; he never noticed his brother's love for Laurence. As to the girl herself, he liked to tease her about her coquetry, – for he confounded that odious defect with the natural desire to please; he was always mistaken in matters of feeling, taste, and the higher ethics. So, whenever this man of the middle-ages appeared on the scene, Laurence immediately made him, unknown to himself, the clown of the play; she amused her cousins by arguing with Robert, and leading him, step by step, into some bog of ignorance and stupidity. She excelled in such clever mischief, which, to be really successful, must leave the victim content with himself. And yet, though his nature was a coarse one, Robert never, during those delightful months (the only happy period in the lives of the three young people) said one virile word which might have brought matters to a crisis between Laurence and her cousins. He was struck with the sincerity of the brothers; he saw how the one could be glad at the happiness of the other and yet suffer anguish in the depths of his heart, and he did perceive how a woman might shrink from showing tenderness to one which would grieve the other. This perception on Robert's part was a just one; it explains a situation which, in times of faith, when the sovereign pontiff had power to intervene and cut the Gordian knot of such

phenomena (allied to the deepest and most impenetrable myster-
ies), would have found its solution. The Revolution had deepened
the Catholic faith in these young hearts, and religion now rendered this crisis in their lives the more severe, because nobility of
character is ever heightened by the grandeur of circumstances. A
sense of this truth kept Monsieur and Madame d'Hauteserre and
the abbe from the slightest fear of any unworthy result on the
part of the brothers or of Laurence.

This private drama, secretly developing within the limits of
the family life where each member watched it silently, ran its
course so rapidly and withal so slowly, it carried with it so many
unhoped-for pleasures, trifling jars, frustrated fancies, hopes re-
versed, anxious waitings, delayed explanations and mute avow-
als that the dwellers at Cinq-Cygne paid no attention to the public drama of the Emperor's coronation. At times these passions
made a truce and sought distraction in the violent enjoyment of
hunting, when weariness of body took from the soul all occasions
to wander in the dangerous meadows of reverie. Neither Laurence nor her cousins had a thought now for public affairs; each
day brought its palpitating and absorbing interests for their
hearts.

"Really," said Mademoiselle Goujet one evening, "I don't
know which of all the lovers loves the most."

Adrien, who happened to be alone in the salon with the four
card-players, raised his eyes and turned pale. For the last few
days his only hold on life had been the pleasure of seeing Laurence and of listening to her.

"I think," said the abbe, "that the countess, being a woman,
loves with the greater abandonment to love."

Laurence, the twins, and Robert entered the room soon after.
The newspapers had just arrived. England, seeing the failure of
all conspiracies attempted within the borders of France, was now
arming all Europe against their common enemy. The disaster at
Trafalgar had overthrown one of the most amazing plans which
human genius ever conceived; by which, if it had succeeded, the
Emperor would have paid the nation for his election by the ruin

of the British power. The camp at Boulogne had just been raised. Napoleon, whose solders were, as always, inferior in numbers to the enemy, was about to carry the war into parts of Europe where he had not before waged it. The whole world was breathless, awaiting the results of the campaign.

"He'll surely be defeated this time," said Robert, laying down the paper.

"The armies of Austria and of Russia are before him," said Marie-Paul.

"He has never fought in Germany," added Paul-Marie.

"Of whom are you speaking?" asked Laurence.

"The Emperor," answered the three gentlemen.

The jealous girl threw a disdainful look at her twin lovers, which humiliated them while it rejoiced the heart of Adrien, who made a gesture of admiration and gave her one proud look, which said plainly that *he* thought only of her, – of Laurence.

"I told you," said the abbe in a low voice, "that love would some day cause her to forget her animosity."

It was the first, last, and only reproach the brothers ever received from her; but certainly at that moment their love, which could still be distracted by national events, was inferior to that of Laurence, which, absorbed her mind so completely that she only knew of the amazing triumph at Austerlitz by overhearing a discussion between Monsieur d'Hauteserre and his sons.

Faithful to his ideas of submission, the old man wished both Robert and Adrien to re-enter the French army and apply for service; they could, he thought, be reinstated in their rank and soon find an opening to military honors. But royalist opinions were now all-powerful at Cinq-Cygne. The four young men and Laurence laughed at their prudent elder, who seemed to foresee a coming evil. Possibly, prudence is less virtue than the exercise of some instinct, or *sense* of the mind (if it is allowable to couple those two words). A day will come, no doubt, when physiologists and philosophers will both admit that the senses are, in some

way, the sheath or vehicle of a keen and penetrative active power
which issues from the mind.

Chapter XI. Wise Counsel

After peace was concluded between France and Austria, towards the end of the month of February, 1806, a relative, whose influence had been employed for the reinstatement of the Simeuse brothers, and who was destined later to give them signal proofs of family attachment, the ci-devant Marquis de Chargeboeuf, whose estates extended from the department of the Seine-et-Marne to that of the Aube, arrived one morning at Cinq-Cygne in a species of caleche which was then named in derision a *berlingot*. When this shabby carriage was driven past the windows the inhabitants of the chateau, who were at breakfast, were convulsed with laughter; but when the bald head of the old man was seen issuing from behind the leather curtain of the vehicle Monsieur d'Hauteserre told his name, and all present rose instantly to receive and do honor to the head of the house of Chargeboeuf.

"We have done wrong to let him come to us," said the Marquis de Simeuse to his brother and the d'Hauteserres; "we ought to have gone to him and made our acknowledgements."

A servant, dressed as a peasant, who drove the horses from a seat on a level with the body of the carriage, slipped his cartman's whip into a coarse leather socket, and got down from the box to assist the marquis from the carriage; but Adrien and the younger de Simeuse prevented him, unbuttoned the leather apron, and helped the old man out in spite of his protestations. This gentleman of the old school chose to consider his yellow *berlingot* with its leather curtains a most convenient and excellent equipage. The servant, assisted by Gothard, unharnessed the stout horses with shining flanks, accustomed no doubt to do as much duty at the plough as in a carriage.

"In spite of this cold weather! Why, you are a knight of the olden time," said Laurence, to her visitor, taking his arm and leading him into the salon.

"What has he come for?" thought old d'Hauteserre.

Monsieur de Chargeboeuf, a handsome old gentleman of sixty-six, in light-colored breeches, his small weak legs encased in colored stockings, wore powder, pigeon-wings and a queue. His green cloth hunting-coat with gold buttons was braided and frogged with gold. His white waistcoat glittered with gold embroidery. This apparel, still in vogue among old people, became his face, which was not unlike that of Frederick the Great. He never put on his three-cornered hat lest he should destroy the effect of the half-moon traced upon his cranium by a layer of powder. His right hand, resting on a hooked cane, held both cane and hat in a manner worthy of Louis XIV. The fine old gentleman took off his wadded silk pelisse and seated himself in an arm-chair, holding the three-cornered hat and the cane between his knees in an attitude the secret of which has never been grasped by any but the roues of Louis XV.'s court, an attitude which left the hands free to play with a snuff-box, always a precious trinket. Accordingly the marquis drew from the pocket of his waistcoat, which was closed by a flap embroidered in gold arabesques, a sumptuous snuff-box. While fingering his own pinch and offering the box around him with another charming gesture accompanied with kindly smiles, he noticed the pleasure which his visit gave. He seemed then to comprehend why these young *emigres* had been remiss in their duty towards him, and to be saying to himself, "When we are making love we can't make visits."

"You will stay with us some days?" said Laurence.

"Impossible," he replied. "If we were not so separated by events (for as to distance, you go farther than that which lies between us) you would know, my dear child, that I have daughters, daughters-in-law, and grand-children. All these dear creatures would be very uneasy if I did not return to them to-night, and I have forty-five miles to go."

"Your horses are in good condition," said the Marquis de Simeuse.

"Oh! I am just from Troyes, where I had business yesterday."

After the customary polite inquiries for the Marquise de Chargeboeuf and other matters really uninteresting but about which politeness assumes that we are keenly interested, it dawned on Monsieur d'Hauteserre that the old gentleman had come to warn his young relatives against imprudence. He remarked that times were changed and no one could tell what the Emperor might now become.

"Oh!" said Laurence, "he'll make himself God."

The Marquis spoke of the wisdom of concession. When he stated, with more emphasis and authority than he put into his other remarks, the necessity of submission, Monsieur d'Hauteserre looked at his sons with an almost supplicating air.

"Would you serve that man?" asked the Marquis de Simeuse.

"Yes, I would, if the interests of my family required it," replied Monsieur de Chargeboeuf.

Gradually the old man made them aware, though vaguely, of some threatened danger. When Laurence begged him to explain the nature of it, he advised the four young men to refrain from hunting and to keep themselves as much in retirement as possible.

"You treat the domain of Gondreville as if it were your own," he said to the Messieurs de Simeuse, "and you are keeping alive a deadly hatred. I see, by the surprise upon your faces, that you are quite unaware of the ill-will against you at Troyes, where your late brave conduct is remembered. They tell of how you foiled the police of the Empire; some praise you for it, but others regard you as enemies of the Emperor; partisans declare that Napoleon's clemency is inexplicable. That, however, is nothing. The real danger lies here; you foiled men who thought themselves cleverer than you; and low-bred men never forgive. Sooner or later justice, which in your department emanates from your enemy, Senator Malin (who has his henchmen everywhere, even in the ministerial offices), – *his* justice will rejoice to see you involved in some annoying scrape. A peasant, for instance, will quarrel with you for riding over his field; your guns are in your hands, you are hot-tempered, and something happens. In your position it is absolutely essential that you should not put yourselves in the wrong. I do not speak to you thus without good reason. The police keep this arrondissement under strict surveillance; they have an agent in that little hole of Arcis expressly to protect the Imperial senator Malin against your attacks. He is afraid of you, and says so openly."

"It is a calumny!" cried the younger Simeuse.

"A calumny, – I am sure of it myself, but will the public believe it? Michu certainly did aim at the senator, who does not forget the danger he was in; and since your return the countess has taken Michu into her service. To many persons, in fact to the majority, Malin will seem to be in the right. You do not understand how delicate the position of an *emigre* is towards those who are now in possession of his property. The prefect, a very intelligent man, dropped a word to me yesterday about you which has made me uneasy. In short, I sincerely wish you would not remain here."

This speech was received in dumb amazement. Marie-Paul rang the bell.

"Gothard," he said, to the little page, "send Michu here."

"Michu, my friend," said the Marquis de Simeuse when the man appeared, "is it true that you intended to kill Malin?"

"Yes, Monsieur le marquis; and when he comes here again I shall lie in wait for him."

"Do you know that we are suspected of instigating it, and that our cousin, by taking you as her farmer is supposed to be furthering your scheme?"

"Good God!" cried Michu, "am I accursed? Shall I never be able to rid you of that villain?"

"No, my man, no!" said Paul-Marie. "But we will always take care of you, though you will have to leave our service and the country too. Sell your property here; we will send you to Trieste to a friend of ours who has immense business connections, and he'll employ you until things are better in this country for all of us."

Tears came into Michu's eyes; he stood rooted to the floor.

"Were there any witnesses when you aimed at Malin?" asked the Marquis de Chargeboeuf.

"Grevin the notary was talking with him, and that prevented my killing him – very fortunately, as Madame la Comtesse knows," said Michu, looking at his mistress.

"Grevin is not the only one who knows it?" said Monsieur de Chargeboeuf, who seemed annoyed at what was said, though none but the family were present.

"That police spy who came here to trap my masters, he knew it too," said Michu.

Monsieur de Chargeboeuf rose as if to look at the gardens, and said, "You have made the most of Cinq-Cygne." Then he left the house, followed by the two brothers and Laurence, who now saw the meaning of his visit.

"You are frank and generous, but most imprudent," said the old man. "It was natural enough that I should warn you of a rumor which was certain to be a slander; but what have you done now? you have let such weak persons as Monsieur and Madame d'Hauteserre and their sons see that there was truth in it. Oh, young men! young men! You ought to keep Michu here and go away yourselves. But if you persist in remaining, at least write a letter to the senator and tell him that having heard the rumors about Michu you have dismissed him from your employ."

"We!" exclaimed the brothers; "what, write to Malin, – to the murderer of our father and our mother, to the insolent plunderer of our property!"

"All true; but he is one of the chief personages at the Imperial court, and the king of your department."

"He, who voted for the death of Louis XVI. in case the army of Conde entered France!" cried Laurence.

"He, who probably advised the murder of the Ducd'Enghien!" exclaimed Paul-Marie.

"Well, well, if you want to recapitulate his titles of nobility," cried Monsieur de Chargeboeuf, "say he who pulled Robespierre by the skirts of his coat to make him fall when he saw that his enemies were stronger than he; he who would have shot Bonaparte if the 18th Brumaire had missed fire; he who manoeuvres now to bring back the Bourbons if Napoleon totters; he whom the strong will ever find on their side to handle either sword or pistol and put an end to an adversary whom they fear! But – all that is only reason the more for what I urge upon you."

"We have fallen very low," said Laurence.

"Children," said the old marquis, taking them by the hand and going to the lawn, then covered by a slight fall of snow; "you will be angry at the prudent advice of an old man, but I am bound to give it, and here it is: If I were you I would employ as go-between some trustworthy old fellow – like myself, for instance; I would commission him to ask Malin for a million of francs for the title-deeds of Gondreville; he would gladly consent if the matter were kept secret. You will then have capital in hand, an income of a hundred thousand francs, and you can buy a fine estate in another part of France. As for Cinq-Cygne, it can safely be left to the management of Monsieur d'Hauteserre, and you can draw lots as to which of you shall win the hand of this dear heiress – But ah! I know the words of an old man in the ears of the young are like the words of the young in the ears of the old, a sound without meaning."

The old marquis signed to his three relatives that he wished no answer, and returned to the salon, where, during their absence, the abbe and his sister had arrived.

The proposal to draw lots for their cousin's hand had offended the brothers, while Laurence revolted in her soul at the bitterness of the remedy the old marquis counselled. All three were now less gracious to him, though they did not cease to be polite. The warmth of their feeling was chilled. Monsieur de Chargeboeuf, who felt the change, cast frequent looks of kindly compassion on these charming young people. The conversation became general, but the old marquis still dwelt on the necessity of submitting to events, and he applauded Monsieur d'Hauteserre for his persistence in urging his sons to take service under the Empire.

"Bonaparte," he said, "makes dukes. He has created Imperial fiefs, he will therefore make counts. Malin is determined to be Comte de Gondreville. That is a fancy," he added, looking at the Simeuse brothers, "which might be profitable to you – "

"Or fatal," said Laurence.

As soon as the horses were put-to the marquis took leave, accompanied to the door by the whole party. When fairly in the carriage he made a sign to Laurence to come and speak to him, and she sprang upon the foot-board with the lightness of a swallow.

"You are not an ordinary woman, and you ought to understand me," he said in her ear. "Malin's conscience will never allow him to leave you in peace; he will set some trap to injure you. I implore you to be careful of all your actions, even the most unimportant. Compromise, negotiate; those are my last words."

The brothers stood motionless behind their cousin and watched the *berlingot* as it turned through the iron gates and took the road to Troyes. Laurence repeated the old man's last words. But sage experience should not present itself to the eyes of youth in a *berlingot*, colored stockings, and a queue. These ardent young hearts had no conception of the change that had passed over France; indignation crisped their nerves, honor boiled with their noble blood through every vein.

"He, the head of the house of Chargeboeuf!" said the Marquis de Simeuse. "A man who bears the motto *Adsit fortior*, the noblest of warcries!"

"We are no longer in the days of Saint-Louis," said the younger Simeuse.

"But 'We die singing,'" said the countess. "The cry of the five young girls of my house is mine!"

"And ours, 'Cy meurs,'" said the elder Simeuse. "Therefore, no quarter, I say; for, on reflection, we shall find that our relative

129

had pondered well what he told us – Gondreville to be the title of a Malin!"

"And his seat!" said the younger.

"Mansart designed it for noble stock, and the populace will get their children in it!" exclaimed the elder.

"If that were to come to pass, I'd rather see Gondreville in ashes!" cried Mademoiselle Cinq-Cygne.

One of the villagers, who had entered the grounds to examine a calf Monsieur d'Hauteserre was trying to sell him, overheard these words as he came from the cow-sheds.

"Let us go in," said Laurence, laughing; "this is very imprudent; we are giving the old marquis a right to blame us. My poor Michu," she added, as she entered the salon, "I had forgotten your adventure; as we are not in the odor of sanctity in these parts you must be careful not to compromise us in future. Have you any other peccadilloes on your conscience?"

"I blame myself for not having killed the murderer of my old masters before I came to the rescue of my present ones – "

"Michu!" said the abbe in a warning tone.

"But I'll not leave the country," Michu continued, paying no heed to the abbe's exclamation, "till I am certain you are safe. I see fellows roaming about here whom I distrust. The last time we hunted in the forest, that keeper who took my place at Gondreville came to me and asked if we supposed we were on our own property. 'Ho! my lad,' I said, 'we can't get rid in two weeks of ideas we've had for centuries.'"

"You did wrong, Michu," said the Marquis de Simeuse, smiling with satisfaction.

"What answer did he make?" asked Monsieur d'Hauteserre.

"He said he would inform the senator of our claims," replied Michu.

"Comte de Gondreville!" repeated the elder Simeuse; "what a

masquerade! But after all, they say 'your Majesty' to Bonaparte!"

"And to the Grand Duc de Berg, 'your Highness!'" said the abbe.

"Who is he?" asked the Marquis de Simeuse.

"Murat, Napoleon's brother-in-law," replied old d'Hauteserre.

"Delightful!" remarked Mademoiselle de Cinq-Cygne. "Do they also say 'your Majesty' to the widow of Beauharnais?"

"Yes, mademoiselle," said the abbe.

"We ought to go to Paris and see it all," cried Laurence.

"Alas, mademoiselle," said Michu, "I was there to put Francois at school, and I swear to you there's no joking with what they call the Imperial Guard. If the rest of the army are like them, the thing may last longer than we."

"They say many of the noble families are taking service," said Monsieur d'Hauteserre.

"According to the present law," added the abbe, "you will be compelled to serve. The conscription makes no distinction of ranks or names."

"That man is doing us more harm with his court than the Revolution did with its axe!" cried Laurence.

"The Church prays for him," said the abbe.

These remarks, made rapidly one after another, were so many commentaries on the wise counsel of the old Marquis de Chargeboeuf; but the young people had too much faith, too much honor, to dream of resorting to a compromise. They told themselves, as all vanquished parties in all times have declared, that the luck of the conquerors would soon be at an end, that the Emperor had no support but that of the army, that the power *de facto* must sooner or later give way to the Divine Right, etc. So, in spite of the wise counsel given to them, they fell into the pitfall, which others, like old d'Hauteserre, more prudent and more amenable to reason, would have been able to avoid. If men were frank they might perhaps admit that misfortunes never overtake them until after they have received either an actual or an occult warning. Many do not perceive the deep meaning of such visible or invisible signs until after the disaster is upon them.

"In any case, Madame la comtesse knows that I cannot leave the country until I have given up a certain trust," said Michu in a low voice to Mademoiselle de Cinq-Cygne.

For all answer she made him a sign of acquiescence, and he left the room.

Chapter XII. The Facts of a Mysterious Affair

Michu sold his farm at once to Beauvisage, a farmer at Bella-che, but he was not to receive the money for twenty days. A month after the Marquis de Chargeboeuf's visit, Laurence, who had told her cousins of their buried fortune, proposed to them to take the day of the Mi-careme to disinter it. The unusual quantity of snow which fell that winter had hitherto prevented Michu from obtaining the treasure, and it now gave him pleasure to undertake the operation with his masters. He was determined to leave the neighborhood as soon as it was over, for he feared himself.

"Malin has suddenly arrived at Gondreville, and no one knows why," he said to his mistress. "I shall never be able to resist putting the property into the market by the death of its owner. I feel I am guilty in not following my inspirations."

"Why should he leave Paris at this season?" said the countess.

"All Arcis is talking about it," replied Michu; "he has left his family in Paris, and no one is with him but his valet. Monsieur Grevin, the notary of Arcis, Madame Marion, the wife of the receiver-general, and her sister-in-law are staying at Gondreville."

Laurence had chosen the mid-lent day for their purpose because it enabled her to give her servants a holiday and so get them out of the way. The usual masquerade drew the peasantry to the town and no one was at work in the fields. Chance made its calculations with as much cleverness as Mademoiselle de Cinq-Cygne made hers. The uneasiness of Monsieur and Madame d'Hauteserre at the idea of keeping eleven hundred thousand francs in gold in a lonely chateau on the borders of a forest was likely to be so great that their sons advised they should know nothing about it. The secret of the expedition was therefore confined to Gothard, Michu, Laurence, and the four gentlemen.

After much consultation it seemed possible to put forty-eight thousand francs in a long sack on the crupper of each of their horses. Three trips would therefore bring the whole. It was

agreed to send all the servants, whose curiosity might be troublesome, to Troyes to see the shows. Catherine, Marthe, and Durieu,
who could be relied on, stayed at home in charge of the house.
The other servants were glad of their holiday and started by daybreak. Gothard, assisted by Michu, saddled the horses as soon as
they were gone, and the party started by way of the gardens to
reach the forest. Just as they were mounting – for the park gate
was so low on the garden side that they led their horses until they
were through it – old Beauvisage, the farmer at Bellache, happened to pass.

"There!" cried Gothard, "I hear some one."

"Oh, it is only I," said the worthy man, coming toward them.
"Your servant, gentleman; are you off hunting, in spite of the new
decrees? *I* don't complain of you; but do take care! though you
have friends you have also enemies."

"Oh, as for that," said the elder Hauteserre, smiling, "God
grant that our hunt may be lucky to-day, – if so, you will get your
masters back again."

These words, to which events were destined to give a totally
different meaning, earned a severe look from Laurence. The elder
Simeuse was confident that Malin would restore Gondreville for
an indemnity. These rash youths were determined to do exactly
the contrary of what the Marquis de Chargeboeuf had advised.
Robert, who shared these hopes, was thinking of them when he
gave utterance to the fatal words.

"Not a word of this, old friend," said Michu to Beauvisage,
waiting behind the others to lock the gate.

It was one of those fine mornings in March when the air is
dry, the earth pure, the sky clear, and the atmosphere a contradiction to the leafless trees; the season was so mild that the eye
caught glimpses here and there of verdure.

"We are seeking treasure when all the while you are the real
treasure of our house, cousin," said the elder Simeuse, gaily.

Laurence was in front, with a cousin on each side of her. The d'Hauteserres were behind, followed by Michu. Gothard had gone forward to clear the way.

"Now that our fortune is restored, you must marry my brother," said the younger in a low voice. "He adores you; together you will be as rich as nobles ought to be in these days."

"No, give the whole fortune to him and I will marry you," said Laurence; "I am rich enough for two."

"So be it," cried the Marquis; "I will leave you, and find a wife worthy to be your sister."

"So you really love me less than I thought you did?" said Laurence looking at him with a sort of jealousy.

"No; I love you better than either of you love me," replied the marquis.

"And therefore you would sacrifice yourself?" asked Laurence with a glance full of momentary preference.

The marquis was silent.

"Well, then, I shall think only of you, and that will be intolerable to my husband," exclaimed Laurence, impatient at his silence.

"How could I live without you?" said the younger twin to his brother.

"But, after all, you can't marry us both," said the marquis, replying to Laurence; "and the time has come," he continued, in the brusque tone of a man who is struck to the heart, "to make your decision."

He urged his horse in advance so that the d'Hauteserres might not overhear them. His brother's horse and Laurence's followed him. When they had put some distance between themselves and the rest of the party Laurence attempted to speak, but tears were at first her only language.

"I will enter a cloister," she said at last.

"And let the race of Cinq-Cygne end?" said the younger

brother. "Instead of one unhappy man, would you make two? No, whichever of us must be your brother only, will resign himself to that fate. It is the knowledge that we are no longer poor that has brought us to explain ourselves," he added, glancing at the marquis. "If I am the one preferred, all this money is my brother's. If I am rejected, he will give it to me with the title of de Simeuse, for he must then take the name and title of Cinq-Cygne. Whichever way it ends, the loser will have a chance of recovery – but if he feels he must die of grief, he can enter the army and die in battle, not to sadden the happy household."

"We are true knights of the olden time, worthy of our fathers," cried the elder. "Speak, Laurence; decide between us."

"We cannot continue as we are," said the younger.

"Do not think, Laurence, that self-denial is without its joys," said the elder.

"My dear loved ones," said the girl, "I am unable to decide. I love you both as though you were one being – as your mother loved you. God will help us. I cannot choose. Let us put it to chance – but I make one condition."

"What is it?"

"Whichever one of you becomes my brother must stay with me until I suffer him to leave me. I wish to be sole judge of when to part."

"Yes, yes," said the brothers, without explaining to themselves her meaning.

"The first of you to whom Madame d'Hauteserre speaks tonight at table after the Benedicite, shall be my husband. But neither of you must practise fraud or induce her to answer a question."

"We will play fair," said the younger, smiling.

Each kissed her hand. The certainty of some decision which both could fancy favorable made them gay.

"Either way, dear Laurence, you create a Comte de Cinq-Cygne – "

"I believe," thought Michu, riding behind them, "that mademoiselle will not long be unmarried. How gay my masters are! If my mistress makes her choice I shall not leave; I must stay and see that wedding."

Just then a magpie flew suddenly before his face. Michu, superstitious like all primitive beings, fancied he heard the muffled tones of a death-knell. The day, however, began brightly enough for lovers, who rarely see magpies when together in the woods. Michu, armed with his plan, verified the spots; each gentleman had brought a pickaxe, and the money was soon found. The part of the forest where it was buried was quite wild, far from all paths or habitations, so that the cavalcade bearing the gold returned unseen. This proved to be a great misfortune. On their way from Cinq-Cygne to fetch the last two hundred thousand francs, the party, emboldened by success, took a more direct way than on their other trips. The path passed an opening from which the park of Gondreville could be seen.

"What is that?" cried Laurence, pointing to a column of blue flame.

"A bonfire, I think," replied Michu.

Laurence, who knew all the by-ways of the forest, left the rest of the party and galloped towards the pavilion, Michu's old home. Though the building was closed and deserted, the iron gates were open, and traces of the recent passage of several horses struck Laurence instantly. The column of blue smoke was rising from a field in what was called the English park, where, as she supposed, they were burning brush.

"Ah! so you are concerned in it, too, are you, mademoiselle?" cried Violette, who came out of the park at top speed on his pony, and pulled up to meet Laurence. "But, of course, it is only a carnival joke? They surely won't kill him?"

"Who?"

"Your cousins wouldn't put him to death?"

"Death! whose death?"

"The senator's."

"You are crazy, Violette!"

"Well, what are you doing here, then?" he demanded.

At the idea of a danger which was threatening her cousins, Laurence turned her horse and galloped back to them, reaching the ground as the last sacks were filled.

"Quick, quick!" she cried. "I don't know what is going on, but let us get back to Cinq-Cygne."

While the happy party were employed in recovering the fortune saved by the old marquis, and guarded for so many years by Michu, an extraordinary scene was taking place in the chateau of Gondreville.

About two o'clock in the afternoon Malin and his friend Grevin were playing chess before the fire in the great salon on the ground-floor. Madame Grevin and Madame Marion were sitting on a sofa and talking together at a corner of the fireplace. All the servants had gone to see the masquerade, which had long been announced in the arrondissement. The family of the bailiff who had replaced Michu had gone too. The senator's valet and Violette were the only persons beside the family at the chateau. The porter, two gardeners, and their wives were on the place, but their lodge was at the entrance of the courtyards at the farther end of the avenue to Arcis, and the distance from there to the chateau is beyond the sound of a pistol-shot. Violette was waiting in the antechamber until the senator and Grevin could see him on business, to arrange a matter relating to his lease. At that moment five men, masked and gloved, who in height, manner, and bearing strongly resembled the Simeuse and d'Hauteserre brothers and Michu, rushed into the antechamber, seized and gagged the valet and Violette, and fastened them to their chairs in a side room. In spite of the rapidity with which this was done, Violette and the servant had time to utter one cry. It was heard in the salon. The two ladies thought it a cry of fear.

"Listen!" said Madame Grevin, "can there be robbers?"

"No, nonsense!" said Grevin, "only carnival cries; the masqueraders must be coming to pay us a visit."

This discussion gave time for the four strangers to close the doors towards the courtyards and to lock up Violette and the valet. Madame Grevin, who was rather obstinate, insisted on knowing what the noise meant. She rose, left the room, and came face to face with the five masked men, who treated her as they had treated the farmer and the valet. Then they rushed into the salon, where the two strongest seized and gagged Malin, and carried him off into the park, while the three others remained behind to gag Madame Marion and Grevin and lash them to their armchairs. The whole affair did not take more than half an hour. The three unknown men, who were quickly rejoined by the two who had carried off the senator, then proceeded to ransack the chateau from cellar to garret. They opened all closets and doors, and sounded the walls; until five o'clock they were absolute masters of the place. By that time the valet had managed to loosen with his teeth the rope that bound Violette. Violette, able then to get the gag from his mouth, began to shout for help. Hearing the shouts the five men withdrew to the gardens, where they mounted horses closely resembling those at Cinq-Cygne and rode away, but not so rapidly that Violette was unable to catch sight of them. After releasing the valet, the two ladies, and the notary, Violette mounted his pony and rode after help. When he reached the pavilion he was amazed to see the gates open and Mademoiselle de Cinq-Cygne apparently on the watch.

Directly after the young countess had ridden off, Violette was overtaken by Grevin and the forester of the township of Gondreville, who had taken horses from the stables at the chateau. The porter's wife was on her way to summon the gendarmerie from Arcis. Violette at once informed Grevin of his meeting with Laurence and the sudden flight of the daring girl, whose strong and decided character was known to all of them.

"She was keeping watch," said Violette.

"Is it possible that those Cinq-Cygne people have done this thing?" cried Grevin.

"Do you mean to say you didn't recognize that stout Michu?" exclaimed Violette. "It was he who attacked me; I knew his fist. Besides, they rode the Cinq-Cygne horses."

Noticing the hoof-marks on the sand of the *rond-point* and along the park road the notary stationed the forester at the gateway to see to the preservation of these precious traces until the justice of peace of Arcis (for whom he now sent Violette) could take note of them. He himself returned hastily to the chateau, where the lieutenant and sub-lieutenant of the Imperial gendarmerie at Arcis had arrived, accompanied by four men and a corporal. The lieutenant was the same man whose head Francois Michu had broken two years earlier, and who had heard from Corentin the name of his mischievous assailant. This man, whose name was Giguet (his brother was in the army, and became one of the finest colonels of artillery), was an extremely able officer of gendarmerie. Later he commanded the squadron of the Aube. The sub-lieutenant, named Welff, had formerly driven Corentin from Cinq-Cygne to the pavilion, and from the pavilion to Troyes. On the way, the spy had fully informed him as to what he called the trickery of Laurence and Michu. The two officers were therefore well inclined to show, and did show, great eagerness against the family at Cinq-Cygne.

Chapter XIII. The Code of Brumaire, Year IV.

Malin and Grevin had both, the latter working for the former, taken part in the construction of the Code called that of Brumaire, year IV., the judicial work of the National Convention, so-called, and promulgated by the Directory. Grevin knew its provisions thoroughly, and was able to apply them in this affair with terrible celerity, under a theory, now converted into a certainty, of the guilt of Michu and the Messieurs de Simeuse and d'Hauteserre. No one in these days, unless it be some antiquated magistrates, will remember this system of justice, which Napoleon was even then overthrowing by the promulgation of his own Codes, and by the institution of his magistracy under the form in which it now rules France.

The Code of Brumaire, year IV., gave to the director of the jury of the department the duty of discovering, indicting, and prosecuting the persons guilty of the delinquency committed at Gondreville. Remark, by the way, that the Convention had eliminated from its judicial vocabulary the word "crime"; *delinquencies* and *misdemeanors* were alone admitted; and these were punished with fines, imprisonment, and penalties "afflictive or infamous." Death was an afflictive punishment. But the penalty of death was to be done away with after the restoration of peace, and twenty-four years of hard labor were to take its place. Thus the Convention estimated twenty-four years of hard labor as the equivalent of death. What therefore can be said for a code which inflicts the punishment of hard labor for life? The system then in process of preparation by the Napoleonic Council of State suppressed the function of the directors of juries, which united many enormous powers. In relation to the discovery of delinquencies and their prosecution the director of the jury was, in fact, agent of police, public prosecutor, municipal judge, and the court itself. His proceedings and his indictments were, however, submitted for signature to a commissioner of the executive power and to the verdict of eight jurymen, before whom he laid the facts of the case, and who examined the witnesses and the accused and rendered the preliminary verdict, called the indictment. The director was, however, in a position to exercise such influence over the jurymen, who met in his private office, that they could not well avoid agreeing with him. These jurymen were called the jury of indictment. There were others who formed the juries of the criminal tribunals whose duty it was to judge the accused; these were called, in contradistinction to the jury of indictment, the judgment jury. The criminal tribunal, to which Napoleon afterwards gave the name of criminal court, was composed of one President or chief justice, four judges, the public prosecutor, and a government commissioner.

Nevertheless, from 1799 to 1806 there were special courts (so-called) which judged without juries certain misdemeanors in certain departments; these were composed of judges taken from the civil courts and formed into a special court. This conflict of special justice and criminal justice gave rise to questions of competence which came before the courts of appeal. If the department of the Aube had had a special court, the verdict on the outrage committed on a senator of the Empire would no doubt have been referred to it; but this tranquil department had never needed unusual jurisdiction. Grevin therefore despatched the sub-lieutenant to Troyes to bring the director of the jury of that town. The emissary went at full gallop, and soon returned in a post-carriage with the all-powerful magistrate.

The director of the Troyes jury was formerly secretary of one of the committees of the Convention, a friend of Malin, to whom he owed his present place. This magistrate, named Lechesneau, had helped Malin, as Grevin had done, in his work on the Code during the Convention. Malin in return recommended him to Cambaceres, who appointed him attorney-general for Italy. Unfortunately for him, Lechesneau had a liaison with a great lady in Turin, and Napoleon removed him to avoid a criminal trial threatened by the husband. Lechesneau, bound in gratitude to Malin, felt the importance of this attack upon his patron, and brought with him a captain of gendarmerie and twelve men.

Before starting he laid his plans with the prefect, who was unable at that late hour, it being after dark, to use the telegraph. They therefore sent a mounted messenger to Paris to notify the minister of police, the chief justice and the Emperor of this extraordinary crime. In the salon of Gondreville, Lechesneau found Mesdames Marion and Grevin, Violette, the senator's valet, and the justice of peace with his clerk. The chateau had already been examined; the justice, assisted by Grevin, had carefully collected the first testimony. The first thing that struck him was the obvious intention shown in the choice of the day and hour for the attack. The hour prevented an immediate search for proofs and traces. At this season it was nearly dark by half-past five, the hour at which Violette gave the alarm, and darkness often means impunity to evil-doers. The choice of a holiday, when most persons had gone to the masquerade at Arcis, and the senator was comparatively alone in the house, showed an obvious intention to get rid of witnesses.

"Let us do justice to the intelligence of the prefecture of police," said Lechesneau; "they have never ceased to warn us to be on our guard against the nobles at Cinq-Cygne; they have always declared that sooner or later those people would play us some dangerous trick."

Sure of the active co-operation of the prefect of the Aube, who sent messengers to all the surrounding prefectures asking them to search for the five abductors and the senator, Lechesneau began his work by verifying the first facts. This was soon done by the help of two such legal heads as those of Grevin and the justice of peace. The latter, named Pigoult, formerly head-clerk in the office where Malin and Grevin had first studied law in Paris, was soon after appointed judge of the municipal court at Arcis. In relation to Michu, Lechesneau knew of the threats the man had made about the sale of Gondreville to Marion, and the danger Malin had escaped in his own park from Michu's gun. These two facts, one being the consequence of the other, were no doubt the precursors of the present successful attack, and they pointed so obviously to the late bailiff as the instigator of the outrage that Grevin, his wife, Violette, and Madame Marion declared that they had recognized among the five masked men one who exactly resembled Michu. The color of the hair and whiskers and the thick-set figure of the man made the mask he wore useless. Besides, who but Michu could have opened the iron gates of the park with a key? The present bailiff and his wife, now returned from the masquerade, deposed to have locked both gates before leaving the pavilion. The gates when examined showed no sign of being forced.

"When we turned him off he must have taken some duplicate keys with him," remarked Grevin. "No doubt he has been meditating a desperate step, for he has lately sold his whole property, and he received the money for it in my office day before yesterday."

"The others have followed his lead!" exclaimed Lechesneau, struck with the circumstances. "He has been their evil genius."

Moreover, who could know as well as the Messieurs de Simeuse the ins and outs of the chateau. None of the assailants seemed to have blundered in their search; they had gone through the house in a confident way which showed that they knew what they wanted to find and where to find it. The locks of none of the opened closets had been forced; therefore the delinquents had keys. Strange to say, however, nothing had been taken; the motive, therefore, was not robbery. More than all, when Violette had followed the tracks of the horses as far as the *rond-point*, he had found the countess, evidently on guard, at the pavilion. From such a combination of facts and depositions arose a presumption as to the guilt of the Messieurs de Simeuse, d'Hauteserre, and Michu, which would have been strong to unprejudiced minds, and to the director of the jury had the force of certainty. What were they likely to do to the future Comte de Gondreville? Did they mean to force him to make over the estate for which Michu declared in 1799 he had the money to pay?

But there was another aspect of the cast to the knowing criminal lawyer. He asked himself what could be the object of the careful search made of the chateau. If revenge were at the bottom of the matter, the assailants would have killed the senator. Perhaps he had been killed and buried. The abduction, however, seemed to point to imprisonment. But why keep their victim imprisoned after searching the castle? It was folly to suppose that the abduction of a dignitary of the Empire could long remain secret. The publicity of the matter would prevent any benefit from it.

To these suggestions Pigoult replied that justice was never able to make out all the motives of scoundrels. In every criminal case there were obscurities, he said, between the judge and the guilty person; conscience had depths into which no human mind could enter unless by the confession of the criminal.

Grevin and Lechesneau nodded their assent, without, however, relaxing their determination to see to the bottom of the present mystery.

"The Emperor pardoned those young men," said Pigoult to Grevin. "He removed their names from the list of *emigres,* though they certainly took part in that last conspiracy against him."

Lechesneau make no delay in sending his whole force of gendarmerie to the forest and to the valley of Cinq-Cygne; telling Giguet to take with him the justice of peace, who, according to the terms of the Code, would then become an auxiliary police-officer. He ordered them to make all preliminary inquiries in the township of Cinq-Cygne, and to take testimony if necessary; and to save time, he dictated and signed a warrant for the arrest of Michu, against whom the charge was evident on the positive testimony of Violette. After the departure of the gendarmes Lechesneau returned to the important question of issuing warrants for the arrest of the Simeuse and d'Hauteserre brothers. According to the Code these warrants would have to contain the charges against the delinquents.

Giguet and the justice of peace rode so rapidly to Cinq-Cygne that they met Laurence's servants returning from the festivities at Troyes. Stopped, and taken before the mayor where they were interrogated, they all stated, being ignorant of the importance of the answer, that their mistress had given them permission to spend the whole day at Troyes. To a question put by the justice of the peace, each replied that Mademoiselle had offered them the amusement which they had not thought of asking for. This testimony seemed so important to the justice of the peace that he sent back a messenger to Gondreville to advise

Lechesneau to proceed himself to Cinq-Cygne and arrest the four gentlemen, while he went to Michu's farm, so that the five arrests might be made simultaneously.

This new element was so convincing that Lechesneau started at once for Cinq-Cygne. He knew well what pleasure would be felt in Troyes at such proceedings against the old nobles, the enemies of the people, now become the enemies of the Emperor. In such circumstances a magistrate is very apt to take mere presumptive evidence for actual proof. Nevertheless, on his way from Gondreville to Cinq-Cygne, in the senator's own carriage, it did occur to Lechesneau (who would certainly have made a fine magistrate had it not been for his love-affair, and the Emperor's sudden morality to which he owed his disgrace) to think the audacity of the young men and Michu a piece of folly which was not in keeping with what he knew of the judgment and character of Mademoiselle de Cinq-Cygne. He imagined in his own mind some other motives for the deed than the restitution of Gondreville. In all things, even in the magistracy, there is what may be called the conscience of a calling. Lechesneau's perplexities came from this conscience, which all men put into the proper performance of the duties they like – scientific men into science, artists into art, judges into the rendering of justice. Perhaps for this reason judges are really greater safeguards for persons accused of wrong-doing than are juries. A magistrate relies only on reason and its laws; juries are floated to and fro by the waves of sentiment. The director of the jury accordingly set several questions before his mind, resolving to find in their solution satisfactory reasons for making the arrests.

Though the news of the abduction was already agitating the town of Troyes, it was still unknown at Arcis, where the inhabitants were supping when the messenger arrived to summon the gendarmes. No one, of course, knew it in the village of Cinq-Cygne, the valley and the chateau of which were now, for the second time, encircled by gendarmes.

Laurence had only to tell Marthe, Catherine, and the Durieus not to leave the chateau, to be strictly obeyed. After each trip to fetch the gold, the horses were fastened in the covered way opposite to the breach in the moat, and from there Robert and Michu, the strongest of the party, carried the sacks through the breach to a cellar under the staircase in the tower called Mademoiselle's. Reaching the chateau with the last load about half-past five o'clock, the four gentlemen and Michu proceeded to bury the treasure in the floor of the cellar and then to wall up the entrance. Michu took charge of the matter with Gothard to help him; the lad was sent to the farm for some sacks of plaster left over when the new buildings were put up, and Marthe went with him to show him where they were. Michu, very hungry, made such haste that by half-past seven o'clock the work was done; and he started for home at a quick pace to stop Gothard, who had been sent for another sack of plaster which he thought he might want. The farm was already watched by the forester of Cinq-Cygne, the justice of peace, his clerk and four gendarmes who, however, kept out of sight and allowed him to enter the house without seeing them.

Michu saw Gothard with the sack on his shoulder and called to him from a distance: "It is all finished, my lad; take that back and stay and dine with us."

Michu, his face perspiring, his clothes soiled with plaster and covered with fragments of muddy stone from the breach, reached home joyfully and entered the kitchen where Marthe and her mother were serving the soup in expectation of his coming.

Just as Michu was turning the faucet of the water-pipe intending to wash his hands, the justice of peace entered the house accompanied by his clerk and the forester.

"What have you come for, Monsieur Pigoult?" asked Michu.

"In the name of the Emperor and the laws, I arrest you," replied the justice.

The three gendarmes entered the kitchen leading Gothard. Seeing the silver lace on their hats Marthe and her mother looked at each other in terror.

"Pooh! why?" asked Michu, who sat down at the table and called to his wife, "Give me something to eat; I'm famished."

"You know why as well as we do," said the justice, making a sign to his clerk to begin the *proces-verbal* and exhibiting the warrant of arrest.

"Well, well, Gothard, you needn't stare so," said Michu. "Do you want some dinner, yes or no? Let them write down their nonsense."

"You admit, of course, the condition of your clothes?" said the justice of peace; "and you can't deny the words you said just now to Gothard?"

Michu, supplied with food by his wife, who was amazed at his coolness, was eating with the avidity of a hungry man. He made no answer to the justice, for his mouth was full and his heart innocent. Gothard's appetite was destroyed by fear.

"Look here," said the forester, going up to Michu and whispering in his ear: "What have you done with the senator? You had better make a clean breast of it, for if we are to believe these people it is a matter of life or death to you."

"Good God!" cried Marthe, who overheard the last words and fell into a chair as if annihilated.

"Violette must have played us some infamous trick," cried Michu, recollecting what Laurence had said in the forest.

"Ha! so you do know that Violette saw you?" said the justice of peace.

Michu bit his lips and resolved to say no more. Gothard imitated him. Seeing the uselessness of all attempts to make them talk, and knowing what the neighborhood chose to call Michu's perversity, the justice ordered the gendarmes to bind his hands and those of Gothard, and take them both to the chateau, whither he now went himself to rejoin the director of the jury.

Chapter XIV. The Arrests

The four young men and Laurence were so hungry and the dinner so acceptable that they would not delay it by changing their dress. They entered the salon, she in her riding-habit, they in their white leather breeches, high-top boots and green-cloth jackets, where they found Monsieur d'Hauteserre and his wife, not a little uneasy at their long absence. The goodman had noticed their goings and comings, and, above all, their evident distrust of him, for Laurence had been unable to get rid of him as she had of her servants. Once when his own sons evidently avoided making any reply to his questions, he went to his wife and said, "I am afraid that Laurence may still get us into trouble!"

"What sort of game did you hunt to-day?" said Madame d'Hauteserre to Laurence.

"Ah!" replied the young girl, laughing, "you'll hear some day what a strange hunt your sons have joined in to-day."

Though said in jest the words made the old lady tremble. Catherine entered to announce dinner. Laurence took Monsieur d'Hauteserre's arm, smiling for a moment at the necessity she thus forced upon her cousins to offer an arm to Madame d'Hauteserre, who, according to agreement, was now to be the arbiter of their fate.

The Marquis de Simeuse took in Madame d'Hauteserre. The situation was so momentous that after the Benedicite was said Laurence and the young men trembled from the violent palpitation of their hearts. Madame d'Hauteserre, who carved, was struck by the anxiety on the faces of the Simeuse brothers and the great alteration that was noticeable in Laurence's lamb-like features.

"Something extraordinary is going on, I am sure of it!" she exclaimed, looking at all of them.

"To whom are you speaking?" asked Laurence.

"To all of you," said the old lady.

"As for me, mother," said Robert, "I am frightfully hungry, and that is not extraordinary."

Madame d'Hauteserre, still troubled, offered the Marquis de Simeuse a plate intended for his brother.

"I am like your mother," she said. "I don't know you apart even by your cravats. I thought I was helping your brother."

"You have helped me better than you thought for," said the youngest, turning pale; "you have made him Comte de Cinq-Cygne."

"What! do you mean to tell me the countess has made her choice?" cried Madame d'Hauteserre.

"No," said Laurence; "we left the decision to fate and you are its instrument."

She told of the agreement made that morning. The elder Simeuse, watching the increasing pallor of his brother's face, was momentarily on the point of crying out, "Marry her; I will go away and die!" Just then, as the dessert was being served, all present heard raps upon the window of the dining-room on the garden side. The eldest d'Hauteserre opened it and gave entrance to the abbe, whose breeches were torn in climbing over the walls of the park.

"Fly! they are coming to arrest you," he cried.

"Why?"

"I don't know yet; but there's a warrant against you."

The words were greeted with general laughter.

"We are innocent," said the young men.

"Innocent or guilty," said the abbe, "mount your horses and make for the frontier. There you can prove your innocence. You could overcome a sentence by default; you will never overcome a sentence rendered by popular passion and instigated by prejudice. Remember the words of President de Harlay, 'If I were accused of carrying off the towers of Notre-Dame the first thing I should do would be to run away.'"

"To run away would be to admit we were guilty," said the Marquis de Simeuse.

"Don't do it!" cried Laurence.

"Always the same sublime folly!" exclaimed the abbe, in despair. "If I had the power of God I would carry you away. But if I am found here in this state they will turn my visit against you, and against me too; therefore I leave you by the way I came. Consider my advice; you have still time. The gendarmes have not yet thought of the wall which adjoins the parsonage; but you are hemmed in on the other sides."

The sound of many feet and the jangle of the sabres of the gendarmerie echoed through the courtyard and reached the dining-room a few moments after the departure of the poor abbe, whose advice had met the same fate as that of the Marquis de Chargeboeuf.

"Our twin existence," said the younger Simeuse, speaking to Laurence, "is an anomaly – our love for you is anomalous; it is that very quality which was won your heart. Possibly, the reason why all twins known to us in history have been unfortunate is that the laws of nature are subverted in them. In our case, see how persistently an evil fate follows us! your decision is now postponed."

Laurence was stupefied; the fatal words of the director of the jury hummed in her ears: – "In the name of the Emperor and the laws, I arrest the Sieurs Paul-Marie and Marie-Paul Simeuse, Adrien and Robert d'Hauteserre – These gentlemen," he added, addressing the men who accompanied him and pointing to the mud on the clothing of the prisoners, "cannot deny that they have spent the greater part of this day on horseback."

"Of what are they accused?" asked Mademoiselle de Cinq-Cygne, haughtily.

"Don't you mean to arrest Mademoiselle?" said Giguet.

"I shall leave her at liberty under bail, until I can carefully examine the charges against her," replied the director.

The mayor offered bail, asking the countess to merely give her word of honor that she would not escape. Laurence blasted him with a look which made him a mortal enemy; a tear started from her eyes, one of those tears of rage which reveal a hell of suffering. The four gentlemen exchanged a terrible look, but remained motionless. Monsieur and Madame d'Hauteserre, dreading lest the young people had practised some deceit, were in a state of indescribable stupefaction. Clinging to their chairs these unfortunate parents, finding their sons torn from them after so many fears and their late hopes of safety, sat gazing before them without seeing, listening without hearing.

"Must I ask you to bail me, Monsieur d'Hauteserre?" cried Laurence to her former guardian, who was roused by the cry, clear and agonizing to his ear as the sound of the last trumpet.

He tried to wipe the tears which sprang to his eyes; he now understood what was passing, and said to his young relation in a quivering voice, "Forgive me, countess; you know that I am yours, body and soul."

Lechesneau, who at first was much struck by the evident tranquillity in which the whole party were dining, now returned to his former opinion of their guilt as he noticed the stupefaction of the old people and the evident anxiety of Laurence, who was seeking to discover the nature of the trap which was set for them.

"Gentlemen," he said, politely, "you are too well-bred to make a useless resistance; follow me to the stables, where I must, in your presence, have the shoes of your horses taken off; they afford important proof of either guilt or innocence. Come, too, mademoiselle."

The blacksmith of Cinq-Cygne and his assistant had been summoned by Lechesneau as experts. While the operation at the stable was going on the justice of peace brought in Gothard and Michu. The work of detaching the shoes of each horse, putting them together and ticketing them, so as to compare them with the hoof-prints in the park, took time. Lechesneau, notified of the

arrival of Pigoult, left the prisoners with the gendarmes and returned to the dining-room to dictate the indictment. The justice of
peace called his attention to the condition of Michu's clothes and
related the circumstances of his arrest.

"They must have killed the senator and plastered the body
up in some wall," said Pigoult.

"I begin to fear it," answered Lechesneau. "Where did you
carry that plaster?" he said to Gothard.

The boy began to cry.

"The law frightens him," said Michu, whose eyes were darting flames like those of a lion in the toils.

The servants, who had been detained at the village by order
of the mayor, now arrived and filled the antechamber where
Catherine and Gothard were weeping. To all the questions of the
director of the jury and the justice of peace Gothard replied by
sobs; and by dint of weeping he brought on a species of convulsion which alarmed them so much that they let him alone. The
little scamp, perceiving that he was no longer watched, looked at
Michu with a grin, and Michu signified his approval by a glance.
Lechesneau left the justice of peace and returned to the stables.

"Monsieur," said Madame d'Hauteserre, at last, addressing
Pigoult; "can you explain these arrests?"

"The gentlemen are accused of abducting the senator by
armed force and keeping him a prisoner; for we do not think they
have murdered him – in spite of appearances," replied Pigoult.

"What penalties are attached to the crime?" asked Monsieur
d'Hauteserre.

"Well, as the old law continues in force, and they are not
amenable under the Code, the penalty is death," replied the justice.

"Death!" cried Madame d'Hauteserre, fainting away.

The abbe now came in with his sister, who stopped to speak
to Catherine and Madame Durieu.

"We haven't even seen your cursed senator!" said Michu.

"Madame Marion, Madame Grevin, Monsieur Grevin, the senator's valet, and Violette all tell another tale," replied Pigoult, with the sour smile of magisterial conviction.

"I don't understand a thing about it," said Michu, dumbfounded by his reply, and beginning now to believe that his masters and himself were entangled in some plot which had been laid against them.

Just then the party from the stables returned. Laurence went up to Madame d'Hauteserre, who recovered her senses enough to say: "The penalty is death!"

"Death!" repeated Laurence, looking at the four gentlemen.

The word excited a general terror, of which Giguet, formerly instructed by Corentin, took immediate advantage.

"Everything can be arranged," he said, drawing the Marquis de Simeuse into a corner of the dining-room. "Perhaps after all it is nothing but a joke; you've been a soldier and soldiers understand each other. Tell me, what have you really done with the senator? If you have killed him – why, that's the end of it! But if you have only locked him up, release him, for you see for yourself your game is balked. Do this and I am certain the director of the jury and the senator himself will drop the matter."

"We know absolutely nothing about it," said the marquis.

"If you take that tone the matter is likely to go far," replied the lieutenant.

"Dear cousin," said the Marquis de Simeuse, "we are forced to go to prison; but do not be uneasy; we shall return in a few hours, for there is some misunderstanding in all this which can be explained."

"I hope so, for your sakes, gentlemen," said the magistrate, signing to the gendarmes to remove the four gentlemen, Michu, and Gothard. "Don't take them to Troyes; keep them in your guardhouse at Arcis," he said to the lieutenant; "they must be

present to-morrow, at daybreak, when we compare the shoes of
their horses with the hoof-prints in the park."

Lechesneau and Pigoult did not follow until they had closely
questioned Catherine, Monsieur and Madame d'Hauteserre, and
Laurence. The Durieus, Catherine, and Marthe declared they had
only seen their masters at breakfast-time; Monsieur d'Hauteserre
said he had seen them at three o'clock.

When, at midnight, Laurence found herself alone with Monsieur and Madame d'Hauteserre, the abbe and his sister, and
without the four young men who for the last eighteen months
had been the life of the chateau and the love and joy of her own
life, she fell into a gloomy silence which no one present dared to
break. No affliction was ever deeper or more complete than hers.
At last a deep sigh broke the stillness, and all eyes turned towards the sound.

Marthe, forgotten in a corner, rose, exclaiming, "Death! They
will kill them in spite of their innocence!"

"Mademoiselle, what is the matter with you?" said the abbe.

Laurence left the room without replying. She needed solitude to recover strength in presence of this terrible unforeseen
disaster.

Chapter XV. Doubts and Fears of Counsel

At a distance of thirty-four years, during which three great revolutions have taken place, none but elderly persons can recall the immense excitement produced in Europe by the abduction of a senator of the French Empire. No trial, if we except that of Trumeaux, the grocer of the Place Saint-Michel, and that of the widow Morin, under the Empire; those of Fualdes and de Castaing, under the Restoration; those of Madame Lafarge and Fieschi, under the present government, ever roused so much curiosity or so deep an interest as that of the four young men accused of abducting Malin. Such an attack against a member of his Senate excited the wrath of the Emperor, who was told of the arrest of the delinquents almost at the moment when he first heard of the crime and the negative results of the inquiries. The forest, searched throughout, the department of the Aube, ransacked from end to end, gave not the slightest indication of the passage of the Comte de Gondreville nor of his imprisonment. Napoleon sent for the chief justice, who, after obtaining certain information from the ministry of police, explained to his Majesty the position of Malin in regard to the Simeuse brothers and the Gondreville estate. The Emperor, at that time pre-occupied with serious matters, considered the affair explained by these anterior facts.

"Those young men are fools," he said. "A lawyer like Malin will escape any deed they may force him to sign under violence. Watch those nobles, and discover the means they take to set the Comte de Gondreville at liberty."

He ordered the affair to be conducted with the utmost celerity, regarding it as an attack on his own institutions, a fatal example of resistance to the results of the Revolution, an effort to open the great question of the sales of "national property," and a hindrance to that fusion of parties which was the constant object of his home policy. Besides all this, he thought himself tricked by these young nobles, who had given him their promise to live peaceably.

"Fouche's prediction has come true," he cried, remembering the words uttered two years earlier by his present minister of police, who said them under the impressions conveyed to him by Corentin's report as to the character and designs of Mademoiselle de Cinq-Cygne.

It is impossible for persons living under a constitutional government, where no one really cares for that cold and thankless, blind, deaf Thing called public interest, to imagine the zeal which a mere word of the Emperor was able to inspire in his political or administrative machine. That powerful will seemed to impress itself as much upon things as upon men. His decision once uttered, the Emperor, overtaken by the coalition of 1806, forgot the whole matter. He thought only of new battles to fight, and his mind was occupied in massing his regiments to strike the great blow at the heart of the Prussian monarchy. His desire for prompt justice in the present case found powerful assistance in the great uncertainty which affected the position of all magistrates of the Empire. Just at this time Cambaceres, as arch-chancellor, and Regnier, chief justice, were preparing to organize *tribunaux de premiere instance* (lower civil courts), imperial courts, and a court of appeal or supreme court. They were agitating the question of a legal garb or costume; to which Napoleon attached, and very justly, so much importance in all official stations; and they were also inquiring into the character of the persons composing the magistracy. Naturally, therefore, the officials of the department of the Aube considered they could have no better recommendation than to give proofs of their zeal in the matter of the abduction of the Comte de Gondreville. Napoleon's suppositions became certainties to these courtiers and also to the populace.

Peace still reigned on the continent; admiration for the Emperor was unanimous in France; he cajoled all interests, persons, vanities, and things, in short, everything, even memories. This attack, therefore, directed against his senator, seemed in the eyes of all an assault upon the public welfare. The luckless and innocent gentlemen were the objects of general opprobrium. A few nobles living quietly on their estates deplored the affair among themselves but dared not open their lips; in fact, how was it possible for them to oppose the current of public opinion. Throughout the department the deaths of the eleven persons killed by the Simeuse brothers in 1792 from the windows of the hotel Cinq-Cygne were brought up against them. It was feared that other returned and now emboldened *emigres* might follow this example of violence against those who had bought their estates from the "national domain," as a method of protesting against what they might call an unjust spoliation.

The unfortunate young nobles were therefore considered as robbers, brigands, murderers; and their connection with Michu was particularly fatal to them. Michu, who was declared, either he or his father-in-law, to have cut off all the heads that fell under the Terror in that department, was made the subject of ridiculous tales. The exasperation of the public mind was all the more intense because nearly all the functionaries of the department owed their offices to Malin. No generous voice uplifted itself against the verdict of the public. Besides all this, the accused had no legal means with which to combat prejudice; for the Code of Brumaire, year IV., giving as it did both the prosecution of a charge and the verdict upon it into the hands of a jury, deprived the accused of the vast protection of an appeal against legal suspicion.

The day after the arrest all the inhabitants of the chateau of Cinq-Cygne, both masters and servants, were summoned to appear before the prosecuting jury. Cinq-Cygne was left in charge of a farmer, under the supervision of the abbe and his sister who moved into it. Mademoiselle de Cinq-Cygne, with Monsieur and Madame d'Hauteserre, went to Troyes and occupied a small house belonging to Durieu in one of the long and wide faubourgs which lead from the little town. Laurence's heart was wrung when she at last comprehended the temper of the populace, the malignity of the bourgeoisie, and the hostility of the administration, from the many little events which happened to them as relatives of prisoners accused of criminal wrong-doing and about to be judged in a provincial town. Instead of hearing encouraging or compassionate words they heard only speeches which called for vengeance; proofs of hatred surrounded them in place of the strict politeness or the reserve required by mere decency; but above all they were conscious of an isolation which every mind must feel, but more particularly those which are made distrustful by misfortune.

Laurence, who had recovered her vigor of mind, relied upon the innocence of the accused, and despised the community too much to be frightened by the stern and silent disapproval they met with everywhere. She sustained the courage of Monsieur and Madame d'Hauteserre, all the while thinking of the judicial struggle which was now being hurried on. She was, however, to receive a blow she little expected, which, undoubtedly, diminished her courage.

In the midst of this great disaster, at the moment when this afflicted family were made to feel themselves, as it were, in a desert, a man suddenly became exalted in Laurence's eyes and showed the full beauty of his character. The day after the indictment was found by the jury, and the prisoners were finally committed for trial, the Marquis de Chargeboeuf courageously appeared, still in the same old caleche, to support and protect his young cousin. Foreseeing the haste with which the law would be administered, this chief of a great family had already gone to Paris and secured the services of the most able as well as the most honest lawyer of the old school, named Bordin, who was for ten years counsel of the nobility in Paris, and was ultimately succeeded by the celebrated Derville. This excellent lawyer chose for his assistant the grandson of a former president of the parliament of Normandy, whose studies had been made under his tuition. This young lawyer, who was destined to be appointed deputy-attorney-general in Paris after the conclusion of the present trial, became eventually one of the most celebrated of French magistrates. Monsieur de Grandville, for that was his name, accepted the defence of the four young men, being glad of an opportunity to make his first appearance as an advocate with distinction.

The old marquis, alarmed at the ravages which troubles had wrought in Laurence's appearance, was charmingly kind and considerate. He made no allusion to his neglected advice; he presented Bordin as an oracle whose counsel must be followed to the letter, and young de Grandville as a defender in whom the utmost confidence might be placed.

Laurence held out her hand to the kind old man, and pressed his with an eagerness which delighted him.

"You were right," she said.

"Will you now take my advice?" he asked.

The young countess bowed her head in assent, as did Monsieur and Madame d'Hauteserre.

"Well, then, come to my house; it is in the middle of town, close to the courthouse. You and your lawyers will be better off there than here, where you are crowded and too far from the field of battle. Here, you would have to cross the town twice a day."

Laurence, accepted, and the old man took her with Madame d'Hauteserre to his house, which became the home of the Cinq-Cygne household and the lawyers of the defence during the whole time the trial lasted. After dinner, when the doors were closed, Bordin made Laurence relate every circumstance of the affair, entreating her to omit nothing, not the most trifling detail. Though many of the facts had already been told to him and his young assistant by the marquis on their journey from Paris to Troyes, Bordin listened, his feet on the fender, without obtruding himself into the recital. The young lawyer, however, could not help being divided between his admiration for Mademoiselle de Cinq-Cygne, and the attention he was bound to give to the facts of his case.

"Is that really all?" asked Bordin when Laurence had related the events of the drama just as the present narrative has given them up to the present time.

"Yes," she answered.

Profound silence reigned for several minutes in the salon of the Chargeboeuf mansion where this scene took place, – one of the most important which occur in life. All cases are judged by the counsellors engaged in them, just as the death or life or a patient is foreseen by a physician, before the final struggle which the one sustains against nature, the other against law. Laurence, Monsieur and Madame d'Hauteserre, and the marquis sat with their eyes fixed on the swarthy and deeply pitted face of the old lawyer, who was now to pronounce the words of life or death. Monsieur d'Hauteserre wiped the sweat from his brow. Laurence looked at the younger man and noted his saddened face.

"Well, my dear Bordin?" said the marquis at last, holding out his snuffbox, from which the old lawyer took a pinch in an absent-minded way.

Bordin rubbed the calf of his leg, covered with thick stockings of black raw silk, for he always wore black cloth breeches and a coat made somewhat in the shape of those which are now termed *a la Francaise*. He cast his shrewd eyes upon his clients with an anxious expression, the effect of which was icy.

"Must I analyze all that?" he said; "am I to speak frankly?"

"Yes; go on, monsieur," said Laurence.

"All that you have innocently done can be converted into proof against you," said the old lawyer. "We cannot save your friends; we can only reduce the penalty. The sale which you induced Michu to make of his property will be taken as evident proof of your criminal intentions against the senator. You sent your servants to Troyes so that you might be alone; that is all the more plausible because it is actually true. The elder d'Hauteserre made an unfortunate speech to Beauvisage, which will be your ruin. You yourself, mademoiselle, made another in your own courtyard, which proves that you have long shown ill-will to the possessor of Gondreville. Besides, you were at the gate of the *rond-point*, apparently on the watch, about the time when the abduction took place; if they have not arrested you, it is solely because they fear to bring a sentimental element into the affair."

"The case cannot be successfully defended," said Monsieur de Grandville.

"The less so," continued Bordin, "because we cannot tell the whole truth. Michu and the Messieurs de Simeuse and d'Hauteserre must hold to the assertion that you merely went for an excursion into the forest and returned to Cinq-Cygne for luncheon. Allowing that we can show you were in the house at three o'clock (the exact hour at which the attack was made), who are our witnesses? Marthe, the wife of one of the accused, the Durieus, and Catherine, your own servants, and Monsieur and Madame d'Hauteserre, father and mother of two of the accused. Such testimony is valueless; the law does not admit it against you, and commonsense rejects it when given in your favor. If, on the other hand, you were to say you went to the forest to recover eleven hundred thousand francs in gold, you would send the accused to the galleys as robbers. Judge, jury, audience, and the whole of France would believe that you took that gold from Gondreville, and abducted the senator that you might ransack his house. The accusation as it now stands is not wholly clear, but tell the truth about the matter and it would become as plain as day; the jury would declare that the robbery explained the mysterious features, – for in these days, you must remember, a royalist means a thief. This very case is welcomed as a legitimate political vengeance. The prisoners are now in danger of the death penalty; but that is not dishonoring under some circumstances. Whereas, if they can be proved to have stolen money, which can never be made to seem excusable, you lose all benefit of whatever interest may attach to persons condemned to death for other crimes. If, at the first, you had shown the hiding-places of the treasure, the plan of the forest, the tubes in which the gold was buried, and the gold itself, as an explanation of your day's work, it is possible you might have been believed by an impartial magistrate, but as it is we must be silent. God grant that none of the prisoners may reveal the truth and compromise the defence; if they do, we must rely on our cross-examinations."

Laurence wrung her hands in despair and raised her eyes to heaven with a despondent look, for she saw at last in all its depths the gulf into which her cousins had fallen. The marquis and the young lawyer agreed with the dreadful view of Bordin. Old d'Hauteserre wept.

"Ah! why did they not listen to the Abbe Goujet and fly!" cried Madame d'Hauteserre, exasperated.

"If they could have escaped, and you prevented them," said Bordin, "you have killed them yourselves. Judgment by default gains time; time enables the innocent to clear themselves. This is the most mysterious case I have ever known in my life, in the course of which I have certainly seen and known many strange things."

"It is inexplicable to every one, even to us," said Monsieur de Grandville. "If the prisoners are innocent some one else has committed the crime. Five persons do not come to a place as if by enchantment, obtain five horses shod precisely like those of the accused, imitate the appearance of some of them, and put Malin apparently underground for the sole purpose of casting suspicion on Michu and the four gentlemen. The unknown guilty parties must have had some strong reason for wearing the skin, as it were, of five innocent men. To discover them, even to get upon their traces, we need as much power as the government itself, as many agents and as many eyes as there are townships in a radius of fifty miles."

"The thing is impossible," said Bordin. "There's no use thinking of it. Since society invented law it has never found a way to give an innocent prisoner an equal chance against a magistrate who is pre-disposed against him. Law is not bilateral. The defence, without spies or police, cannot call social power to the rescue of its innocent clients. Innocence has nothing on her side but reason, and reasoning which may strike a judge is often powerless on the narrow minds of jurymen. The whole department is against you. The eight jurors who have signed the indictment are each and all purchasers of national domain. Among the trial jurors we are certain to have some who have either sold or bought the same property. In short, we can get nothing but a Malin jury. You must therefore set up a consistent defence, hold fast to it, and perish in your innocence. You will certainly be condemned. But there's a court of appeal; we will go there and try to remain there as long as possible. If in the mean time we can collect proofs in your favor you must apply for pardon. That's the anatomy of the business, and my advice. If we triumph (for everything is possible in law) it will be a miracle; but your advocate Monsieur de Grandville is the most likely man among all I know to produce that miracle, and I'll do my best to help him."

"The senator has the key to the mystery," said Monsieur de Grandville; "for a man knows his enemies and why they are so. Here we find him leaving Paris at the close of the winter, coming to Gondreville alone, shutting himself up with his notary, and delivering himself over, as one might say, to five men who seize him."

"Certainly," said Bordin, "his conduct seems inexplicable. But how could we, in the face of a hostile community, become accusers when we ourselves are the accused? We should need the help and good-will of the government and a thousand times more proof than is wanted in ordinary circumstances. I am convinced there was premeditation, and subtle premeditation, on the part of our mysterious adversaries, who must have known the situation of Michu and the Messieurs de Simeuse towards Malin. Not to utter one word; not to steal one thing! – remarkable prudence! I see something very different from ordinary evil-doers behind those masks. But what would be the use of saying so to the sort of jurors we shall have to face?"

This insight into hidden matters which gives such power to certain lawyers and certain magistrates astonished and confounded Laurence; her heart was wrung by that inexorable logic.

"Out of every hundred criminal cases," continued Bordin, "there are not ten where the law really lays bare the truth to its full extent; and there is perhaps a good third in which the truth is never brought to light at all. Yours is one of those cases which are inexplicable to all parties, to accused and accusers, to the law and to the public. As for the Emperor, he has other fish to fry than to consider the case of these gentlemen, supposing even that they had not conspired against him. But who the devil *is* Malin's enemy? and what has really been done with him?"

Bordin and Monsieur de Grandville looked at each other; they seemed in doubt as to Laurence's veracity. This evident suspicion was the most cutting of all the many pangs the girl had suffered in the affair; and she turned upon the lawyers a look which effectually put an end to their distrust.

The next day the indictment was handed over to the defence,

and the lawyers were then enabled to communicate with the prisoners. Bordin informed the family that the six accused men were "well supported," – using a professional term.

"Monsieur de Grandville will defend Michu," said Bordin.

"Michu!" exclaimed the Marquis de Chargeboeuf, amazed at the change.

"He is the pivot of the affair – the danger lies there," replied the old lawyer.

"If he is more in danger than the others, I think that is just," cried Laurence.

"We see certain chances," said Monsieur de Grandville, "and we shall study them carefully. If we are able to save these gentlemen it will be because Monsieur d'Hauteserre ordered Michu to repair one of the stone posts in the covered way, and also because a wolf has been seen in the forest; in a criminal court everything depends on discussions, and discussions often turn on trivial matters which then become of immense importance."

Laurence sank into that inward dejection which humiliates the soul of all thoughtful and energetic persons when the uselessness of thought and action is made manifest to them. It was no longer a matter of overthrowing a usurper, or of coming to the help of devoted friends, – fanatical sympathies wrapped in a shroud of mystery. She now saw all social forces full-armed against her cousins and herself. There was no taking a prison by assault with her own hands, no deliverance of prisoners from the midst of a hostile population and beneath the eyes of a watchful police. So, when the young lawyer, alarmed at the stupor of the generous and noble girl, which the natural expression of her face made still more noticeable, endeavored to revive her courage, she turned to him and said: "I must be silent; I suffer, – I wait."

The accent, gesture, and look with which the words were said made this answer one of those sublime things which only need a wider stage to make them famous.

A few moments later old d'Hauteserre was saying to the

Marquis de Chargeboeuf: "What efforts I have made for my two unfortunate sons! I have already laid by in the Funds enough to give them eight thousand francs a year. If they had only been willing to serve in the army they would have reached the higher grades by this time, and could now have married to advantage. Instead of that, all my plans are scattered to the winds!"

"How can you," said his wife, "think of their interests when it is a question of their honor and their lives?"

"Monsieur d'Hauteserre thinks of everything," said the marquis.

Chapter XVI. Marthe Inveigled

While the masters of Cinq-Cygne were waiting at Troyes for the opening of the trial before the Criminal court and vainly soliciting permission to see the prisoners, an event of the utmost importance had taken place at the chateau.

Marthe returned to Cinq-Cygne as soon as she had given her testimony before the indicting jury. This testimony was so insignificant that it was not thought necessary to summon her before the Criminal court. Like all persons of extreme sensibility, the poor woman sat silent in the salon, where she kept company with Mademoiselle Goujet, in a pitiable state of stupefaction. To her, as to the abbe, and indeed to all others who did not know how the accused had been employed on that day, their innocence seemed doubtful. There were moments when Marthe believed that Michu and his masters and Laurence had executed vengeance on the senator. The unhappy woman now knew Michu's devotion well enough to be certain that he was the one who would be most in danger, not only because of his antecedents, but because of the part he was sure to have taken in the execution of the scheme.

The Abbe Goujet and his sister and Marthe were bewildered among the possibilities to which this opinion gave rise; and yet, in the process of thinking them over, their minds insensibly took hold of them in a certain way. The absolute doubt which Descartes demands can no more exist in the brain of a man than a vacuum can exist in nature, and the mental operation required to produce it would, like the effect of a pneumatic machine, be exceptional and anomalous. Whatever a case may be, the mind believes in something. Now Marthe was so afraid that the accused were guilty that her fear became equivalent to belief; and this condition of her mind proved fatal to her.

Five days after the arrests, just as she was in the act of going to bed about ten o'clock at night, she was called from the courtyard by her mother, who had come from the farm on foot.

"A laboring man from Troyes wants to speak to you; he is sent by Michu, and is waiting in the covered way," she said to

Marthe.

They passed through the breach so as to take the shortest path. In the darkness it was impossible for Marthe to distinguish anything more than the form of a person which loomed through the shadows.

"Speak, madame; so that I may be certain you are really Madame Michu," said the person, in a rather anxious voice.

"I am Madame Michu," said Marthe; "what do you want of me?"

"Very good," said the unknown, "give me your hand; do not fear me. I come," he added, leaning towards her and speaking low, "from Michu with a note for you. I am employed at the prison, and if my superiors discover my absence we shall all be lost. Trust me; your good father placed me where I am. For that reason Michu counted on my helping him."

He put the letter into Marthe's hand and disappeared toward the forest without waiting for an answer. Marthe trembled at the thought that she was now to hear the secret of the mystery. She ran to the farm with her mother and shut herself up to read the following letter: –

My dear Marthe, – You can rely on the discretion of the man who will give you this letter; he does not know how to read or to write. He is a stanch Republican, and shared in Baboeuf's conspiracy; your father often made use of him, and he regards the senator as a traitor. Now, my dear wife, attend to my directions. The senator has been shut up by us in the cave where our masters were hidden. The poor creature had provisions for only five days, and as it is our interest that he should live, I wish you, as soon as you receive this letter, to take him food for at least five days more. The forest is of course watched; therefore take as many precautions as we formerly did for our young masters. Don't say a word to Malin; don't speak to him; and put on one of our masks which you will find on the steps which lead down to the cave. Unless you wish to compromise our heads you must be absolutely silent about this letter and the secret I have now confided to you. Don't say a word to Mademoiselle de Cinq-Cygne, who might tell of it. Don't fear for me. We are certain that the matter will turn out well; when the time comes Malin himself will save us. I don't need to tell you to burn this letter as soon as you have read it, for it would cost me my head if a line of it were seen. I kiss you for now and always,

Michu.

The existence of the cave was known only to Marthe, her son, Michu, the four gentlemen, and Laurence; or rather, Marthe, to whom her husband had not related the incident of his meeting with Peyrade and Corentin, believed it was known only to them. Had she consulted her mistress and the two lawyers, who knew the innocence of the prisoners, the shrewd Bordin would have gained some light upon the perfidious trap which was evidently laid for his clients. But Marthe, acting like most women under a first impulse, was convinced by this proof which came to her own eyes, and flung the letter into the fire as directed. Nevertheless, moved by a singular gleam of caution, she caught a portion of it from the flames, tore off the five first lines, which compromised no one, and sewed them into the hem of her dress. Terrified at the thought that the prisoner had been without food for twenty-four hours, she resolved to carry bread, meat, and wine to him at once; curiosity was well as humanity permitting no delay. Accordingly, she heated her oven and made, with her mother's help, a *pate* of hare and ducks, a rice cake, roasted two fowls, selected three bottles of wine, and baked two loaves of bread. About two in the morning she started for the forest, carrying the load on her back, accompanied by Couraut, who in all such expeditions showed wonderful sagacity as a guide. He scented strangers at immense distances, and as soon as he was certain of their presence he returned to his mistress with a low growl, looking at her fixedly and turning his muzzle in the direction of the danger.

Marthe reached the pond about three in the morning, and left the dog as sentinel on the bank. After half an hour's labor in clearing the entrance she came with a dark lantern to the door of the cave, her face covered with a mask, which she had found, as directed, on the steps. The imprisonment of the senator seemed to have been long premeditated. A hole about a foot square, which Marthe had never seen before, was roughly cut in the upper part of the iron door which closed the cave; but in order to prevent Malin from using the time and patience all prisoners have at their command in loosening the iron bar which held the door, it was securely fastened with a padlock.

The senator, who had risen from his bed of moss, sighed when he saw the masked face and felt that there was no chance then of his deliverance. He examined Marthe, as much as he could by the unsteady light of her dark lantern, and he recognized her by her clothes, her stoutness, and her motions. When she passed the *pate* through the door he dropped it to seize her hand and then, with great swiftness, he tried to pull the rings from her fingers, – one her wedding-ring, the other a gift from Mademoiselle de Cinq-Cygne.

"You cannot deny that it is you, my dear Madame Michu," he said.

Marthe closed her fist the moment she felt his fingers, and gave him a vigorous blow in the chest. Then, without a word, she turned away and cut a stick, at the end of which she held out to the senator the rest of the provisions.

"What do they want of me?" he asked.

Marthe departed giving him no answer. By five o'clock she had reached the edge of the forest and was warned by Couraut of the presence of strangers. She retraced her steps and made for the pavilion where she had lived so long; but just as she entered the avenue she was seen from afar by the forester of Gondreville, and she quickly reflected that her best plan was to go straight up to him.

"You are out early, Madame Michu," he said, accosting her.

"We are so unfortunate," she replied, "that I am obliged to do a servant's work myself. I am going to Bellache for some grain."

"Haven't you any at Cinq-Cygne?" said the forester.

Marthe made no answer. She continued on her way and reached the farm at Bellache, where she asked Beauvisage to give her some seed-grain, saying that Monsieur d'Hauteserre advised her to get it from him to renew her crop. As soon as Marthe had left the farm, the forester went there to find out what she asked for.

Six days later, Marthe, determined to be prudent, went at midnight with her provisions so as to avoid the keepers who were evidently patrolling the forest. After carrying a third supply to the senator she suddenly became terrified on hearing the abbe read aloud the public examination of the prisoners, – for the trial was by that time begun. She took the abbe aside, and after obliging him to swear that he would keep the secret she was about to reveal as though it was said to him in the confessional, she showed him the fragments of Michu's letter, told him the contents of it, and also the secret of the hiding-place where the senator then was.

The abbe at once inquired if she had other letters from her husband that he might compare the writing. Marthe went to her home to fetch them and there found a summons to appear in court. By the time she returned to the chateau the abbe and his sister had received a similar summons on behalf of the defence. They were obliged therefore to start for Troyes immediately. Thus all the personages of our drama, even those who were only, as it were, supernumeraries, were collected on the spot where the fate of the two families was about to be decided.

Chapter XVII. The Trial

There are but few localities in France where Law derives from outward appearance the dignity which ought always to accompany it. Yet it surely is, after religion and royalty, the greatest engine of society. Everywhere, even in Paris, the meanness of its surroundings, the wretched arrangement of the courtrooms, their barrenness and want of decoration in the most ornate and showy nation upon earth in the matter of its public monuments, lessens the action of the law's mighty power. At the farther end of some oblong room may be seen a desk with a green baize covering raised on a platform; behind it sit the judges on the commonest of arm-chairs. To the left, is the seat of the public prosecutor, and beside him, close to the wall, is a long pen filled with chairs for the jury. Opposite to the jury is another pen with a bench for the prisoners and the gendarmes who guard them. The clerk of the court sits below the platform at a table covered with the papers of the case. Before the imperial changes in the administration of justice were instituted, a commissary of the government and the director of the jury each had a seat and a table, one to the right, the other to the left of the baize-covered desk. Two sheriffs hovered about in the space left in front of the desk for the station of witnesses. Facing the judges and against the wall above the entrance, there is always a shabby gallery reserved for officials and for women, to which admittance is granted only by the president of the court, to whom the proper management of the courtroom belongs. The non-privileged public are compelled to stand in the empty space between the door of the hall and the bar. This normal appearance of all French law courts and assize-rooms was that of the Criminal court of Troyes.

In April, 1806, neither the four judges nor the president (or chief-justice) who made up the court, nor the public prosecutor, the director of the jury, the commissary of the government, nor the sheriffs or lawyers, in fact no one except the gendarmes, wore any robes or other distinctive sign which might have relieved the nakedness of the surroundings and the somewhat meagre aspect of the figures. The crucifix was suppressed; its example was no longer held up before the eyes of justice and of guilt. All was dull and vulgar. The paraphernalia so necessary to excite social interest is perhaps a consolation to criminals. On this occasion the eagerness of the public was what it has ever been and ever will be in trials of this kind, so long as France refuses to recognize that the admission of the public to the courts involves publicity, and that the publicity given to trials is a terrible penalty which would never have been inflicted had legislators reflected on it. Customs are often more cruel than laws. Customs are the deeds of men, but laws are the judgment of a nation. Customs in which there is often no judgment are stronger than laws.

Crowds surrounded the courtroom; the president was obliged to station squads of soldiers to guard the doors. The audience, standing below the bar, was so crowded that persons suffocated. Monsieur de Grandville, defending Michu, Bordin, defending the Simeuse brothers, and a lawyer of Troyes who appeared for the d'Hauteserres, were in their seats before the opening of the court; their faces wore a look of confidence. When the prisoners were brought in, sympathetic murmurs were heard at the appearance of the young men, whose faces, in twenty days' imprisonment and anxiety, had somewhat paled. The perfect likeness of the twins excited the deepest interest. Perhaps the spectators thought that Nature would exercise some special protection in the case of her own anomalies, and felt ready to join in repairing the harm done to them by destiny. Their noble, simple faces, showing no signs of shame, still less of bravado, touched the women's hearts. The four gentlemen and Gothard wore the clothes in which they had been arrested; but Michu, whose coat and trousers were among the "articles of testimony," so-called, had put on his best clothes, – a blue surtout, a brown velvet waistcoat *a la* Robespierre, and a white cravat. The poor man paid the penalty of his dangerous-looking face. When he cast a glance of his yellow eye, so clear and so profound upon the audience, a murmur of repulsion answered it. The assembly chose to see the finger of God bringing him to the dock where his father-in-law had sacrificed so many victims. This man, truly great, looked at his masters, repressing a smile of scorn. He seemed to say to them, "I am injuring your cause." Five of the prisoners exchanged greetings with their counsel. Gothard still played the part of an idiot.

After several challenges, made with much sagacity by the defence under advice of the Marquis de Chargeboeuf, who boldly took a seat beside Bordin and de Grandville, the jury were empanelled, the indictment was read, and the prisoners were brought up separately to be examined. They answered every question with remarkable unanimity. After riding about the forest all the morning they had returned to Cinq-Cygne for breakfast at one o'clock. After that meal, from three to half-past five in the afternoon, they had returned to the forest. That was the basis of each testimony; any variations were merely individual circumstances. When the president asked the Messieurs de Simeuse why they had ridden out so early, they both declared that wishing, since their return, to buy back Gondreville and intending to make an offer to Malin who had arrived the night before, they had gone out early with their cousin and Michu to make certain examinations of the property on which to base their offer. During that time the Messieurs d'Hauteserre, their cousin, and Gothard had chased a wolf which was reported in the forest by the peasantry. If the director of the jury had sought for the prints of their horses' feet in the forest as carefully as in the park of Gondreville, he would have found proof of their presence at long distances from the house.

The examination of the Messieurs d'Hauteserre corroborated this testimony, and was in harmony with their preliminary dispositions. The necessity of some reason for their ride suggested to each of them the excuse of hunting. The peasants had given warning, a few days earlier, of a wolf in the forest, and on that they had fastened as a pretext.

The public prosecutor, however, pointed out a discrepancy between the first statements of the Messieurs d'Hauteserre, in which they mentioned that the whole party hunted together, and the defence now made by the Messieurs de Simeuse that their purpose on that day was the valuation of the forest.

Monsieur de Grandville here called attention to the fact that as the crime was not committed until after two o'clock in the afternoon, the prosecution had no ground to question their word when they stated the manner in which they had employed their morning.

The prosecutor replied that the prisoners had an interest in concealing their preparations for the abduction of the senator.

The remarkable ability of the defence was now felt. Judges, jurors, and audience became aware that victory would be hotly contested. Bordin and Monsieur de Grandville had studied their ground and foreseen everything. Innocence is required to render a clear and plausible account of its actions. The duty of the defence is to present a consistent and probable tale in opposition to an insufficient and improbable accusation. To counsel who regard their client as innocent, an accusation is false. The public examination of the four gentlemen sufficiently explained the matter in their favor. So far all was well. But the examination of Michu was more serious; there the real struggle began. It was now clear to every one why Monsieur de Grandville had preferred to take charge of the servant's defence rather than that of his masters.

Michu admitted his threats against Marion; but denied that he had made them violently. As for the ambush in which he was supposed to have watched for his enemy, he said he was merely making his rounds in his park; the senator and Monsieur Grevin might perhaps have been alarmed at the sight of his gun and have thought his intentions hostile when they were really inoffensive. He called attention to the fact that in the dusk a man who was not in the habit of hunting might easily fancy a gun was pointed at him, whereas, in point of fact, it was held in his hand at half-cock. To explain the condition of his clothes when arrested, he said he had slipped and fallen in the breach on his way home. "I could scarcely see my way," he said, "and the loose stones slipped from under me as I climbed the bank." As for the plaster which Gothard was bringing him, he replied as he had done in all previous examinations, that he wanted it to secure one of the stone posts of the covered way.

The public prosecutor and the president asked him to explain how he could have been at the top of the covered way engaged in mending a stone post and at the same time in the breach of the moat leading to the chateau; more especially as the justice of peace, the gendarmes and the forester all declared they had heard him approach them from the lower road. To this Michu replied that Monsieur d'Hauteserre had blamed him for not having mended the post, – which he was anxious to have finished because there were difficulties about that road with the township, – and he had therefore gone up to the chateau to report that the work was done.

Monsieur d'Hauteserre had, in fact, put up a fence above the covered way to prevent the township from taking possession of it. Michu seeing the important part which the state of his clothes was likely to play, invented this subterfuge. If, in law, truth is often like falsehood, falsehood on the other hand has a very great resemblance to truth. The defence and the prosecution both attached much importance to this testimony, which became one of the leading points of the trial on account of the vigor of the defence and the suspicions of the prosecution.

Gothard, instructed no doubt by Monsieur de Grandville, for up to that time he had only wept when they questioned him, admitted that Michu had told him to carry the plaster.

"Why did neither you nor Gothard take the justice of peace and the forester to the stone post and show them your work?" said the public prosecutor, addressing Michu.

"Because," replied the man, "I didn't believe there was any serious accusation against us."

All the prisoners except Gothard were now removed from the courtroom. When Gothard was left alone the president adjured him to speak the truth for his own sake, pointing out that his pretended idiocy had come to an end; none of the jurors believed him imbecile; if he refused to answer the court he ran the risk of serious penalty; whereas by telling the truth at once he would probably be released. Gothard wept, hesitated, and finally ended by saying that Michu had told him to carry several sacks of plaster; but that each time he had met him near the farm. He was asked how many sacks he had carried.

"Three," he replied.

An argument hereupon ensued as to whether the three sacks included the one which Gothard was carrying at the time of the arrest (which reduced the number of the other sacks to two) or whether there were three without the last. The debate ended in favor of the first proposition, the jury considering that only two sacks had been used. They appeared to have a foregone conviction on that point, but Bordin and Monsieur de Grandville judged it best to surfeit them with plaster, and weary them so thoroughly with the argument that they would no longer comprehend the question. Monsieur de Grandville made it appear that experts ought to have been sent to examine the stone posts.

"The director of the jury," he said, "has contented himself with merely visiting the place, less for the purpose of making a careful examination than to trap Michu in a lie; this, in our opinion, was a failure of duty, but the blunder is to our advantage."

On this the Court appointed experts to examine the posts and see if one of them had been really mended and reset. The public prosecutor, on his side, endeavored to make capital of the affair before the experts could testify.

"You seem to have chosen," he said to Michu, who was now brought back into the courtroom, "an hour when the daylight was waning, from half-past five to half-past six o'clock, to mend this post and to cement it all alone."

"Monsieur d'Hauteserre had blamed me for not doing it," replied Michu.

"But," said the prosecutor, "if you used that plaster on the post you must have had a trough and a trowel. Now, if you went to the chateau to tell Monsieur d'Hauteserre that you had done the work, how do you explain the fact that Gothard was bringing you more plaster. You must have passed your farm on your way to the chateau, and you would naturally have left your tools at home and stopped Gothard."

This overwhelming argument produced a painful silence in the courtroom.

"Come," said the prosecutor, "you had better admit at once that what you buried was *not a stone post*."

"Do you think it was the senator?" said Michu, sarcastically.

Monsieur de Grandville hereupon demanded that the public prosecutor should explain his meaning. Michu was accused of abduction and the concealment of a person, but not of murder. Such an insinuation was a serious matter. The code of Brumaire, year IV., forbade the public prosecutor from presenting any fresh count at the trial; he must keep within the indictment or the proceedings would be annulled.

The public prosecutor replied that Michu, the person chiefly concerned in the abduction and who, in the interests of his masters, had taken the responsibility on his own shoulders, might have thought it necessary to plaster up the entrance of the hiding-place, still undiscovered, where the senator was now immured.

Pressed with questions, hampered by the presence of Gothard, and brought into contradiction with himself, Michu struck his fist upon the edge of the dock with a resounding blow and said: "I have had nothing whatever to do with the abduction of the senator. I hope and believe his enemies have merely imprisoned him; when he reappears you'll find out that the plaster was put to no such use."

"Good!" said de Grandville, addressing the public prosecutor; "you have done more for my client's cause than anything I could have said."

The first day's session ended with this bold declaration, which surprised the judges and gave an advantage to the defence. The lawyers of the town and Bordin himself congratulated the young advocate. The prosecutor, uneasy at the assertion, feared that he had fallen into some trap; in fact he was really caught in a snare that was cleverly set for him by the defence and admirably played off by Gothard. The wits of the town declared that he had white-washed the affair and splashed his own cause, and had made the accused as white as the plaster itself. France is the domain of satire, which reigns supreme in our land; Frenchmen jest on a scaffold, at the Beresina, at the barricades, and some will doubtless appear with a quirk upon their lips at the grand assizes of the Last Judgment.

Chapter XVIII. Trial Continued: Cruel Vicissitudes

On the morrow the witnesses for the prosecution were examined, – Madame Marion, Madame Grevin, Grevin himself, the senator's valet, and Violette, whose testimony can readily be imagined from the facts already told. They all identified the five prisoners, with more or less hesitation as to the four gentlemen, but with absolute certainty as to Michu. Beauvisage repeated Robert d'Hauteserre's speech when he met them at daybreak in the park. The peasant who had bought Monsieur d'Hauteserre's calf testified to overhearing that of Mademoiselle de Cinq-Cygne. The experts, who had compared the hoof-prints with the shoes on the horses ridden by the five prisoners and found them absolutely alike, confirmed their previous depositions. This point was naturally one of vehement contention between Monsieur de Grandville and the prosecuting officer. The defence called the blacksmith at Cinq-Cygne and succeeded in proving that he had sold several horseshoes of the same pattern to strangers who were not known in the place. The blacksmith declared, moreover, that he was in the habit of shoeing in this particular manner not only the horses of the chateau de Cinq-Cygne, but those from other places in the canton. It was also proved that the horse which Michu habitually rode was always shod at Troyes, and the mark of that shoe was not among the hoof-prints found in the park.

"Michu's double was not aware of this circumstance, or he would have provided for it," said Monsieur de Grandville, looking at the jury. "Neither has the prosecution shown what horses our clients rode."

He ridiculed the testimony of Violette so far as it concerned a recognition of the horses, seen from a long distance, from behind, and after dusk. Still, in spite of all his efforts, the body of the evidence was against Michu; and the prosecutor, judge, jury, and audience were impressed with a feeling (as the lawyers for the defence had foreseen) that the guilt of the servant carried with it that of the masters. So the vital interest centred on all that concerned Michu. His bearing was noble. He showed in his answers the sagacity with which nature had endowed him; and the public, seeing him on his mettle, recognized his superiority. And yet, strange to say, the more they understood him the more certainty they felt that he was the instigator of the outrage.

The witnesses for the defence, always less important in the eyes of a jury and of the law than the witnesses for the prosecution, seemed to testify as in duty bound, and were listened to with that allowance. In the first place neither Marthe, nor Monsieur and Madame d'Hauteserre took the oath. Catherine and the Durieus, in their capacity as servants, did not take it. Monsieur d'Hauteserre stated that he had ordered Michu to replace and mend the stone post which had been thrown down. The deposition of the experts sent to examine the fence, which was now read, confirmed his testimony; but they helped the prosecution by declaring they could not fix the exact time at which the repairs had been made; it might have been several weeks or no more than twenty days.

The appearance of Mademoiselle de Cinq-Cygne excited the liveliest curiosity; but the sight of her cousins in the prisoners' dock after three weeks' separation affected her so much that her emotions gave the audience an impression of guilt. She felt an overwhelming desire to stand beside the twins, and was obliged, as she afterwards admitted, to use all her strength to repress the longing that came into her mind to kill the prosecutor so as to stand in the eyes of the world as a criminal beside them. She testified, with simplicity, that riding from Cinq-Cygne and seeing smoke in the park of Gondreville, she had supposed there was a fire; at first she thought they were burning weeds or brush; "but later," she added, "I observed a circumstance which I offer to the attention of the Court. I found in the frogging of my habit and in the folds of my collar small fragments of what appeared to be burned paper which were floating in the air."

"Was there much smoke?" asked Bordin.

"Yes," replied Mademoiselle de Cinq-Cygne, "I feared a conflagration."

"This is enough to change the whole inquiry," remarked

Bordin. "I request the Court to order an immediate examination of that region of the park where the fire occurred."

The president ordered the inquiry.

Grevin, recalled by the defence and questioned on this circumstance, declared he knew nothing about it. But Bordin and he exchanged looks which mutually enlightened them.

"The gist of the case is there," thought the old notary.

"They've laid their finger on it," thought the notary.

But each shrewd head considered the following up of this point useless. Bordin reflected that Grevin would be silent as the grave; and Grevin congratulated himself that every sign of the fire had been effaced.

To settle this point, which seemed a mere accessory to the trial and somewhat puerile (but which is really essential in the justification which history owes to these young men), the experts and Pigoult, who were despatched by the president to examine the park, reported that they could find no traces of a bonfire.

Bordin summoned two laborers, who testified to having dug over, under the direction of the forester, a tract of ground in the park where the grass had been burned; but they declared they had not observed the nature of the ashes they had buried.

The forester, recalled by the defence, said he had received from the senator himself, as he was passing the chateau of Gondreville on his way to the masquerade at Arcis, an order to dig over that particular piece of ground which the senator had remarked as needing it.

"Had papers, or herbage been burned there?"

"I could not say. I saw nothing that made me think that papers had been burned there," replied the forester.

"At any rate," said Bordin, "if, as it appears, a fire was kindled on that piece of ground some one brought to the spot whatever was burned there."

The testimony of the abbe and that of Mademoiselle Goujet made a favorable impression. They said that as they left the church after vespers and were walking towards home, they met the four gentlemen and Michu leaving the chateau on horseback and making their way to the forest. The character, position, and known uprightness of the Abbe Goujet gave weight to his words.

The summing up of the public prosecutor, who felt sure of obtaining a verdict, was in the nature of all such speeches. The prisoners were the incorrigible enemies of France, her institutions and laws. They thirsted for tumult and conspiracy. Though they had belonged to the army of Conde and had shared in the late attempts against the life of the Emperor, that magnanimous sovereign had erased their names from the list of *emigres*. This was the return they made for his clemency! In short, all the oratorical declamations of the Bourbons against the Bonapartists, which in our day are repeated against the republicans and the legitimists by the Younger Branch, flourished in the speech. These trite commonplaces, which might have some meaning under a fixed government, seem farcical in the mouth of administrators of all epochs and opinions. A saying of the troublous times of yore is still applicable: "The label is changed, but the wine is the same as ever." The public prosecutor, one of the most distinguished legal men under the Empire, attributed the crime to a fixed determination on the part of returned *emigres* to protest against the sale of their estates. He made the audience shudder at the probable condition of the senator; then he massed together proofs, half-proofs, and probabilities with a cleverness stimulated by a sense that his zeal was certain of its reward, and sat down tranquilly to await the fire of his opponents.

Monsieur de Grandville never argued but this one criminal case; and it made his reputation. In the first place, he spoke with the same glowing eloquence which to-day we admire in Berryer. He was profoundly convinced of the innocence of his clients, and that in itself is a most powerful auxiliary of speech. The following are the chief points of his defence, which was reported in full by all the leading newspapers of the period. In the first place he exhibited the character and life of Michu in its true light. He made it a noble tale, ringing with lofty sentiments, and it awakened the sympathies of many. When Michu heard himself vindicated by that eloquent voice, tears sprang from his yellow eyes and rolled down his terrible face. He appeared then for what he really was, – a man as simple and as wily as a child; a being whose whole existence had but one thought, one aim. He was suddenly explained to the minds of all present, more especially by his tears, which produced a great effect upon the jury. His able defender seized that moment of strong interest to enter upon a discussion of the charges: –

"Where is the body of the person abducted? Where is the senator?" he asked. "You accuse us of walling him up with stones and plaster. If so, we alone know where he is; you have kept us twenty-three days in prison, and the senator must be dead by this time for want of food. We are therefore murderers, but you have not accused us of murder. On the other hand, if he still lives, we must have accomplices. If we have them, and if the senator is living, we should assuredly have set him at liberty. The scheme in relation to Gondreville which you attribute to us is a failure, and only aggravates our position uselessly. We might perhaps obtain a pardon for an abortive attempt by releasing our victim; instead of that we persist in detaining a man from whom we can obtain no benefit whatever. It is absurd! Take away your plaster; the effect is a failure," he said, addressing the public prosecutor. "We are either idiotic criminals (which you do not believe) or the innocent victims of circumstances as inexplicable to us as they are to you. You ought rather to search for the mass of papers which were burned at Gondreville, which will reveal motives stronger far than yours or ours and put you on the track of the causes of this abduction."

The speaker discussed these hypotheses with marvellous ability. He dwelt on the moral character of the witnesses for the defence, whose religious faith was a living one, who believed in a future life and in eternal punishment. He rose to grandeur in this part of his speech and moved his hearers deeply: –

"Remember!" he said; "these criminals were tranquilly dining when told of the abduction of the senator. When the officer of gendarmes intimated to them the best means of ending the whole affair by giving up the senator, they refused, for they did not understand what was asked of them!"

Then, reverting to the mystery of the matter, he declared that its solution was in the hands of time, which would eventually reveal the injustice of the charge. Once on this ground, he boldly and ingeniously supposed himself a juror; related his deliberations with his colleagues; imagined his distress lest, having condemned the innocent, the error should be known too late, and drew such a picture of his remorse, dwelling on the grave doubts which the case presented, that he brought the jury to a condition of intense anxiety.

Juries were not in those days so blase to this sort of allocution as they are now; Monsieur de Grandville's appeal had the power of things new, and the jurors were evidently shaken. After this passionate outburst they had to listen to the wily and specious prosecutor, who went over the whole case, brought out the darkest points against the prisoners and made the rest inexplicable. His aim was to reach the minds and the reasoning faculties of his hearers just as Monsieur de Grandville had aimed at the heart and the imagination. The latter, however, had seriously entangled the convictions of the jury, and the public prosecutor found his well-laid arguments ineffectual. This was so plain that the counsel for the Messieurs d'Hauteserre and Gothard appealed to the judgment of the jury, asking that the case against their clients be abandoned. The prosecutor demanded a postponement till the next day in order that he might prepare an answer. Bordin, who saw acquittal in the eyes of the jury if they deliberated on the case at once, opposed the delay of even one night by arguments of legal right and justice to his innocent clients; but in vain, – the court allowed it.

"The interests of society are as great as those of the accused," said the president. "The court would be lacking in equity if it denied a like request when made by the defence; it ought therefore to grant that of the prosecution."

"All is luck or ill-luck!" said Bordin to his clients when the session was over. "Almost acquitted tonight you may be condemned to-morrow."

"In either case," said the elder de Simeuse, "we can only admire your skill."

Mademoiselle de Cinq-Cygne's eyes were full of tears. After the doubts and fears of the counsel for the defence, she had not expected this success. Those around her congratulated her and predicted the acquittal of her cousins. But alas! the matter was destined to end in a startling and almost theatrical event, the most unexpected and disastrous circumstance which ever changed the face of a criminal trial.

At five in the morning of the day after Monsieur de Grandville's speech, the senator was found on the high road to Troyes, delivered from captivity during his sleep, unaware of the trial that was going on or of the excitement attaching to his name in Europe, and simply happy in being once more able to breathe the fresh air. The man who was the pivot of the drama was quite as amazed at what was now told to him as the persons who met him on his way to Troyes were astounded at his reappearance. A farmer lent him a carriage and he soon reached the house of the prefect at Troyes. The prefect notified the director of the jury, the commissary of the government, and the public prosecutor, who, after a statement made to them by Malin, arrested Marthe, while she was still in bed at the Durieu's house in the suburbs. Mademoiselle de Cinq-Cygne, who was only at liberty under bail, was also snatched from one of the few hours of slumber she had been able to obtain at rare intervals in the course of her ceaseless anxiety, and taken to the prefecture to undergo an examination. An order to keep the accused from holding any communication with each other or with their counsel was sent to the prison. At ten o'clock the crowd which assembled around the courtroom were informed that the trial was postponed until one o'clock in the afternoon of the same day.

This change of hour, following on the news of the senator's deliverance, Marthe's arrest, and that of Mademoiselle de Cinq-Cygne, together with the denial of the right to communicate with the prisoners carried terror to the hotel de Chargeboeuf. The whole town and the spectators who had come to Troyes to be present at the trial, the short-hand writers for the daily journals, even the populace were in a ferment which can readily be imagined. The Abbe Goujet came at ten o'clock to see Monsieur and Madame d'Hauteserre and the counsel for the defence, who were breakfasting – as well as they could under the circumstances. The abbe took Bordin and Monsieur Grandville apart, told them what Marthe had confided to him the day before, and gave them the fragment of the letter she had received. The two lawyers exchanged a look, after which Bordin said to the abbe: "Not a word of all this! The case is lost; but at any rate let us show a firm front."

Marthe was not strong enough to evade the cross-questioning of the director of the jury and the public prosecutor. Moreover the proof against her was too overwhelming. Lechesneau had sent for the under crust of the last loaf of bread she had carried to the cavern, also for the empty bottles and various other articles. During the senator's long hours of captivity he had formed conjectures in his own mind and had looked for indications which might put him on the track of his enemies. These he now communicated to the authorities. Michu's farmhouse, lately built, had, he supposed, a new oven; the tiles or bricks on which the bread was baked would show their jointed lines on the bottom of the loaves, and thus afford a proof that the bread supplied to him was baked on that particular oven. So with the wine brought in bottles sealed with green wax, which would probably be found identical with other bottles in Michu's cellar. These shrewd observations, which Malin imparted to the justice of peace, who made the first examination (taking Marthe with him), led to the results foreseen by the senator.

Marthe, deceived by the apparent friendliness of Lechesneau and the public prosecutor, who assured her that complete confession could alone save her husband's life, admitted that the cavern where the senator had been hidden was known only to her husband and the Messieurs de Simeuse and d'Hauteserre, and that she herself had taken provisions to the senator on three separate occasions at midnight.

Laurence, questioned about the cavern, was forced to acknowledge that Michu had discovered it and had shown it to her at the time when the four young men evaded the police and were hidden in it.

As soon as these preliminary examinations were ended, the jury, lawyers, and audience were notified that the trial would be resumed. At three o'clock the president opened the session by announcing that the case would be continued under a new aspect. He exhibited to Michu three bottles of wine and asked him if he recognized them as bottles from his own cellar, showing him at the same time the identity between the green wax on two empty bottles with the green wax on a full bottle taken from his cellar that morning by the justice of peace in presence of his wife. Michu refused to recognize anything as his own. But these proofs for the prosecution were understood by the jurors, to whom the president explained that the empty bottles were found in the place where the senator was imprisoned.

Each prisoner was questioned as to the cavern or cellar beneath the ruins of the old monastery. It was proved by all witnesses for the prosecution, and also for the defence, that the existence of this hiding-place discovered by Michu was known only to him and his wife, and to Laurence and the four gentlemen. We may judge of the effect in the courtroom when the public prosecutor made known the fact that this cavern, known only to the accused and to their two witnesses, was the place where the senator had been imprisoned.

Marthe was summoned. Her appearance caused much excitement among the spectators and keen anxiety to the prisoners. Monsieur de Grandville rose to protest against the testimony of a wife against her husband. The public prosecutor replied that Marthe by her own confession was an accomplice in the outrage; that she had neither sworn nor testified, and was to be heard solely in the interests of truth.

"We need only submit her preliminary examination to the jury," remarked the president, who now ordered the clerk of the court to read the said testimony aloud.

"Do you now confirm your own statement?" said the president, addressing Marthe.

Michu looked at his wife, and Marthe, who saw her fatal error, fainted away and fell to the floor. It may be truly said that a thunderbolt had fallen upon the prisoners and their counsel.

"I never wrote to my wife from prison, and I know none of the persons employed there," said Michu.

Bordin passed to him the fragments of the letter Marthe had received. Michu gave but one glance at it. "My writing has been imitated," he said.

"Denial is your last resource," said the public prosecutor.

The senator was introduced into the courtroom with all the ceremonies due to his position. His entrance was like a stage scene. Malin (now called Comte de Gondreville, without regard to the feelings of the late owners of the property) was requested by the president to look at the prisoners, and did so with great attention and for a long time. He stated that the clothing of his abductors was exactly like that worn by the four gentlemen; but he declared that the trouble of his mind had been such that he could not be positive that the accused were really the guilty parties.

"More than that," he said, "it is my conviction that these four gentlemen had nothing to do with it. The hands that blindfolded me in the forest were coarse and rough. I should rather suppose," he added, looking at Michu, "that my old enemy took charge of that duty; but I beg the gentlemen of the jury not to give too much weight to this remark. My suspicions are very slight, and I feel no certainty whatever – for this reason. The two men who seized me put me on horseback behind the man who blindfolded me, and whose hair was red like Michu's. However singular you may consider the observation I am about to make, it is necessary to make it because it is the ground of an opinion favorable to the accused – who, I hope, will not feel offended by it. Fastened to the man's back I would naturally have been affected by his odor – yet

I did not perceive that which is peculiar to Michu. As to the person who brought me provisions on three several occasions, I am certain it was Marthe, the wife of Michu. I recognized her the first time she came by a ring she always wore, which she had forgotten to remove. The Court and jury will please allow for the contradictions which appear in the facts I have stated, which I myself am wholly unable to reconcile."

A murmur of approval followed this testimony. Bordin asked permission of the Court to address a few questions to the witness.

"Does the senator think that his abduction was due to other causes than the interests respecting property which the prosecution attributes to the prisoners?"

"I do," replied the senator, "but I am wholly ignorant of what the real motives were; for during a captivity of twenty days I saw and heard no one."

"Do you think," said the public prosecutor, "that your chateau at Gondreville contains information, title-deeds, or other papers of value which would induce a search on the part of the Messieurs de Simeuse?"

"I do not think so," replied Malin; "I believe those gentlemen to be incapable of attempting to get possession of such papers by violence. They had only to ask me for them to obtain them."

"You burned certain papers in the park, did you not?" said Monsieur de Gondreville, abruptly.

Malin looked at Grevin. After exchanging a rapid glance with the notary, which Bordin intercepted, he replied that he had not burned any papers. The public prosecutor having asked him to describe the ambush to which he had so nearly fallen a victim two years earlier, the senator replied that he had seen Michu watching him from the fork of a tree. This answer, which agreed with Grevin's testimony, produced a great impression.

The four gentlemen remained impassible during the examination of their enemy, who seemed determined to overwhelm them with generosity. Laurence suffered horrible agony. From time to time the Marquis de Chargeboeuf held her by the arm, fearing she might dart forward to the rescue. The Comte de Gondreville retired from the courtroom and as he did so he bowed to the four gentlemen, who did not return the salutation. This trifling matter made the jury indignant.

"They are lost now," whispered Bordin to the Marquis de Chargeboeuf.

"Alas, yes! and always through the nobility of their sentiments," replied the marquis.

"My task is now only too easy, gentlemen," said the prosecutor, rising to address the jury.

He explained the use of the cement by the necessity of securing an iron frame on which to fasten a padlock which held the iron bar with which the gate of the cavern was closed; a description of which was given in the *proces-verbal* made that morning by Pigoult. He put the falsehoods of the accused into the strongest light, and pulverized the arguments of the defence with the new evidence so miraculously obtained. In 1806 France was still too near the Supreme Being of 1793 to talk about divine justice; he therefore spared the jury all reference to the intervention of heaven; but he said that earthly justice would be on the watch for the mysterious accomplices who had set the senator at liberty, and he sat down, confidently awaiting the verdict.

The jury believed there was a mystery, but they were all persuaded that it came from the prisoners, who were probably concealing some matter of a private interest of great importance to them.

Monsieur de Grandville, to whom a plot or machination of some kind was quite evident, rose; but he seemed discouraged, – less, however, by the new evidence than by the manifest opinion of the jury. He surpassed, if anything, his speech of the previous evening; his argument was more compact and logical; but he felt his fervor repelled by the coldness of the jury; he spoke ineffectually, and he knew it, – a chilling situation for an advocate. He called attention to the fact that the release of the senator, as if by magic and clearly without the aid of any of the accused or of Marthe, corroborated his previous argument. Yesterday the prisoners could most surely rely on acquittal, and if they had, as the prosecution claimed, the power to hold or to release the senator, they certainly would not have released him until after their acquittal. He endeavored to bring before the minds of the Court and jury the fact that mysterious enemies, undiscovered as yet, could alone have struck the accused this final blow.

Strange to say, the only minds Monsieur de Grandville reached with this argument were those of the public prosecutor and the judges. The jury listened perfunctorily; the audience, usually so favorable to prisoners, were convinced of their guilt. In a court of justice the sentiments of the crowd do unquestionably weigh upon the judges and the jury, and *vice versa*. Seeing this condition of the minds about him, which could be felt if not defined, the counsel uttered his last words in a tone of passionate excitement caused by his conviction: –

"In the name of the accused," he cried, "I forgive you for the fatal error you are about to commit, and which nothing can repair! We are the victims of some mysterious and Machiavellian power. Marthe Michu was inveigled by vile perfidy. You will discover this too late, when the evil you now do will be irreparable."

Bordin simply claimed the acquittal of the prisoners on the testimony of the senator himself.

The president summed up the case with all the more impartiality because it was evident that the minds of the jurors were already made up. He even turned the scales in favor of the prisoners by dwelling on the senator's evidence. This clemency, however, did not in the least endanger the success of the prosecution. At eleven o'clock that night, after the jury had replied through their foreman to the usual questions, the Court condemned Michu to death, the Messieurs de Simeuse to twenty-four years' and the Messieurs d'Hauteserre to ten years, penal servitude at hard labor. Gothard was acquitted.

The whole audience was eager to observe the bearing of the five guilty men in this supreme moment of their lives. The four gentlemen looked at Laurence, who returned them, with dry eyes, the ardent look of the martyrs.

"She would have wept had we been acquitted," said the younger de Simeuse to his brother.

Never did convicted men meet an unjust fate with serener brows or countenances more worthy of their manhood than these five victims of a cruel plot.

"Our counsel has forgiven you," said the eldest de Simeuse to the Court.

* * * * *

Madame d'Hauteserre fell ill, and was three months in her bed at the hotel de Chargeboeuf. Monsieur d'Hauteserre returned patiently to Cinq-Cygne, inwardly gnawed by one of those sorrows of old age which have none of youth's distractions; often he was so absent-minded that the abbe, who watched him, knew the poor father was living over again the scene of the fatal verdict. Marthe passed away from all blame; she died three weeks after the condemnation of her husband, confiding her son to Laurence, in whose arms she died.

The trial once over, political events of the utmost importance effaced even the memory of it, and nothing further was discovered. Society is like the ocean; it returns to its level and its specious calmness after a disaster, effacing all traces of it in the tide of its eager interests.

Without her natural firmness of mind and her knowledge of her cousins' innocence, Laurence would have succumbed; but she gave fresh proof of the grandeur of her character; she astonished Monsieur de Grandville and Bordin by the apparent serenity which these terrible misfortunes called forth in her noble soul. She nursed Madame d'Hauteserre and went daily to the prison, saying openly that she would marry one of the cousins when they were taken to the galleys.

"To the galleys!" cried Bordin, "Mademoiselle! our first endeavor must be to wring their pardon from the Emperor."

"Their pardon! – *from a Bonaparte*?" cried Laurence in horror.

The spectacles of the old lawyer jumped from his nose; he caught them as they fell and looked at the young girl who was now indeed a woman; he understood her character at last in all its bearings; then he took the arm of the Marquis de Chargeboeuf, saying: –

"Monsieur le Marquis, let us go to Paris instantly and save them without her!"

The appeal of the Messieurs de Simeuse and d'Hauteserre and that of Michu was the first case to be brought before the new court. Its decision was fortunately delayed by the ceremonies attending its installation.

Chapter XIX. The Emperor's Bivouac

Towards the end of September, after three sessions of the Court of Appeals in which the lawyers for the defence pleaded, and the attorney-general Merlin himself spoke for the prosecution, the appeal was rejected. The Imperial Court of Paris was by this time instituted. Monsieur de Grandville was appointed assistant attorney-general, and the department of the Aube coming under the jurisdiction of this court, it became possible for him to take certain steps in favor of the convicted prisoners, among them that of importuning Cambaceres, his protector. Bordin and Monsieur de Chargeboeuf came to his house in the Marais the day after the appeal was rejected, where they found him in the midst of his honeymoon, for he had married in the interval. In spite of all these changes in his condition, Monsieur de Chargeboeuf saw very plainly that the young lawyer was faithful to his late clients. Certain lawyers, the artists of their profession, treat their causes like mistresses. This is rare, however, and must not be depended on.

As soon as they were alone in his study, Monsieur de Grandville said to the marquis: "I have not waited for your visit; I have already employed all my influence. Don't attempt to save Michu; if you do, you cannot obtain the pardon of the Messieurs de Simeuse. The law will insist on one victim."

"Good God!" cried Bordin, showing the young magistrate the three petitions for mercy; "how can I take upon myself to withdraw the application for that man. If I suppress the paper I cut off his head."

He held out the petition; de Grandville took it, looked it over, and said: –

"We can't suppress it; but be sure of one thing, if you ask all you will obtain nothing."

"Have we time to consult Michu?" asked Bordin.

"Yes. The order for execution comes from the office of the attorney-general; I will see that you have some days. We kill men," he said with some bitterness, "but at least we do it formally, especially in Paris."

Monsieur de Chargeboeuf had already received from the chief justice certain information which added weight to these sad words of Monsieur de Grandville.

"Michu is innocent, I know," continued the young lawyer, "but what can we do against so many? Remember, too, that my present influence depends on my keeping silent. I must order the scaffold to be prepared, or my late client is certain to be beheaded."

Monsieur de Chargeboeuf knew Laurence well enough to be certain she would never consent to save her cousins at the expense of Michu; he therefore resolved on making one more effort. He asked an audience of the minister of foreign affairs to learn if salvation could be looked for through the influence of the great diplomat. He took Bordin with him, for the latter knew the minister and had done him some service. The two old men found Talleyrand sitting with his feet stretched out, absorbed in contemplation of his fire, his head resting on his hand, his elbow on the table, a newspaper lying at his feet. The minister had just read the decision of the Court of Appeals.

"Pray sit down, Monsieur le marquis," said Talleyrand, "and you, Bordin," he added, pointing to a place at the table, "write as follows: – "

Sire, – Four innocent gentlemen, declared guilty by a jury have just had their condemnation confirmed by your Court of Appeals.

Your Imperial Majesty can now only pardon them. These gentlemen ask this pardon of your august clemency, in the hope that they may enter your army and meet their death in battle before your eyes; and thus praying, they are, of your Imperial and Royal Majesty, with reverence, etc.

"None but princes can do such prompt and graceful kindness," said the Marquis de Chargeboeuf, taking the precious draft of the petition from the hands of Bordin that he might have it signed by the four gentlemen; resolving in his own mind that he would also obtain the signatures of several august names.

"The life of your young relatives, Monsieur le marquis," said the minister, "now depends on the turn of a battle. Endeavor to reach the Emperor on the morning after a victory and they are saved."

He took a pen and himself wrote a private and confidential letter to the Emperor, and another of ten lines to Marechal Duroc. Then he rang the bell, asked his secretary for a diplomatic passport, and said tranquilly to the old lawyer, "What is your honest opinion of that trial?"

"Do you know, monseigneur, who was at the bottom of this cruel wrong?"

"I presume I do; but I have reasons to wish for certainty," replied Talleyrand. "Return to Troyes; bring me the Comtesse de Cinq-Cygne, here, to-morrow at the same hour, but secretly; ask to be ushered into Madame de Talleyrand's salon; I will tell her you are coming. If Mademoiselle de Cinq-Cygne, who shall be placed where she can see a man who will be standing before me, recognizes that man as an individual who came to her house during the conspiracy of de Polignac and Riviere, tell her to remember that, no matter what I say or what he answers me, she must not utter a word nor make a gesture. One thing more, think only of saving the de Simeuse brothers; don't embarrass yourself with that scoundrel of a bailiff – "

"A sublime man, monseigneur!" exclaimed Bordin.

"Enthusiasm! in you, Bordin! The man must be remarkable. Our sovereign has an immense self-love, Monsieur le marquis," he said, changing the conversation. "He is about to dismiss me that he may commit follies without warning. The Emperor is a great soldier who can change the laws of time and distance, but he cannot change men; yet he persists in trying to run them in his own mould! Now, remember this; the young men's pardon can be obtained by one person only – Mademoiselle de Cinq-Cygne."

The marquis went alone to Troyes and told the whole matter

to Laurence. She obtained permission from the authorities to see Michu, and the marquis accompanied her to the gates of the prison, where he waited for her. When she came out her face was bathed in tears.

"Poor man!" she said; "he tried to kneel to me, praying that I would not think of him, and forgetting the shackles that were on his feet! Ah, marquis, I *will* plead his cause. Yes, I'll kiss the boot of their Emperor. If I fail – well, the memory of that man shall live eternally honored in our family. Present his petition for mercy so as to gain time; meantime I am resolved to have his portrait. Come, let us go."

The next day, when Talleyrand was informed by a sign agreed upon that Laurence was at her post, he rang the bell; his orderly came to him, and received orders to admit Monsieur Corentin.

"My friend, you are a very clever fellow," said Talleyrand, "and I wish to employ you."

"Monsiegneur – "

"Listen. In serving Fouche you will get money, but never honor nor any position you can acknowledge. But in serving me, as you have lately done at Berlin, you can win credit and repute."

"Monseigneur is very good."

"You displayed genius in that late affair at Gondreville."

"To what does Monseigneur allude?" said Corentin, with a manner that was neither too reserved nor too surprised.

"Ah, Monsieur!" observed the minister, dryly, "you will never make a successful man; you fear – "

"What, monseigneur?"

"Death!" replied Talleyrand, in his fine, deep voice. "Adieu, my good friend."

"That is the man," said the Marquis de Chargeboeuf entering the room after Corentin was dismissed; "but we have nearly killed the countess."

"He is the only man I know capable of playing such a trick," replied the minister. "Monsieur le marquis, you are in danger of not succeeding in your mission. Start ostensibly for Strasburg; I'll send you double passports in blank to be filled out. Provide yourself with substitutes; change your route and above all your carriage; let your substitutes go on to Strasburg, and do you reach Prussia through Switzerland and Bavaria. Not a word – prudence! The police are against you; and you do not know what the police are – "

Mademoiselle de Cinq-Cygne offered the then celebrated Robert Lefebvre a sufficient sum to induce him to go to Troyes and take Michu's portrait. Monsieur de Grandville promised to afford the painter every possible facility. Monsieur de Chargeboeuf then started in the old *berlingot*, with Laurence and a servant who spoke German. Not far from Nancy they overtook Mademoiselle Goujet and Gothard, who had preceded them in an excellent carriage, which the marquis took, giving them in exchange the *berlingot*.

Talleyrand was right. At Strasburg the commissary-general of police refused to countersign the passport of the travellers, and gave them positive orders to return. By that time the marquis and Laurence were leaving France by way of Besancon with the diplomatic passport.

Laurence crossed Switzerland in the first days of October, without paying the slightest attention to that glorious land. She lay back in the carriage in the torpor which overtakes a criminal on the eve of his execution. To her eyes all nature was shrouded in a seething vapor; even common things assumed fantastic shapes. The one thought, "If I do not succeed they will kill themselves," fell upon her soul with reiterated blows, as the bar of the executioner fell upon the victim's members when tortured on the wheel. She felt herself breaking; she lost her energy in this terrible waiting for the cruel moment, short and decisive, when she should find herself face to face with that man on whom the fate of the condemned depended. She chose to yield to her depression rather than waste her strength uselessly. The marquis, who was incapable of understanding this resolve of firm minds, which often assumes quite diverse aspects (for in such moments of tension certain superior minds give way to surprising gaiety), began to fear that he might never bring Laurence alive to the momentous interview, solemn to them only, and yet beyond the ordinary limits of private life. To Laurence, the necessity of humiliating herself before that man, the object of her hatred and contempt, meant the sacrifice of all her noblest feelings.

"After this," she said, "the Laurence who survives will bear no likeness to her who is now to perish."

The travellers could not fail to be aware of the vast movement of men and material which surrounded them the moment they entered Prussia. The campaign of Jena had just begun. Laurence and the marquis beheld the magnificent divisions of the French army deploying and parading as if at the Tuileries. In this display of military power, which can be adequately described only with the words and images of the Bible, the proportions of the Man whose spirit moved these masses grew gigantic to Laurence's imagination. Soon, the cry of victory resounded in her ears. The Imperial arms had just obtained two signal advantages. The Prince of Prussia had been killed the evening before the day on which the travellers arrived at Saalfeld on their endeavor to overtake Napoleon, who was marching with the rapidity of lightning.

At last, on the 13th of October (date of ill-omen) Mademoiselle de Cinq-Cygne was skirting a river in the midst of the Grand Army, seeing nought but confusion, sent hither and thither from one village to another, from division to division, frightened at finding herself alone with one old man tossed about in an ocean of a hundred and fifty thousand armed men facing a hundred and fifty thousand more. Weary of watching the river through the hedges of the muddy road which she was following along a hillside, she asked its name of a passing soldier.

"That's the Saale," he said, showing her the Prussian army, grouped in great masses on the other side of the stream.

Night came on. Laurence beheld the camp-fires lighted and

the glitter of stacked arms. The old marquis, whose courage was chivalric, drove the horses himself (two strong beasts bought the evening before), his servant sitting beside him. He knew very well he should find neither horses nor postilions within the lines of the army. Suddenly the bold equipage, an object of great astonishment to the soldiers, was stopped by a gendarme of the military gendarmerie, who galloped up to the carriage, calling out to the marquis: "Who are you? where are you going? what do you want?"

"The Emperor," replied the Marquis de Chargeboeuf; "I have an important dispatch for the Grand-marechal Duroc."

"Well, you can't stay here," said the gendarme.

Mademoiselle de Cinq-Cygne and the marquis were, however, compelled to remain where they were on account of the darkness.

"Where are we?" she asked, stopping two officers whom she saw passing, whose uniforms were concealed by cloth overcoats.

"You are among the advanced guard of the French army," answered one of the officers. "You cannot stay here, for if the enemy makes a movement and the artillery opens you will be between two fires."

"Ah!" she said, with an indifferent air.

Hearing that "Ah!" the other officer turned and said: "How did that woman come here?"

"We are waiting," said Laurence, "for a gendarme who has gone to find General Duroc, a protector who will enable us to speak to the Emperor."

"Speak to the Emperor!" exclaimed the first officer; "how can you think of such a thing – on the eve of a decisive battle?"

"True," she said; "I ought to speak to him on the morrow – victory would make him kind."

The two officers stationed themselves at a little distance and sat motionless on their horses. The carriage was now surrounded by a mass of generals, marshals, and other officers, all extremely brilliant in appearance, who appeared to pay deference to the carriage merely because it was there.

"Good God!" said the marquis to Mademoiselle de Cinq-Cygne; "I am afraid you spoke to the Emperor."

"The Emperor?" said a colonel, beside them, "why there he is!" pointing to the officer who had said, "How did that woman get here?" He was mounted on a white horse, richly caparisoned, and wore the celebrated gray top-coat over his green uniform. He was scanning with a field-glass the Prussian army massed beyond the Saale. Laurence understood then why the carriage remained there, and why the Emperor's escort respected it. She was seized with a convulsive tremor – the hour had come! She heard the heavy sound of the tramp of men and the clang of their arms as they arrived at a quick step on the plateau. The batteries had a language, the caissons thundered, the brass glittered.

"Marechal Lannes will take position with his whole corps in the advance; Marechal Lefebvre and the Guard will occupy this hill," said the other officer, who was Major-general Berthier.

The Emperor dismounted. At his first motion Roustan, his famous mameluke, hastened to hold his horse. Laurence was stupefied with amazement; she had never dreamed of such simplicity.

"I shall pass the night on the plateau," said the Emperor.

Just then the Grand-marechal Duroc, whom the gendarme had finally found, came up to the Marquis de Chargeboeuf and asked the reason of his coming. The marquis replied that a letter from the Prince de Talleyrand, of which he was the bearer, would explain to the marshal how urgent it was that Mademoiselle de Cinq-Cygne and himself should obtain an audience of the Emperor.

"His Majesty will no doubt dine at his bivouac," said Duroc, taking the letter, "and when I find out what your object is, I will let you know if you can see him. Corporal," he said to the gendarme, "accompany this carriage, and take it close to that hut at the rear."

Monsieur de Chargeboeuf followed the gendarme and stopped his horses behind a miserable cabin, built of mud and branches, surrounded by a few fruit-trees, and guarded by pickets of infantry and cavalry.

It may be said that the majesty of war appeared here in all its grandeur. From this height the lines of the two armies were visible in the moonlight. After an hour's waiting, the time being occupied by the incessant coming and going of the aides-de-camp, Duroc himself came for Mademoiselle de Cinq-Cygne and the marquis, and made them enter the hut, the floor of which was of battened earth like that of a stable.

Before a table with the remains of dinner, and before a fire made of green wood which smoked, Napoleon was seated in a clumsy chair. His muddy boots gave evidence of a long tramp across country. He had taken off the famous top-coat; and his equally famous green uniform, crossed by the red cordon of the Legion of honor and heightened by the white of his kerseymere breeches and of his waistcoat, brought out vividly his pale and terrible Caesarian face. One hand was on a map which lay unfolded on his knees. Berthier stood near him in the brilliant uniform of the vice-constable of the Empire. Constant, the valet, was offering the Emperor his coffee from a tray.

"What do you want?" said Napoleon, with a show of roughness, darting his eye like a flash through Laurence's head. "You are no longer afraid to speak to me before the battle? What is it about?"

"Sire," she said, looking at him with as firm an eye, "I am Mademoiselle de Cinq-Cygne."

"Well?" he replied, in an angry voice, thinking her look braved him.

"Do you not understand? I am the Comtesse de Cinq-Cygne, come to ask mercy," she said, falling on her knees and holding out to him the petition drawn up by Talleyrand, endorsed by the Empress, by Cambaceres and by Malin.

The Emperor raised her graciously, and said with a keen look: "Have you come to your senses? Do you now understand what the French Empire is and must be?"

"Ah! at this moment I understand only the Emperor," she said, vanquished by the kindly manner with which the man of destiny had said the words that foretold to her ears success.

"Are they innocent?" asked the Emperor.

"Yes, all of them," she said with enthusiasm.

"All? No, that bailiff is a dangerous man, who would have killed my senator without taking your advice."

"Ah, Sire," she said, "if you had a friend devoted to you, would you abandon him? Would you not rather – "

"You are a woman," he said, interrupting her in a faint tone of ridicule.

"And you, a man of iron!" she replied with a passionate sternness which pleased him.

"That man has been condemned to death by the laws of his country," he continued.

"But he is innocent!"

"Child!" he said.

He took Mademoiselle de Cinq-Cygne by the hand and led her from the hut to the plateau.

"See," he continued, with that eloquence of his which changed even cowards to brave men, "see those three hundred thousand men – all innocent. And yet to-morrow thirty thousand of them will be lying dead, dead for their country! Among those Prussians there is, perhaps, some great mathematician, a man of genius, an idealist, who will be mown down. On our side we shall assuredly lose many a great man never known to fame. Perhaps even I shall see my best friend die. Shall I blame God? No. I shall bear it silently. Learn from this, mademoiselle, that a man must die for the laws of his country just as men die here for her

glory." So saying, he led her back into the hut. "Return to France,"
he said, looking at the marquis; "my orders shall follow you."

Laurence believed in a commutation of Michu's punishment,
and in her gratitude she knelt again before the Emperor and
kissed his hand.

"You are the Marquis de Chargeboeuf?" said Napoleon, addressing the marquis.

"Yes, Sire."

"You have children?"

"Many children."

"Why not give me one of your grandsons? he shall be my
page."

"Ah!" thought Laurence, "there's the sub-lieutenant after all;
he wants to be paid for his mercy."

The marquis bowed without replying. Happily at this moment General Rapp rushed into the hut.

"Sire, the cavalry of the Guard, and that of the Grand-duc de
Berg cannot be set up before midday to-morrow."

"Never mind," said Napoleon, turning to Berthier, "we, too,
get our reprieves; let us profit by them."

At a sign of his hand the marquis and Laurence retired and
again entered their carriage; the corporal showed them their road
and accompanied them to a village where they passed the night.
The next day they left the field of battle behind them, followed by
the thunder of the cannon, – eight hundred pieces, – which pur-
sued them for ten hours. While still on their way they learned of
the amazing victory of Jena.

Eight days later, they were driving through the faubourg of
Troyes, where they learned that an order of the chief justice,
transmitted through the *procureur imperial* of Troyes, commanded
the release of the four gentlemen on bail during the Emperor's
pleasure. But Michu's sentence was confirmed, and the warrant

for his execution had been forwarded from the ministry of police. These orders had reached Troyes that very morning. Laurence went at once to the prison, though it was two in the morning, and obtained permission to stay with Michu, who was about to undergo the melancholy ceremony called "the toilet." The good abbe, who had asked permission to accompany him to the scaffold, had just given absolution to the man, whose only distress in dying was his uncertainty as to the fate of his young masters. When Laurence entered his cell he uttered a cry of joy.

"I can die now," he said.

"They are pardoned," she said; "I do not know on what conditions, but they are pardoned. I did all I could for you, dear friend – against the advice of others. I thought I had saved you; but the Emperor deceived me with his graciousness."

"It was written above," said Michu, "that the watch-dog should be killed on the spot where his old masters died."

The last hour passed rapidly. Michu, at the moment of parting, asked to kiss her hand, but Laurence held her cheek to the lips of the noble victim that he might sacredly kiss it. Michu refused to mount the cart.

"Innocent men should go afoot," he said.

He would not let the abbe give him his arm; resolutely and with dignity he walked alone to the scaffold. As he laid his head on the plank he said to the executioner, after asking him to turn down the collar of his coat, "My clothes belong to you; try not to spot them."

* * * * *

The four gentlemen had hardly time to even see Mademoiselle de Cinq-Cygne. An orderly of the general commanding the division to which they were assigned, brought them their commissions as sub-lieutenants in the same regiment of cavalry, with orders to proceed at once to Bayonne, the base of supplies for its particular army-corps. After a scene of heart-rending farewells, for they all foreboded what the future should bring forth, Mademoiselle de Cinq-Cygne returned to her desolate home.

The two brothers were killed together under the eyes of the Emperor at Sommo-Sierra, the one defending the other, both being already in command of their troop. The last words of each were, "Laurence, *cy meurs!*"

The elder d'Hauteserre died a colonel at the attack on the redoubt at Moscow, where his brother took his place.

Adrien d'Hauteserre, appointed brigadier-general at the battle of Dresden, was dangerously wounded there and was sent to Cinq-Cygne for proper nursing. While endeavoring to save this relic of the four gentlemen who for a few brief months had been so happy around her, Laurence, then thirty-two years of age, married him. She offered him a withered heart, but he accepted it; those who truly love doubt nothing or doubt all.

The Restoration found Laurence without enthusiasm. The Bourbons returned too late for her. Nevertheless, she had no cause for complaint. Her husband, made peer of France with the title of Marquis de Cinq-Cygne, became lieutenant-general in 1816, and was rewarded with the blue ribbon for the eminent services which he then performed.

Michu's son, of whom Laurence took care as though he were her own child, was admitted to the bar in 1817. After practising two years he was made assistant-judge at the court of Alencon, and from there he became *procureur-du-roi* at Arcis in 1827. Laurence, who had also taken charge of Michu's property, made over to the young man on the day of his majority an investment in the public Funds which yielded him an income of twelve thousand francs a year. Later, she arranged a marriage for him with Mademoiselle Girel, an heiress at Troyes.

The Marquis de Cinq-Cygne died in 1829, in the arms of his wife, surrounded by his father and mother, and his children who adored him. At the time of his death no one had ever fathomed the mystery of the senator's abduction. Louis XVIII. did not neglect to repair, as far as possible, the wrongs done by that affair; but he was silent as to the causes of the disaster. From that time forth the Marquise de Cinq-Cygne believed him to have been an accomplice in the catastrophe.

"You have been here since nine o'clock this morning, haven't you?" said Corentin to Violette.

"No, beg your pardon, since last night I haven't left the place, and I've gained nothing after all; the more he makes me drink the more he puts up the price."

"In all markets he who raises his elbow raises a price," said Corentin.

A dozen empty bottles ranged along the table proved the truth of the old woman's words. Just then the gendarme who had driven him made a sign to Corentin, who went to the door to speak to him.

"There is no horse in the stable," said the man.

"You sent your boy on horseback to the chateau, didn't you?" said Corentin, returning to the kitchen. "Will he be back soon?"

"No, monsieur," said Michu, "he went on foot."

"What have you done with your horse, then?"

"I have lent him," said Michu, curtly.

"Come out here, my good fellow," said Corentin; "I've a word for your ear."

Corentin and Michu left the house.

"The gun which you were loading yesterday at four o'clock you meant to use in murdering the Councillor of State; but we can't take you up for that – plenty of intention, but no witnesses. You managed, I don't know how, to stupefy Violette, and you and your wife and that young rascal of yours spent the night out of doors to warn Mademoiselle de Cinq-Cygne and save her cousins, whom you are hiding here, – though I don't as yet know where. Your son or your wife threw the corporal off his horse cleverly enough. Well, you've got the better of us just now; you're a devil of a fellow. But the end is not yet, and you won't have the last word. Hadn't you better compromise? your masters would be the better for it."

"Come this way, where we can talk without being over-heard," said Michu, leading the way through the park to the pond.

When Corentin saw the water he looked fixedly at Michu, who was no doubt reckoning on his physical strength to fling the spy into seven feet of mud below three feet of water. Michu replied with a look that was not less fixed. The scene was absolutely as if a cold and flabby boa constrictor had defied one of those tawny, fierce leopards of Brazil.

"I am not thirsty," said Corentin, stopping short at the edge of the field and putting his hand into his pocket to feel for his dagger.

"We shall never come to terms," said Michu, coldly.

"Mind what you're about, my good fellow; the law has its eye upon you."

"If the law can't see any clearer than you, there's danger to every one," said the bailiff.

"Do you refuse?" said Corentin, in a significant tone.

"I'd rather have my head cut off a thousand times, if that could be done, than come to an agreement with such a villain as you."

Corentin got into his vehicle hastily, after one more comprehensive look at Michu, the lodge, and Couraut, who barked at him. He gave certain orders in passing through Troyes, and then returned to Paris. All the brigades of gendarmerie in the neighborhood received secret instructions and special orders.

During the months of December, January, and February the search was active and incessant, even in remote villages. Spies were in all the taverns. Corentin learned some important facts: a horse like that of Michu had been found dead in the neighborhood of Lagny; the five horses burned in the forest of Nodesme had been sold, for five hundred francs each, by farmers and millers to a man who answered to the description of Michu. When the decree against the accomplices and harborers of Georges was put in force Corentin confined his search to the forest of Nodesme. After Moreau, the royalists, and Pichegru were arrested no strangers were ever seen about the place.

Michu lost his situation at that time; the notary of Arcis brought him a letter in which Malin, now made senator, requested Grevin to settle all accounts with the bailiff and dismiss him. Michu asked and obtained a formal discharge and became a free man. To the great astonishment of the neighborhood he went to live at Cinq-Cygne, where Laurence made him the farmer of all the reserved land about the chateau. The day of his installation as farmer coincided with the fatal day of the death of the Duc d'Enghien, when nearly the whole of France heard at the same time of the arrest, trial, condemnation, and death of the prince, – terrible reprisals, which preceded the trial of Polignac, Riviere, and Moreau.

Chapter XX. The Mystery Solved

The late Marquis de Cinq-Cygne had used his savings, as
well as those of his father and mother, in the purchase of a fine
house in the rue de Faubourg-du-Roule, entailing it on heirs male
for the support of the title. The sordid economy of the marquis
and his parents, which had often troubled Laurence, was then
explained. After this purchase the marquise, who lived at Cinq-
Cygne and economized on her own account for her children,
spent her winters in Paris, – all the more willingly because her
daughter Berthe and her son Paul were now of an age when their
education required the resources of Paris.

Madame de Cinq-Cygne went but little into society. Her
husband could not be ignorant of the regrets which lay in her
tender heart; but he showed her always the most exquisite delicacy, and died having loved no other woman. This noble soul, not
fully understood for a period of time but to which the generous
daughter of the Cinq-Cygnes returned in his last years as true a
love as that he gave to her, was completely happy in his married
life. Laurence lived for the joys of home. No woman has ever
been more cherished by her friends or more respected. To be received in her house is an honor. Gentle, indulgent, intellectual,
above all things simple and natural, she pleases choice souls and
draws them to her in spite of her saddened aspect; each longs to
protect this woman, inwardly so strong, and that sentiment of
secret protection counts for much in the wondrous charm of her
friendship. Her life, so painful during her youth, is beautiful and
serene towards evening. Her sufferings are known, and no one
asks who was the original of that portrait by Lefebvre which is
the chief and sacred ornament of her salon. Her face has the ma-
turity of fruits that have ripened slowly; a hallowed pride digni-
fies that long-tried brow.

At the period when the marquise came to Paris to open the
new house, her fortune, increased by the law of indemnities, gave
her some two hundred thousand francs a year, not counting her
husband's salary; besides this, Laurence had inherited the money
guarded by Michu for his young masters. From that time forth

she made a practice of spending half her income and of laying by the rest for her daughter Berthe.

Berthe is the living image of her mother, but without her warrior nerve; she is her mother in delicacy, in intellect, – "more a woman," Laurence says, sadly. The marquise was not willing to marry her daughter until she was twenty years of age. Her savings, judiciously invested in the Funds by old Monsieur d'Hauteserre at the moment when consols fell in 1830, gave Berthe a dowry of eighty thousand francs a year in 1833, when she was twenty.

About that time the Princesse de Cadignan, who was seeking to marry her son, the Duc de Maufrigneuse, brought him into intimate relations with Madame de Cinq-Cygne. Georges de Maufrigneuse dined with the marquise three times a week, accompanied the mother and daughter to the Opera, and curvetted in the Bois around their carriage when they drove out. It was evident to all the world of the Faubourg Saint-Germain that Georges loved Berthe. But no one could discover to a certainty whether Madame de Cinq-Cygne was desirous of making her daughter a duchess, to become a princess later, or whether it was only the princess who coveted for her son the splendid dowry. Did the celebrated Diane court the noble provincial house? and was the daughter of the Cinq-Cygnes frightened by the celebrity of Madame de Cadignan, her tastes and her ruinous extravagance? In her strong desire not to injure her son's prospects the princess grew devout, shut the door on her former life, and spent the summer season at Geneva in a villa on the lake.

One evening there were present in the salon of the Princesse de Cadignan, the Marquise d'Espard, and de Marsay, then president of the Council (on this occasion the princess saw her former lover for the last time, for he died the following year), Eugene de Rastignac, under-secretary of State attached to de Marsay's ministry, two ambassadors, two celebrated orators from the Chamber of Peers, the old dukes of Lenoncourt and de Navarreins, the Comte de Vandenesse and his young wife, and d'Arthez, – who formed a rather singular circle, the composition of which can be thus explained. The princess was anxious to obtain from the prime minister of the crown a permit for the return of the Prince de Cadignan. De Marsay, who did not choose to take upon himself the responsibility of granting it came to tell the princess the matter had been entrusted to safe hands, and that a certain political manager had promised to bring her the result in the course of that evening.

Madame and Mademoiselle de Cinq-Cygne were announced. Laurence, whose principles were unyielding, was not only surprised but shocked to see the most illustrious representatives of Legitimacy talking and laughing in a friendly manner with the prime minister of the man whom she never called anything but Monsieur le Duc d'Orleans. De Marsay, like an expiring lamp, shone with a last brilliancy. He laid aside for the moment his political anxieties, and Madame de Cinq-Cygne endured him, as they say the Court of Austria endured de Saint-Aulaire; the man of the world effaced the minister of the citizen-king. But she rose to her feet as though her chair were of red-hot iron when the name was announced of "Monsieur le Comte de Gondreville."

"Adieu, madame," she said to the princess in a curt tone.

She left the room with Berthe, measuring her steps to avoid encountering that fatal being.

"You may have caused the loss of Georges' marriage," said the princess to de Marsay, in a low voice. "Why did you not tell me your agent's name?"

The former clerk of Arcis, former Conventional, former Thermidorien, tribune, Councillor of State, count of the Empire and senator, peer of the Restoration, and now peer of the monarchy of July, made a servile bow to the princess.

"Fear nothing, madame," he said; "we have ceased to make war on princes. I bring you an assurance of the permit," he added, seating himself beside her.

Malin was long in the confidence of Louis XVIII., to whom his varied experience was useful. He had greatly aided in overthrowing Decazes, and had given much good advice to the ministry of Villele. Coldly received by Charles X., he had adopted all the rancors of Talleyrand. He was now in high favor under the twelfth government he had served since 1789, and which in turn he would doubtless betray. For the last fifteen months he had broken the long friendship which had bound him for thirty-six years to our greatest diplomat, the Prince de Talleyrand. It was in the course of this very evening that he made answer to some one who asked why the Prince showed such hostility to the Duc de Bordeaux, "The Pretender is too young!"

"Singular advice to give young men," remarked Rastignac.

De Marsay, who grew thoughtful after Madame de Cadignan's reproachful speech, took no notice of these jests. He looked askance at Gondreville and was evidently biding his time until that now old man, who went to bed early, had taken leave. All present, who had witnessed the abrupt departure of Madame de Cinq-Cygne (whose reasons were well-known to them), imitated de Marsay's conduct and kept silence. Gondreville, who had not recognized the marquise, was ignorant of the cause of the general reticence, but the habit of dealing with public matters had given him a certain tact; he was moreover a clever man; he saw that his presence was embarrassing to the company and he took leave. De Marsay, standing with his back to the fire, watched the slow departure of the old man in a manner which revealed the gravity of his thoughts.

"I did wrong, madame, not to tell you the name of my negotiator," said the prime minister, listening for the sound of Malin's wheels as they rolled away. "But I will redeem my fault and give you the means of making your peace with the Cinq-Cygnes. It is now thirty years since the affair I am about to speak of took place; it is as old to the present day as the death of Henri IV. (which between ourselves and in spite of the proverb is still a mystery, like so many other historical catastrophes). I can, however, assure you that even if this affair did not concern Madame de Cinq-Cygne it would be none the less curious and interesting. Moreover, it throws light on a celebrated exploit in our modern annals, – I mean that of the Mont Saint-Bernard. Messieurs les Ambassadeurs," he added, bowing to the two diplomats, "will see that in the element of profound intrigue the political men of the present day are far behind the Machiavellis whom the waves of the popular will lifted, in 1793, above the storm, – some of whom have 'found,' as the old song says, 'a haven.' To be anything in France in these days a man must have been tossed in those tempests."

"It seems to me," said the princess, smiling, "that from that point of view the present state of things under your regime leaves nothing to be desired."

A well-bred laugh went round the room, and even the prime minister himself could not help smiling. The ambassadors seemed impatient for the tale; de Marsay coughed dryly and silence was obtained.

"On a June night in 1800," began the minister, "about three in the morning, just as daylight was beginning to pale the brilliancy of the wax candles, two men tired of playing at *bouillotte* (or who were playing merely to keep others employed) left the salon of the ministry of foreign affairs, then situated in the rue du Bac, and went apart into a boudoir. These two men, of whom one is dead and the other has *one* foot in the grave, were, each in his own way, equally extraordinary. Both had been priests; both had abjured religion; both were married. One had been merely an Oratorian, the other had worn the mitre of a bishop. The first was named Fouche; I shall not tell you the name of the second;[*] both were then mere simple citizens – with very little simplicity. When they were seen to leave the salon and enter the boudoir, the rest of the company present showed a certain curiosity. A third person followed them, – a man who thought himself far stronger than the other two. His name was Sieyes, and you all know that he too had been a priest before the Revolution. The one who *walked with difficulty* was then the minister of foreign affairs; Fouche was minister of police; Sieyes had resigned the consulate.

[*] Talleyrand was still living when de Marsay related these circumstances.

"A small man, cold and stern in appearance, left his seat and followed the three others, saying aloud in the hearing of the person from whom I have the information, 'I mistrust the gambling of priests.' This man was Carnot, minister of war. His remark did

215

not trouble the two consuls who were playing cards in the salon. Cambaceres and Lebrun were then at the mercy of their ministers, men who were infinitely stronger than they.

"Nearly all these statesmen are dead, and no secrecy is due to them. They belong to history; and the history of that night and its consequences has been terrible. I tell it to you now because I alone know it; because Louis XVIII. never revealed the truth to that poor Madame de Cinq-Cygne; and because the present government which I serve is wholly indifferent as to whether the truth be known to the world or not.

"All four of these personages sat down in the boudoir. The lame man undoubtedly closed the door before a word was said; it is even thought that he ran the bolt. It is only persons of high rank who pay attention to such trifles. The three priests had the livid, impassible faces which you all remember. Carnot alone was ruddy. He was the first to speak. 'What is the point to be discussed?' he asked. 'France,' must have been the answer of the Prince (whom I admire as one of the most extraordinary men of our time). 'The Republic,' undoubtedly said Fouche. 'Power,' probably said Sieyes."

All present looked at each other. With voice, look, and gesture de Marsay had wonderfully represented the three men.

"The three priests fully understood one another," he continued, resuming his narrative. "Carnot no doubt looked at his colleagues and the ex-consul in a dignified manner. He must, however, have felt bewildered in his own mind.

"'Do you believe in the success of the army?' Sieyes said to him.

"'We may expect everything from Bonaparte,' replied the minister of war; 'he has crossed the Alps.'

"'At this moment,' said the minister of foreign affairs, with deliberate slowness, 'he is playing his last stake.'

"'Come, let's speak out,' said Fouche; 'what shall we do if the First Consul is defeated? Is it possible to collect another army?

Must we continue his humble servants?'

"'There is no republic now,' remarked Sieyes; 'Bonaparte is consul for ten years.'

"'He has more power than ever Cromwell had,' said the former bishop, 'and he did not vote for the death of the king.'

"'We have a master,' said Fouche; 'the question is, shall we continue to keep him if he loses the battle or shall we return to a pure republic?'

"'France,' replied Carnot, sententiously, 'cannot resist except she reverts to the old Conventional *energy*.'

"'I agree with Carnot,' said Sieyes; 'if Bonaparte returns defeated we must put an end to him; he has let us know him too well during the last seven months.'

"'The army is for him,' remarked Carnot, thoughtfully.

"'And the people for us!' cried Fouche.

"'You go fast, monsieur,' said the Prince, in that deep bass voice which he still preserves and which now drove Fouche back into himself.

"'Be frank,' said a voice, as a former Conventional rose from a corner of the boudoir and showed himself; 'if Bonaparte returns a victor, we shall adore him; if vanquished, we'll bury him!'

"'So you were there, Malin, were you?' said the Prince, without betraying the least feeling. 'Then you must be one of us; sit down'; and he made him a sign to be seated.

"It is to this one circumstance that Malin, a Conventional of small repute, owes the position he afterwards obtained and, ultimately, that in which we see him at the present moment. He proved discreet, and the ministers were faithful to him; but they made him the pivot of the machine and the cat's-paw of the machination. To return to my tale.

"'Bonaparte has never yet been vanquished,' cried Carnot, in a tone of conviction, 'and he has just surpassed Hannibal.'

"'If the worst happens, here is the Directory,' said Sieyes, artfully, indicating with a wave of his hand the five persons present.

"'And,' added the Prince, 'we are all committed to the maintenance of the French republic; we three priests have literally unfrocked ourselves; the general, here, voted for the death of the king; and you,' he said, turning to Malin, 'have got possession of the property of *emigres*.'

"'Yes, we have all the same interests,' said Sieyes, dictatorially, 'and our interests are one with those of the nation.'

"'A rare thing,' said the Prince, smiling.

"'We must act,' interrupted Fouche. 'In all probability the battle is now going on; the Austrians outnumber us; Genoa has surrendered; Massena has committed the great mistake of embarking for Antibes; it is very doubtful if he can rejoin Bonaparte, who will then be reduced to his own resources.'

"'Who gave you that news?' asked Carnot.

"'It is sure,' replied Fouche. 'You will have the courier when the Bourse opens.'

"Those men didn't mince their words," said de Marsay, smiling, and stopping short for a moment.

"'Remember,' continued Fouche, 'it is not when the news of a disaster comes that we can organize clubs, rouse the patriotism of the people, and change the constitution. Our 18th Brumaire ought to be prepared beforehand.'

"'Let us leave the care of that to the minister of police,' said the Prince, bowing to Fouche, 'and beware ourselves of Lucien.' (Lucien Bonaparte was then minister of the interior.)

"'I'll arrest him,' said Fouche.

"'Messieurs!' cried Sieyes, 'our Directory ought not to be subject to anarchical changes. We must organize a government of the few, a Senate for life, and an elective chamber the control of which shall be in our hands; for we ought to profit by the blunders of the past.'

"'With such a system, there would be peace for me,' remarked the ex-bishop.

"'Find me a sure man to negotiate with Moreau; for the Army of the Rhine will be our sole resource,' cried Carnot, who had been plunged in meditation.

"Ah!" said de Marsay, pausing, "those men were right. They were grand in this crisis. I should have done as they did"; then he resumed his narrative.

"'Messieurs!' cried Sieyes, in a grave and solemn tone.

"That word 'Messieurs!' was perfectly understood by all present; all eyes expressed the same faith, the same promise, that of absolute silence, and unswerving loyalty to each other in case the First Consul returned triumphant.

"'We all know what we have to do,' added Fouche.

"Sieyes softly unbolted the door; his priestly ear had warned him. Lucien entered the room.

"'Good news!' he said. 'A courier has just brought Madame Bonaparte a line from the First Consul. The campaign has opened with a victory at Montebello.'

"The three ministers exchanged looks.

"'Was it a general engagement?' asked Carnot.

"'No, a fight, in which Lannes has covered himself with glory. The affair was bloody. Attacked with ten thousand men by eighteen thousand, he was only saved by a division sent to his support. Ott is in full retreat. The Austrian line is broken.'

"'When did the fight take place?' asked Carnot.

"'On the 8th,' replied Lucien.

"'And this is the 13th,' said the sagacious minister. 'Well, if that is so, the destinies of France are in the scale at the very moment we are speaking.'"

(In fact, the battle of Marengo did begin at dawn of the 14th.)

"'Four days of fatal uncertainty!' said Lucien.

"'Fatal?' said the minister of foreign affairs, coldly and interrogatively.

"'Four days,' echoed Fouche.

"An eye-witness told me," said de Marsay, continuing the narrative in his own person, "that the consuls, Cambaceres and Lebrun, knew nothing of this momentous news until after the six personages returned to the salon. It was then four in the morning. Fouche left first. That man of dark and mysterious genius, extraordinary, profound, and little understood, but who undoubtedly had the gifts of a Philip the Second, a Tiberius and a Borgia, went at once to work with an infernal and secret activity. His conduct at the time of the affair at Walcheren was that of a consummate soldier, a great politician, a far-seeing administrator. He was the only real minister that Napoleon ever had. And you all know how he then alarmed him.

"Fouche, Massena and the Prince," continued de Marsay, reflectively, "are the three greatest men, the wisest heads in diplomacy, war, and government, that I have ever known. If Napoleon had frankly allied them with his work there would no longer be a Europe, only a vast French Empire. Fouche did not finally detach himself from Napoleon until he saw Sieyes and the Prince de Talleyrand shoved aside.

"He now went to work, and in three days (all the while hiding the hand that stirred the ashes of the Montagne) he had organized that general agitation which then arose all over France and revived the republicanism of 1793. As it is necessary that I should explain this obscure corner of our history, I must tell you that this agitation, starting from Fouche's own hand (which held the wires of the former Montagne), produced republican plots against the life of the First Consul, which was in peril from this cause long after the victory of Marengo. It was Fouche's sense of the evil he had thus brought about which led him to warn Napoleon, who held a contrary opinion, that republicans were more concerned than royalists in the various conspiracies.

"Fouche was an admirable judge of men; he relied on Sieyes because of his thwarted ambition, on Talleyrand because he was a great *seigneur*, on Carnot for his perfect honesty; but the man he dreaded was the one whom you have seen here this evening. I will now tell how he entangled that man in his meshes.

"Malin was only Malin in those days, – a secret agent and correspondent of Louis XVIII. Fouche now compelled him to reduce to writing all the proclamations of the proposed revolutionary government, its warrants and edicts against the factions of the 18th Brumaire. An accomplice against his own will, Malin was required to have these documents secretly printed, and the copies held ready in his own house for distribution if Bonaparte were defeated. The printer was subsequently imprisoned and detained two months; he died in 1816, and always believed he had been employed by a Montagnard conspiracy.

"One of the most singular scenes ever played by Fouche's police was caused by the blunder of an agent, who despatched a courier to a famous banker of that day with the news of a defeat at Marengo. Victory, you will remember, did not declare itself for Napoleon until seven o'clock in the evening of the battle. At midday the banker's agent, considering the day lost and the French army about to be annihilated, hastened to despatch the courier. On receipt of that news Fouche was about to put into motion a whole army of bill-posters and cries, with a truck full of proclamations, when the second courier arrived with the news of the triumph which put all France beside itself with joy. There were heavy losses at the Bourse, of course. But the criers and posters who were gathered to announce the political death of Bonaparte and to post up the new proclamations were only kept waiting awhile till the news of the victory could be struck off!

"Malin, on whom the whole responsibility of the plot of which he had been the working agent was likely to fall if it ever became known, was so terrified that he packed the proclamations and other papers in carts and took them down to Gondreville in the night-time, where no doubt they were hidden in the cellars of that chateau, which he had bought in the name of another man – who was it, by the bye? he had him made chief-justice of an Imperial court – Ah! Marion. Having thus disposed of these damning proofs he returned to Paris to congratulate the First Consul on his victory. Napoleon, as you know, rushed from Italy to Paris after the battle of Marengo with alarming celerity. Those who know the secret history of that time are well aware that a message from Lucien brought him back. The minister of the interior had foreseen the attitude of the Montagnard party, and though he had no idea of the quarter from which the wind really blew, he feared a storm. Incapable of suspecting the three ministers and Carnot, he attributed the movement which stirred all France to the hatred his brother had excited by the 18th Brumaire, and to the confident belief of the men of 1793 that defeat was certain in Italy.

"The battle of Marengo detained Napoleon on the plains of Lombardy until the 25th of June, but he reached Paris on the 2nd of July. Imagine the faces of the five conspirators as they met the First Consul at the Tuileries, and congratulated him on the victory. Fouche on that very occasion at the palace told Malin to have patience, for *all was not over yet*. The truth was, Talleyrand and Fouche both held that Bonaparte was not as much bound to the principles of the Revolution as they were, and as he ought to be; and for this reason, as well as for their own safety, they subsequently, in 1804, buckled him irrevocably, as they believed, to its cause by the affair of the Duc d'Enghien. The execution of that prince is connected by a series of discoverable ramifications with the plot which was laid on that June evening in the boudoir of the ministry of foreign affairs, the night before the battle of Marengo. Those who have the means of judging, and who have known persons who were well-informed, are fully aware that Bonaparte was handled like a child by Talleyrand and Fouche, who were determined to alienate him irrevocably from the House of Bourbon, whose agents were even then, at the last moment, endeavoring to negotiate with the First Consul."

"Talleyrand was playing whist in the salon of Madame de Luynes," said a personage who had been listening attentively to de Marsay's narrative. "It was about three o'clock in the morning, when he pulled out his watch, looked at it, stopped the game, and asked his three companions abruptly and without any preface whether the Prince de Conde had any other children than the Duc d'Enghien. Such an absurd inquiry from the lips of Talleyrand caused the utmost surprise. 'Why do you ask us what you know perfectly well yourself?' they said to him. 'Only to let you know that the House of Conde comes to an end at this moment.' Now Monsieur de Talleyrand had been at the hotel de Luynes the entire evening, and he must have known that Bonaparte was absolutely unable to grant the pardon."

"But," said Eugene de Rastignac, "I don't see in all this any connection with Madame de Cinq-Cygnes and her troubles."

"Ah, you were so young at that time, my dear fellow; I forgot to explain the conclusion. You all know the affair of the abduction of the Comte de Gondreville, then senator of the Empire, for which the Simeuse brothers and the two d'Hauteserres were condemned to the galleys, – an affair which did, in fact, lead to their death."

De Marsay, entreated by several persons present to whom the circumstances were unknown, related the whole trial, stating that the mysterious abductors were five sharks of the secret service of the ministry of the police, who were ordered to obtain the proclamations of the would-be Directory which Malin had surreptitiously taken from his house in Paris, and which he had himself come to Gondreville for the express purpose of destroying, being convinced at last that the Empire was on a sure foundation and could not be overthrown. "I have no doubt," added de Marsay, "that Fouche took the opportunity to have the house searched for the correspondence between Malin and Louis XVIII., which was always kept up, even during the Terror. But in this cruel affair there was a private element, a passion of revenge in the mind of the leader of the party, a man named Corentin, who is still living, and who is one of those subaltern agents whom nothing can replace and who makes himself felt by his amazing ability. It appears that Madame, then Mademoiselle de Cinq-Cygne, had ill-treated him on a former occasion when he attempted to arrest the Simeuse brothers. What happened afterwards in connection with the senator's abduction was the result of his private vengeance.

223

"These facts were known, of course, to Malin, and through
him to Louis XVIII. You may therefore," added de Marsay, turning to the Princesse de Cadignan, "explain the whole matter to the
Marquise de Cinq-Cygne, and show her why Louis XVIII.
thought fit to keep silence."